To: Betty

D.C. Ben

Chronicles of Angels

KISMET

Books 1 and 2 of the Chronicles of Angels Series

By: D.C. Bennett

ISBN: 145282309X
ISBN-13: 9781452823096
Library of Congress Control Number: 2010905961

CONTENTS

It has been said that Heaven,
Hell, and the World of Man
all exist in the same place
and time ... but in separate
dimensions ... dimensions that
lay just beyond the ridged
edges of a man-made world.

Few men have seen such
dimensions, and those who
have, were thought mad.

This is the story of such a
man and his journey through
a Celestial dimension unlike
any other ...

"The Cherubim Fields"

BOOK 1 "THE CHERUBIM FIELDS"

CHAPTER I

TOLLHOUSE ROAD

⚜

Our story begins on 'Tollhouse Road' in the oak and sycamore-tree-covered foothills of Central California, miles away from the hustle and bustle of city life. Tollhouse is a narrow road not easily traveled at speeds exceeding twenty-five miles per hour as it winds whimsically through the hilly terrain. It is a foggy, drizzly day with visibility less than a quarter mile.

As we make our way through the trees and rolling hills, we are flanked by a shallow creek with many pools and falls. The locals call it 'Granite Creek', named after its natural granite outcroppings that blanket the creek bed and speckle the surrounding foothills. While it is dry throughout the summer months, in early autumn, it is teeming with the runoff of the Sierra's first snow.

Wrapping snuggly around the backside of Black Mountain, Tollhouse merges into Lodge Road, which leads to Sierra High School. The school is a vision from the past, with its high steeple rooftops and lap-siding construction. Old-fashion bleachers of maroon and white surround the small but well used football stadium. Directly behind the stadium, at the very end of the football field, graze neighboring livestock that roam the surrounding hillsides overlooking the school.

Built in a simpler time, the high school hasn't undergone significant change or modification in many years, literally standing still for half a century while the world went on without it. It is nestled at the base of Black Mountain, not quite the Sierra-Nevadas but much larger than a foothill. Due to the terrain, the school's facilities rest on several elevation levels adding to its early California charm.

Upon entering the metal double doors of the school, there is a plethora of glass bookcases hosting countless trophies, cups, ribbons and awards, most of which were achieved in football. The school is decorated in a perpetual state of "Pep Rally" with banners and streamers lining the narrow hallways.

Past the sea of gray metal lockers and administrative offices is the door to Professor Goodwin's Theology 101 class. It is a large, semi-circle-shaped room with red stadium seats that cascade down to an altar-like desk at the bottom of the arena. The walls are covered on one side with large portraits of the Presidents, and on the other, inexpensive prints of scriptural passages and regional maps of ancient earth. Between the oversized desk and the black board stands the Professor.

He is a man of medium build, roughly five-foot-ten-inches tall and one hundred and seventy-five pounds. Uncombed, ash-brown hair frames his long, slender face. A square chin and well-defined jaw offers an illusion of strength, while dark-brown, deep-set eyes exudes vulnerability. He is a fair-skinned man who tans well in the summer months. Approaching his late thirties, Professor Goodwin is a handsome but unkempt man, as for many years his passion has been the study of religion with little emphasis on himself.

Clean, but disheveled, his clothes are baggy as if handed down to him by an older sibling. He wears a brown hound's-tooth coat with a charcoal tie and cream-colored shirt. His keen fashion sense is further illustrated by his brown corduroy pants that don't quite match the coat. His shoes are a generic brand of loafer with holes worn through under each big toe.

He leans on his desk in a confidently relaxed posture while fielding questions from his students regarding a recent dig in Cairo. But despite many years of lecturing, he hasn't fully overcome his fear of speaking in front of large crowds.

"Did you find anything in Cairo that could prove or disprove the existence of God, Professor?" asked one student.

"Oh my . . . Talk about getting right to the point. Well let's see," he answered. "My experience has been that ancient cultures often times point to the existence of a more advanced civilization. But if The Holy Grail is what you are referring to, then I would have to say that the answer is no . . . Not yet."

In a soft but fluid voice yet another question is posed, only this time, it comes from the Professor's new aid. It is her first day, and although she is seated at the front of the class, she quietly entered with the students, seemingly unnoticed by the Professor. She is a graduate student working on her masters in Theology, and by interning in Professor Goodwin's classroom; she will earn extra credit towards her credentials.

Her name is Amena Benjamin. She is a simple girl, blessed with poverty at a young age and surrounded by the love and support of an immigrant family whose sole goal in life was to see her do well.

She'd remained silent throughout the lecture but can no longer contain herself:

"So if you were to find concrete proof of the existence of God, wouldn't that eliminate the need for faith?" Amena asked.

The Professor had briefly turned his back to the class to erase some illustrations from the black board. Upon hearing the question, he turned slowly toward his class and said:

"Who said that?"

"I did," answered Amena, with her hand half raised.

The Professor studied her face for what felt like several minutes, when in fact, it was only a second or two. She was sitting upright with her legs crossed, and her hands folded firmly upon the desk-top in a proper English manner. She looked out of place somehow as her beauty was much more profound than any student he'd ever had the pleasure of teaching. Her skin was white and smooth like a porcelain doll. Her eyes were the shape of almonds, light green with a dark blue border. Her hair was golden brown and flowed gently onto the nape of her neck. She wore very little makeup, though it was clear that she needed none.

She was wearing a navy blue interview suit with a crisp white shirt buttoned up to her collar. The matching skirt was straight, hemmed just above the knee and ironed, or dry-cleaned, to perfection. Her natural-tone stockings flowed effortlessly into her navy blue short-healed pumps. And although her attire vaguely resembled a Transatlantic Stewardess, she presented like a single, spring daisy in a field of dormant Bermuda grass. Her face seemed familiar to the Professor, as her striking beauty could not easily have been forgotten.

He tried not to appear too eager:

"Yes," he said quickly, immediately lowering his voice and slowing the pace of his speech, in a failing effort to appear less animated. "I mean, you are correct. Surely it would change everything."

Just then the bell rang which startled the Professor. Sensing his innocent demeanor, Amena smiled somewhat confidently while gathering her books and placing them into her shinny black-leather book bag. The Professor turned to the class a bit frazzled but determined:

"Think about the ramifications of the discovery of concrete proof of God's existence and be ready to discuss during Monday's lecture. Have a great weekend and be safe . . . the roads are slick this time of year."

But when he turned back to Amena, she was gone. She had exited with the students as quietly as she'd entered.

The Professor remained still and quiet for several seconds while facing the door. His mind raced as he attempted to recall the exact facts surrounding his brief acquaintance with her. He knew she'd been a student in his class somewhere in the last five or six years, but only for a short while as he couldn't recall grading her or even seeing a name that would fit the face on any official roster.

He walked slowly down the clearing corridor with his eyes on the floor in front of him, hardly aware of anything else in his general vicinity. He couldn't quite process why she was in his class after all this time. Upon opening the door to his office, he felt a tap on his shoulder; he turned with enthusiasm only to see the back of one of his students hustling off to football practice.

"Have a good weekend Professor!" the boy shouted as he exited the rear double doors of the school.

"You too," he replied, somewhat disappointedly.

And with the door already half open behind him, he turned to enter. And there . . . on his chair, in the middle of the closet-sized office, sat Amena.

Trying not to show too much enthusiasm, he spoke:

"May I help you?"

And after a brief, uncomfortable pause, she said:

"You don't remember me, do you?"

The Professor inquisitively tilted his head to one side, and with a puzzled look responded:

"Should I?"

"Six years ago, in your Advanced Theology class. I was a student at Stanislaus High, visiting here to study Sierra High's Ag Program before going on to Veterinary school. I was able to sit in on a few of your classes, as Theology had always been an interest of mine," she replied.

She had a presence that was not easily forgotten, as the pieces of the puzzle began to come together. He quickly calculated her age to be twenty-four or twenty-five.

"Ah yes . . . the aspiring animal doctor. If my memory serves me correctly, you challenged my knowledge of the great Assyrian Empire," he said.

"I apologize for that. My family is Assyrian and have somewhat inundated me with their history for as long as I can remember," she said.

"No need to apologize," he responded. "What a fascinating heritage."

"So you DO remember me," she said.

"It's all coming back now," he replied. "I remember finding your knowledge of religion to be quite extensive for a soon-to-be veterinarian."

"Shortly after my visit to Sierra High School, I changed my major to Theology. Your lectures had, let's just say . . . an affect on me," she said.

Realizing that he'd made a positive impression on her, his confidence was boosted, as words seemed to flow a bit easier:

"So you've decided to join us in the search for the Holy Grail as it were. A noble profession filled with underpaid and overworked, socially inept hermits such as myself," chuckled the Professor.

"I take it the search for the Holy Grail isn't going so well?" she said.

"For me, the Holy Grail is not necessarily a chalice or goblet, but rather, any material finding that would transcend faith, by proving the existence of God," he answered.

"And what then? I mean, give me some insight into the lecture on Monday. What happens if we do find, for lack of better terms, The Holy Grail?"

"I'm afraid that such a discovery would signify the end of times. For just as you stated so eloquently in class today, irrefutable proof of God's existence would eliminate the need for faith and remove Man's freedom of choice setting off an unstoppable chain of events," said the Professor.

"Revelations," she said.

"Exactly," he replied.

"Well, although I am looking forward to meeting God in person, I'd rather it be later than sooner, if you know what I mean," she said.

"I'll do my best to refrain from any and all apocalyptic discoveries in the near future," smiled the Professor.

Amena then stood up and extended her hand, confidently yet softly saying:

"By the way . . . I'm Amena Benjamin."

He took her hand and gently squeezed it, genuinely responding:

"Please call me Don."

And as he shook her hand, he felt a sense of calming
security he hadn't felt since he was a child. She had
an innocence and sweetness about her that was not
lost on the Professor.

"So, enough of the doom and gloom, to what do I
owe the pleasure of your company today Ms. or is it
Mrs. Amena Benjamin?" he asked in a pitiful attempt
to inquire into her marital status. The Professor
looked down at his shoes in an embarrassed effort to
avoid her reaction.

"You don't read your memos, do you?" she said.
"I'm your aid for the semester."

The Professor immediately tried to cover for his
rudeness.

"Yes, Yes, of course you are. There's been so much on
my mind lately that I'd completely forgotten about
you, or I mean, about the aid position . . . I uh . . ."

"It's ok Professor," she disappointedly said while
grabbing her bag and standing up to leave. "Thank
you for your time, I'll let you get back to your busy
schedule."

The Professor realized that he'd hurt her feelings
by implying that her presence was not significant,
covering up for his own boyish enthusiasm.

He lacked experience engaging in coy conversation
with a woman, let alone one as beautiful as Amena.

Stumbling and grasping for words, he did his best to recover:

"No, No . . . Did I mention being socially inept? Forgive my rudeness, please," he continued.

He grabbed his jacket and briefcase and rushed to catch up to her as she headed for the door.

"At least let me walk you to your car. I promise not to be rude," appealed the Professor.

"Well, I suppose there's no law against allowing you to grovel a bit for not decorating the halls with bells and whistles in preparation for my arrival," joked Amena.

And as he leaned out into the hall to hold the door open for her, she slowly passed, and in a soft whispering voice she said:

"And no . . . it's not Mrs."

The Professor's face turned bright red, and without even an attempt at pro-quo, he locked the door behind him and rushed to join her.

Fumbling with his materials, and with uncharted, nervous excitement, the Professor finally managed to catch up to her. They exited the rear double-doors of the building and while heading toward the employee parking lot, he searched unsuccessfully for the right words or coy banter that would extend their conversation.

Walking briskly and without breaking stride, Amena said:

"And you . . . when do I get to meet your wife and kids?"

The Professor was now in a position he was not at all accustomed to:

"Uh, No . . . You can't . . . I mean, there isn't any," he stuttered.

"You mean there aren't any," she corrected.

"Yes, or no, I mean . . ." he stammered, unable to find the words.

And by some small miracle, just as he was about to make a complete fool of himself, a student, suited up in light-practice football gear, shouted from the adjacent soccer field:

"Hey, Professor! They say you hold the unofficial record for the fastest forty in the history of Sierra High. How about it? I could use the warm up!" the boy shouted while walking onto the track.

The Professor knew the boy. He was an eighteen-year old senior, enrolled in one of the Professor's religion classes. He was a starter in virtually every sport, and by no coincidence, the fastest runner at Sierra High. The boy sat down on his helmet at the edge of the track and waited for the Professor. By this time the

Professor, being of relatively sound mind, attempted in earnest to avoid such a futile engagement.
"Oh no . . . Track and loafers don't mix," he said. "Besides, aren't I almost twice your age?"

"Oh come on. You can't let a little thing like OLD-AGE stand between you and a challenge, can you? Mister Record Holder." prodded Amena, giggling, with her hand over her mouth.

Inspired by the moment, the Professor seized the opportunity and said:

"OLD-AGE huh? Well let's just see about that."

He then walked confidently onto the track, kicked off his well-used loafers and said:

"Alright son, take your shoes off."

"Age before beauty, Professor," boldly boasted the student.

And in the blink of an eye, the Professor took off from a full stand with the boy right on his heels.

He pulled nearly three strides away from the boy, as watching teammates yelled and cheered:

"Catch 'em! Come on, get 'em!"

The Professor, now nearing the forty-yard mark, shouted over his shoulder to the boy:

"I'll give you a passing grade if you catch me!" as he glided smoothly down the track.

The student surged forward only to cause the Professor to pull even further away. After breezing past the sixty-yard mark, the Professor slowed to a stop, bent down with his hands on his knees and huffed and puffed for life.

"No fair!" exclaimed the boy, "I'm wearing shoulder pads!"

"Well, let's just suffice it to say, slacks and a tie aren't exactly track and field." panted the Professor.

The student agreed and patted the Professor on the back, "You still got it Goodwin. That is for an OLD dude."

The Professor and the student walked laughing arm in arm off the field, and as the boy grabbed his helmet and ran to join the others, the Professor shouted:

"See you tonight! But you better run faster than that if you wanna win . . . And you're still not passing my class!"

Amena, pleasantly surprised by the Professor's hidden talents, patted him on the shoulder while sliding her hand over his upper arm giving it a quick squeeze.

"Wow . . . Not bad! Not bad at all . . . I mean, for an OLD guy," she said.

"Haven't you heard . . . thirty is the new twenty," he said.

"Oh please," she responded, confidently tossing her hair over her shoulder.

And as they reached the end of the parking lot, Amena slowed and turned to her car. It was a nineteen-seventies, white V.W. Bug, with black interior, and completely stock. The inoperable AM/FM radio and cracked front windshield were things she'd planed on fixing when her student loans were paid off. She inserted the key to open the car door with the Professor standing several feet behind her in an apparent loss for words. Sensing his intentions, but somewhat frustrated by his ambivalence, she opened the door, tossed her book bag onto the passenger seat, turned and exhaled out loud:

"Well, are you going to just stand there, or are you going to ask me to tonight's football game?"

In an effort to clarify her intentions he replied:

"Doesn't the employee handbook say something about staff and dating?"

"Well, technically, I'm not staff. I get credit towards my credentials . . . but if it makes you uncomfortable then . . ."

The Professor quickly interrupted in a desperate attempt to avoid making the same mistake twice.

"Oh my Gosh, No! It would be my honor to escort you to tonight's game . . . Ms. Benjamin."

"Well that's more like it . . . "Don"," she said softly with a smile.

Now with a sense of accomplishment and added familiarity, he asked:

"What time should I pick you up?"

"I'm staying with a friend, and she's kind of a slob, so why don't I just meet you here?" she asked.

"Alright then. I'll see you here at seven, and if you like ice cream, the local Mexican food restaurant makes a great bananas foster," he added.

"I think that would be perfect," she said with a smile.

"It's a date then?" he asked.

"Absolutely," she replied.

Amena started her thirty-something-year-old Bug, and attempting to minimize any further embarrassment, she hand cranked down her window and shouted through the smoke and backfire:

"We're taking your car to ice cream!"

The Professor laughed and waived as he headed slowly to his 1982 silver-oxidized, four-door Volvo.

He boyishly kicked loose bedrock in the school
parking lot, while thinking back to a time in grade
school when he kissed a girl for the first time. He
recognized the feelings of nervous excitement
that filled the lingering minutes of carefree days.
They were feelings he'd misplaced long ago, but
subconsciously longed for in their dormancy.

And as he slowly made his way down Lodge Road,
just a few miles from the High School, the Professor
made a turn onto a path that would change his life
forever . . . Tollhouse Road.

CHAPTER II
GRANITE CREEK
※

It was early afternoon when Professor Goodwin slowly made his way down Tollhouse Road, heading home after a full day of lecturing. His thoughts were on Amena; their reaquaintance earlier that day, and their first date later that evening.

It had been quite some time since he'd been on a date:

"Where will we go . . . what will I wear?" he thought, as he rolled his window down oblivious to the misty fog.

He leaned his head out to better absorb the sweet-smelling sycamores as they passed. He'd always enjoyed the fragrances of the foothills, but on this day, they seemed exceptionally pleasing to him.

Although he preferred talk radio, he would sometimes turn to the local classic-rock station in hopes of hearing some Boston or Credence Clearwater Revival.

Today he was in luck; it was CCR's Green River. In uninhibited, childlike bliss, he turned the radio up and sang along loudly. He stretched for every note, oblivious to the fact that he was somewhat off key.

The music was blasting, and he was unabashedly singing like a rock star, sharing his joy with the empty hillside that surrounded the otherwise lonely road. He took for granted that like every other day, this moment would last.

While rounding a tight corner, not far down from the High School, his path was blocked by a logging truck jackknifed sideways in the road. His emotions shifted instantly from glee to panic as the tranquility of the scenic countryside was replaced by the rigid edges of twisted steel and burning rubber. With no time to think, the Professor instinctively slammed on his brakes, desperately attempting to avoid the impending collision.

Not unexpectedly, the slick road, moist from the day's drizzly fog, gave way to centrifugal force. With no recourse to the conditions, his vehicle slid sideways as he struggled to regain control. Time stood still in a cruel satire, enabling him to fully experience the brief moments of life that hung tenuously in the balance. Trees, glass, and metal swirled by slowly in an unnatural state of suspended animation.

Veering off the road, the Professor hit broad-side into a massive oak tree, and was instantly ejected through the very window out of which he was so joyfully singing just moments before. Somehow, as though watching the events unfold from afar, he saw himself tumble lifelessly through the air, striking twigs and oak branches as he flew. Eventually, landing over twenty yards from the initial crash site, he was brought to a sudden standstill with the back of his head impacting a large boulder at the edge of Granite Creek . . .

Within seconds of the crash, the Professor found himself laying half in and half out of the shallow rushing stream with cold water flowing briskly over his lower body. The clamor of twisting metal and breaking glass subsided, and despite the wreckage, oddly the radio was unaffected as the sounds of CCR's Green River eerily filled the air.

Although dazed and somewhat confused, he was relieved to hear the same song as before the accident, indicating that he was still alive and hadn't lost consciousness. Attempting to assess his injuries, he slowly lifted his head and upper shoulders when a strong throbbing sensation filled and engulfed his brain. His ears were ringing, and his head pounded and throbbed with each beat of his heart. He opened his eyes slowly, carefully wiggling each finger and toe in the hopes that his appendages were still operable.

He sat up with his waist and legs completely submerged in the icy cold waters of the snow's first run-off. Slowly pivoting his head and neck from side to side, he meticulously evaluated the condition of his spinal cord. While inspecting his legs and trying to regain his composure, he noticed an object moving in the stream. It was a rainbow trout slowly swimming by, ostensibly unaware of the Professor's presence. As he admired the beauty of the shiny, silvery fish, his mind drifted back to his childhood.

He remembered vividly a time when he and his family traveled north to Lake Tahoe for some fishing and white-water rafting. They stayed in a cabin in the woods close to a nearby stream teeming with rainbow trout indigenous to northern California.

Preparations were made as he and his older brother excitedly situated their gear the night before. They laid out their clothes, readied their tackle boxes, and leaned their poles against the back door of the cabin like a tiny armory awaiting battle.

The next morning he awoke with the sun and crawled out of his army-green sleeping bag in anticipation of his day with THE MEN. As he slowly walked about the cabin, his anxiety began to build. He searched the house in a panic finding only his sleeping mother and toddler sister. He ran with quiet desperation into the woods in front of the cabin only to find his father's car gone . . .

After all these years he'd completely forgotten or compartmentalized the pain he felt upon realizing that he'd been left behind. Maybe he was too young, or that he hadn't shown enough enthusiasm leading up to the excursion to be included. It's possible that the men had tried unsuccessfully to wake him, ultimately deciding to let him sleep.

Whatever the reason, what remained was an eight-year-old boy, left behind and overwhelmed by the solitary feeling of unwantedness, which oddly enough after all these years had resurfaced in the freezing waters of Granite Creek.

He wasn't quite sure what triggered the memory of the fishing trip. Maybe it was the fish, the stream, or the feeling of helplessness he was experiencing after being hurled through the air against his will.

After just a few short minutes of sitting in the icy brook, the Professor's legs began to burn with the stinging sensation of frostbite. He likened the feeling to a thousand tiny piranha nipping at his flesh. And just as it would have been with the miniature carnivores, he knew that if he didn't move now . . . he might not be able to.

He slowly pulled his feet up under his body and deliberately pushed against the sandy creek bed to stand. He felt dizzy and nauseous, but was able to keep his balance. Now confident that there were no broken bones or potential for paralysis, he turned to assess the crash site.

He stood and faced the scene of the accident like a fawn looking back on its pursuer after cheating death. Standing knee high in the stream, he was perplexed by the awkwardness of what appeared to be his car wrapped around an enormous oak tree. His confusion was exacerbated by the abnormal condition of his vehicle. It was oddly semitransparent, like an image that was not entirely in focus. The music that was blasting, out of his twenty-year-old, six-by-nine Jensen Healy speakers just seconds before, was fading.

In an attempt to improve his vision, he squinted and rubbed his eyes, only to witness his car disappear completely, leaving only the majestic oak tree standing firm and unscarred.

The music was gone, and the hillside was bare. There was no traffic noise; no sirens in the distance; not even the knocking hum of the semi truck's diesel engine, as it too was gone. The Professor stood alone and in complete silence, one second being thankful for having survived the accident, and the next wondering if, in fact, he'd survived it at all.

He bent down and splashed several handfuls of cold water into his eyes in an effort to clear his vision, but with no reward. The images did not reappear.

He stood peering at the empty hillside that just moments before was a pile of twisted metal and glass. He pondered in silent disbelief, the possibility and probability that he'd suffered significant brain damage, since for all intents and purposes, HIS world had vanished.

Unable to put a handle on his situation, he knew in the event of any head injury, that he had to remain conscious for as long as possible until help arrived.

Now unsure of his condition and surroundings, he began to hear noises that sounded like branches breaking in the trees on the other side of the stream. He turned to look but was puzzled by the unfamiliar scenery.

The landscape appeared more lush and more dense than he'd remembered, like a forest, but with many varieties of trees unfamiliar to him. He noticed that some trees and underbrush on the nearby hillside had been burned. But curiously, the burned trees stood alone amongst clusters of healthy trees as though individually and deliberately destroyed.

Standing waist high in the current, he felt the water pulling strongly against his legs. The stream was faster and deeper with eight to ten-foot waterfalls every hundred yards or so. He studied the stream that he'd driven passed for over half his life, as it was noticeably deeper and faster than before. The only thing that appeared unchanged was the foggy mist that drizzled heavily onto his already soaked body.

In the few seconds it took to process the unfamiliar environment, the Professor became increasingly aware of the sounds of snapping branches and falling trees growing louder and louder.

Suddenly, a large animal exited the thick underbrush and violently entered the stream sixty to seventy yards upstream from the Professor's position. He could see the animal as it thrashed about the stream. Its center of attention was focused on something in the water, evidently unaware of anything else in its immediate vicinity. Peering intently into the icy creek, it grappled viciously in what appeared to be an awkward attempt at catching fish.

The Professor had assumed it was an animal, but then upon further evaluation realized that it was different from any animal he'd ever seen. It possessed the upper torso of a man, but moved more like a large gorilla as it pounded at the water in a fisted rage. Its shoulders and arms were massive with large veins close to the outer epidermis exposing the deep purple blood surging just beneath the surface. Forming its neck were thick strands of muscle, banding together between its upper jaw and shoulders, giving it the appearance of having no neck at all. It was massive, easily weighing close to a ton and a good ten-feet tall.

The creature's skin was white and clammy closely resembling the underside of an alligator. Its upper body was thick and enormously muscular with very little hair. Its face and head were peering down and away from the Professor, making it difficult to ascertain exactly what kind of animal it was. From the side, it appeared that it was heavily furred from the waist down, covering its mid section and enormously muscular legs.

As it thrashed within the stream, it caught fish
with inconsistent accuracy, ripping and tearing the
fish with its massively oversized claws, clearly more
interested in killing than eating. Regardless of
the animal's origin, or genus family species, it was
obviously something the Professor needed to avoid at
all cost.

The Professor stood completely still, trying with
every ounce of his being not to move a muscle,
part paralyzed with fear and part trying to remain
unnoticed by the large creature.

Without warning, the beast rose up in an alert
position. It squatted with a straight-back, knee deep
in the stream as if ready to lunge or leap. With its
head up, it surveyed the banks of the stream and the
hillsides that surrounded its position, but did not
notice the Professor. At this time, it became clear
to the Professor that this was no gorilla, nor was it
anything he'd ever seen or heard of in all his years
of study. Although more than seventy yards away, its
face could now clearly be seen.

It was some sort of horribly disfigured amalgamation
of animal and human. It had the head and face of a
man with the exception of two, 2-3 foot long horns
that protruded outward and away from the skull,
then forward to a sharp point, similar to those of a
bull. Its nose was either upturned like that of a bat,
or possibly no nose at all, just nasal openings where
a nose should have been. Its face was long and
triangular. Its eyes were deep, black, and wide set,

affording it greater peripheral vision. It had short legs in relation to its upper torso, possibly enabling it to travel on all fours with ease.

The Professor's heart began to race as he struggled to keep from moving. He deduced that his immobility had allowed him to remain unnoticed by the monster.

Just then a single drop of blood betrayed the Professor's anonymity by exiting his scalp and traveling slowly down his forehead. The creature sniffed the air twice and smelled the blood instantly. It then jerked its head and looked immediately and directly at the Professor.

The beast dropped to all fours in the stream and roared, like a freight train. The deafening sound pierced and vibrated the Professor's eardrum. In mid roar it charged, beating its chest and pounding at the water like a grizzly as it came.

Still in shock and disbelief, the Professor slowly began stepping backwards in retreat as the monster closed-in on his location. It seemed like an eternity before the fear, which was now in control, would give way to panic and release his legs to run. All rational thought was expunged by survival instincts and his will to live another day.

The Professor turned to run back to the road for help, but the road was no longer there, or for that matter, anything that would remotely resemble the world as he knew it. Confused and feeling very much alone, he turned and frantically ran in the opposite direction of the creature. In full run and heading downstream at water's edge, the Professor deduced that the blood, now dripping profusely down his face, must have given away his position and that the smell of it would only put the creature into a dangerous frenzy, surely tearing him to pieces like a fish in the stream. But in the Professor's favor, the beast's pursuit was hindered by the waist deep stream its massive body was crazily trudging through.

The Professor was quickly approaching a large waterfall when the beast stopped in the icy stream, reached down and lifted an automobile size granite boulder over its head and hurled it at its fleeing victim. Despite the accident, and with panic driven adrenaline, the Professor was able to dodge the projectile, but as the boulder hit the stream only feet away, the wall of water it displaced picked him up and over the waterfall he was hoping to avoid.

After plunging more than thirty feet, he found himself being swept down rolling white-water rapids, tumbling and twisting at the whim of the stream, eventually floating to a stop onto the banks of a calm pool. But oddly, what appeared to have been yet another unfortunate event, turned to the Professor's favor as his water emersion confused the beast . . . at least temporarily.

The creature stopped and stood at the top of the falls, franticly sniffing the air to regain the scent of its prey. The Professor remained still, hoping that like most large carnivores, the beast would have poor long-range vision and would have to rely on movement to recalibrate its victim's position.

The beast, now turning his attention back to the stream, had evidently given up the pursuit. The Professor was unsure if it was his motionlessness that eluded the beast, or if the cold waters of the stream aided in concealing his position. Many animals of prey possess a keen sense of thermal vision enabling them to track and spot their kill by seeing the heat trail as it radiates off of their victim's bodies, but such a gift limits their ability to hunt cold-blooded animals. Nevertheless, it was clear that remaining motionless in the icy-cold waters of the stream was his only chance for survival; unfortunately, this was a short-term solution, as the nearly frozen stream would surely render him helpless if he remained in it much longer.

Confident that the creature's attention was diverted, the Professor turned his focus downstream to deeper waters where he might be able to swim for help.

He slowly began to move his hand to push himself up from the stream, when he sensed a presence directly in front of him. As he slowly raised his eyes, he beheld a curious sight.

A few feet ahead and perched on a branch of a burned-out-ancient oak was a completely different kind of creature. Standing utterly still like a statue, slender, and close to twelve-feet tall was a sight the

Professor thought he would never see, at least not in this lifetime.

It was a manlike being with six wings, two were covering its face, and two were covering its feet, while the other two were poised behind, ready to take flight. The Professor immediately recognized the creature as a celestial being. A being the likes of which he'd only read about . . . an Angel. More specifically, it was what the Professor believed to be a Seraph, as described in the Bible and other ancient books.[1] And although thought to be peaceful in nature, it was capable of mass destruction.

After seeing the Angel, the Professor now considered that he was undoubtedly dead and in some sort of middle realm. But being a Christian man with a deep understanding and belief in the Scripture, he did not believe that he would spend any time in hell, or be tested in the afterlife.

"So then, what was this place?" he pondered. "Could this all be in my mind? Is it possible that I've been imagining the whole thing?"

For a moment, the Professor felt a secure, calming sensation at the feet of the Holy Creature, but then quickly reasoned that the Seraph could just as easily destroy him, as could the beast in the stream.

Suddenly, the beast regained the scent of the Professor and began to grunt and foam at the mouth with excitement while clambering violently down the granite boulders at the edge of the falls.

The Professor began to initiate his planned escape downstream, when the Angel slowly and purposefully raised one hand out from beneath its wing. It placed it in front of its man-like face, now visible through its wings and with its index finger to its lips, softly and deliberately whispered the universal sound:

"Shhhh!"

It then turned its hand, palm down, and lowered it slowly, motioning to the Professor to stay down. The Professor fought to remain still despite every ounce of his being urging him to run for life from the advancing creature. But trusting in the Angel, he lowered himself slowly back into the water and looked back to see if the beast was still in pursuit.

Now at the bottom of the falls, a mere twenty to thirty yards from its kill, the beast was able to target the Professor, and in doing so, saw the Seraph perched above him. Upon spotting the Angel, the creature went crazy. The Professor suddenly became inconsequential when the beast, while locking eyes with the Seraph, let out a violent roar.

Within seconds and before the beast concluded its manic roar, the entire mountain came alive with beasts. They seemed out of their minds with anger and rage as they charged toward the stream like un-caged animals. They crashed down trees and ripped out bushes as they stormed the Professor's location.

The perching Seraph unfurled all six of its wings and met the beast's battle cry with one of its own. It was a loud screeching sound, similar to that of a bird of prey descending fiercely upon its victim. Its cry was immediately echoed as hundreds of Angels approached from the skies above.

They flew in formation in groups of six. Traveling much faster than flapping wings could possibly propel them; they converged on the creek in seconds. As the descending squadrons neared the Professor's location, he could clearly make out that these creatures were quite different from the Seraph in the tree.

In appearance, their form was that of a man, but with the most obvious exception being that they were flying. Each creature had four wings, spanning at least fifteen feet from tip to tip.[2] Their wings were tarnished and shaped like the wings of doves, one pair originating from the center of their shoulder blades and the other just above the small of their backs.

The sounds of their wings were deafening as they flapped in rapid succession enabling them to hover, ascend, or descend in any direction. Clearly more than thirteen feet tall, they were outfitted in Roman Gladiator-style light armor, strong enough to withstand heavy debris but thin enough to allow them to fly unimpeded into battle. In their left hands they carried circular shields made of ancient bronze, razor sharp on edge with the Cross of Golgotha burned onto the shield faces.[3]

Along their left arm they wore manica[4] to protect them from grazing blows that escaped the shield. In their right hand was a sica[5], fashioned similar to a small broadsword or large machete, but with a slightly curved blade, possibly for less wind resistance in flight. They seemed specialized in their battle duties seeing that some carried small arsenals of archer weaponry.

Their faces were manlike in nature, but depending on the angle, they appeared to take on a different facade, either that of an ox, lion, or eagle, possibly to confuse and/or intimidate their enemies in battle.[6]

Upon seeing their faces, the Professor knew that he was witnessing Cherubim; Mighty Angels of the Lord in all their glory and splendor in the likes that he'd never imagined. He recalled passages in the Bible where Cherubim are described, but mostly in the context of wall carvings and adornment but never in a combat situation such as this.[7]

The first squadron to arrive immediately split into two parties of three. The volume of air displaced by their wings caused a whirlwind that whisked moisture from the stream's surface temporarily confusing their opponent. The three nearest the beast in the stream immediately began firing arrows from crossbows striking the creature with deadly accuracy.

The first Cherub to arrive at the beast unsheathed from behind its back what appeared to be a large hatchet or small ax with a slightly curved blade. Without touching the ground, the Cherub made short work of cutting the creature in half just below the rib cage. A fountain of dark red blood spewed upward, covering the small party of Cherubim, further mottling their already blood stained wings. Flying like giant hummingbirds, they backed away from the death throes of the flailing carcass and flew straight up to rejoin their squadron.

Arrows were flying and metal was clanging as the Cherubim hewed away at the beasts. With surgical precision, they separated creatures from their appendages seemingly effortlessly. They attacked each beast with deliberate and calculated strikes, inflicting as much mortal damage as possible with the fewest number of passes.

The Angels showed no clemency while hurling their razor-sharp shields like discuses, beheading and dismembering beasts at will. Then in a circular motion, the weaponized shields boomeranged back into the hands of the Cherubim. They were clearly driven and intent on the very task of killing as many beasts as possible . . . as quickly as possible. And though they were experts in their work . . . they exhibited no signs of sport or joy in their butchery.

Although the Angels were skilled to perfection, the battle was not one sided. Many fell to the beasts' overpowering strength.

After managing to divide the Cherubim into smaller more vulnerable groups, the beasts would double up and distract their victims, pulling them down from the sky, one by one with their massive bone-crushing arms and claws. But even within the death grip of the larger and more powerful beasts, the Angels continued to hack away, swords drawn, at the tough hide of the monsters.

The Cherubim seemed pure in thought, with only one mission or purpose . . . to stop the beasts at any cost. The beasts appeared equally as determined to push forward relentlessly.

As the battle raged, the Professor grew weaker. The terror and horror of combat and significant loss of blood made it too difficult to remain focused on the gruesome mêlée. Without the energy to swim, he slowly turned over onto his back and quietly pushed himself away from the banks of the once clear pool now darkened by the blood of battle, and gradually began to drift downstream.

Gazing up into the crimson and orange-colored setting sky, he saw hovering over him the same Seraph from the tree who helped him once before. Floating slowly downstream with his arms stretched out widely, the Professor marveled at God's creature. It was suspended in the air, just a few feet above the

Professor, mirroring his position and looking down on him in apparent confusion, not knowing what to make of this small, helpless creature and seemingly assessing the differences between them.

Its wings were flapping at a rate that could not be seen with the naked eye. Due to the size and force of their enormous wingspan, they created a roaring hum that all but drowned out the awful sounds of killing and dying as the battle raged on across the surrounding hillsides.

He considered that maybe this was all a struggle over his eternal soul, and since he was a God-loving Christian, the Seraph had come to take him to Heaven.

As his consciousness slowly faded, the deafening sound of the Seraph's fluttering wings steadily turned into the unmistakable "whap, whap, whapping" sound of rotor blades, as the Angel blurred into the form of a Rescue Helicopter. And as the image grew clearer, the Angel's face transformed into the orange-helmeted face of a rescue worker rappelling from the belly of the chopper on a long, rope-like ladder, attempting to reach the Professor's remote location as he drifted slowly downstream.

Fading in and out of consciousness, he could faintly hear stopped motorists yelling:

"There he is!"

"They found him!"

And after a brief short-haul, the rescue team carefully managed to load the Professor aboard the Rescue Helicopter and slowly began to rise away from the crash site.

The Professor struggled to remain conscious while the chopper made a bee-line toward the nearest urgent care facility. Despite his best efforts, the hum and vibration of the massive rotor blades made it impossible to stay awake. While fighting to stay conscious, the Professor managed to look out an open window and down onto the foothills below, seeing only roads, traffic, and his car wrapped around a two hundred year old Blue Oak Tree . . . but no sign of the horrors he had witnessed . . .

CHAPTER III
SAINT MARY'S PEDIATRIC

In the time it took to transport and admit the Professor, night had fallen, and the foothills were quiet. The Professor now lay in a hospital bed at a state of the art children's facility. Originally designed for patients a fraction of his age, it was the nearest head trauma center with helicopter access. He remains unconscious with his head wrapped in bandages and a cervical collar around his neck. He is surrounded by an overabundance of machinery, monitoring everything from his heart rate to his brain activity.

At his bedside is Professor Numier, a close friend and colleague of the Professor's, who although has the appropriate credentials to instruct at any major University in the country, chooses to teach at the nearby Foothill Junior College. He has a PHD in anthropology, as well as an extensive knowledge of history and theology.

Numier is a rather distinguished looking gentleman in his early to mid sixties. He enjoys playing the part of a scholar down to his wardrobe, with a Sherlock-Holmes type hat, heavy-duty brown, camelhair coat, tie, and matching trousers. The hat and usually smoldering, mahogany-wood pipe leave nothing to the imagination regarding his profession. He is a man of average height and slightly above average width, as many years of fine dining and good wine have all but enhanced his abdominal region. He has white, collar-length hair that curls up in the back, and a white mustache and goatee, yellowed by years of tobacco smoke. His pale-pink complexion set off his striking blue eyes and tarnished, yellow teeth.

He was on his way to the football game when the radio reported details of an accident involving a Sierra High teacher. Almost instinctively, he headed down Tollhouse Road only to discover his best friend's totaled vehicle on the back of a flatbed tow truck heading in the opposite direction. He slowed to a stop just short of flares still burning, and spotted an emergency crew shoveling glass and metal off the pavement. They told him that the med-evac team had transported the Professor to Saint Mary's Pediatric Hospital.

It was a forty-minute drive to the hospital, but Numier made it in twenty. On the way to the hospital, he recalled the time when he first met Don Goodwin. It was on a dig site in Cairo. Don was a young college student with aspirations of someday changing the world through his unearthened-anthropological discoveries. While they shared the same love for buried history, they were on the dig for entirely different reasons. Numier was in search of ancient cultures hoping to uncover advance civilizations and the missing link that would conjoin the caveman with modern-day man. On the other hand, Don seemed to be in search of something far more illusive. Numier remembered being immediately impressed by his colleague's enthusiasm and dedication to his work. Ultimately, their collective passion for the struggle would prove to be conducive to a long-lasting friendship.

Just as Numier was hurriedly driving into the hospital parking lot, on his radio he heard the faint buzzing of the emergency broadcast system. At first he was sure it was the usual test; nevertheless, with curiosity getting the better of him, he turned up the volume just in case. He rushed impatiently through the stations and was surprised to hear that every station in the area was buzzing. Now concerned, he sat in his parked car, despite his eagerness to enter the hospital, and awaited the broadcast.

It was breaking news. China had deployed two million troops west toward its border with India. Three million troops moved east toward its borders with Korea, and a garrison five million strong were advancing toward its northern border with Russia.

In response to the massive troop movement, India was taking an immediate nuclear posture with Missile silos opening on all of China's borders. Korea mobilized its war machine equal in numbers to the advancing Chinese, while Russia, much less concerned due to the violent terrain at its southern borders, was on high alert in a wait-and-see posture.

Numier, although very concerned with the situations unfolding in the East, refocused his thoughts on Don and the images of the twisted metal wreckage that was once his friend's automobile.

Upon entering the hospital, Numier was directed to the Intensive Care Unit on the fourth floor. He walked tentatively - fearing for the worst. He entered through the glass double doors of the I.C.U. and immediately saw Don. He was unconscious with his head thoroughly bandaged and tubes protruding from his mouth. Numier approached his bedside feeling somewhat uncomfortable in seeing that Don had been intubated. The respirator was breathing for him through a long tube running down his throat. There were I.V.s and many wires attached to his head and upper chest.

Still not entirely comfortable with the outward appearance of his friend, Numier's mind raced with questions regarding the accident and Don's injuries.

As Numier waited to speak with the attending physician, his eye drifted to the corner of the room where he noticed a black, book-bag resting neatly on a chair. He assumed that it belonged to the doctor, nurse, or family member of another patient.

At that moment, Amena entered the room, with a cup of coffee in her right hand and the attending physician to her left. He was a relatively young doctor in his early to mid fifties. He wore a white, lab-coat with a stethoscope draped over his shoulder signifying that he was in fact a doctor. They approached the Professor's bedside where Numier anxiously awaited word of Don's condition.

"Hello. My name is Doctor Packer, I am the attending physician caring for Donald Goodwin." he said while extending his hand to Numier.

"Oh . . . Yes of course. I'm Professor Eugene Numier, a colleague and close personal friend of Professor Goodwin's."

After dispensing with the obligatory introductions, Numier looked at Amena, while lowering his chin and lifting his eyebrows in anticipation of her introduction.

"My name is Amena Benjamin, also a friend," she said, extending her hand and firmly shaking Numier's.

Not recognizing her, Numier tilted his head and nodded, while puckering his mouth in a mildly chauvinistic manner, clearly approving of Don's beautiful new friend.

After all introductions were made, Numier wasted no time in deposing the doctor.

"What exactly happened?"

"What is your prognosis?"

"Will he be alright?"

"It's really too early to tell," said Dr. Packer. "Your friend was involved in an automobile accident and has suffered a significant head injury. Most people would not have survived the initial impact. I think the icy cold water in the stream may have played a part in reducing the cranial swelling and prolonging his survival."

"Are you saying he's dying?" barked Numier.

"No, No," said Dr. Packer.

"So then he'll be O.K.?" asked Amena.

"To tell you the truth Miss, I'm not quite sure . . . The first seventy-two hours are the most critical," answered the doctor.

The doctor then looked around the room and asked in a firm manner:

"Do you think I could speak with his family?"

"Unfortunately for the good Professor," said Numier, "I'm the closest thing to family he has. You see, he's made the study of theology his life's work, leaving very little time for family, or anything else for that matter. So what you need to say, you might as well say to us . . . Assuming your O.K. with that, Miss. Benjamin?" as he looked at her with lifted brow.

"I'd like to stay . . . if it's alright?" she replied while looking up to the men for approval.

Numier's eyebrows relaxed as he politely nodded.

"Well, the hospital requires that we follow strict protocol when it comes to patients' rights to privacy. Our insurance carrier prevents us from disclosing a patient's medical condition to anyone other than family, unless in a John Doe situation, and even then, there's a waiting period."

Numier realized that the seriousness of Don's condition would probably warrant contacting his family, and although they lived nearby, he was clear on his friend's wishes in such a situation.

"Don and I embark on somewhat regular anthropological excursions that can, at times, be dangerous. They require that we carry in our possession, contact information as well as a current will and testament. We named each other mutual executors of each others' living wills. I carry the paperwork in my brief case in the car."

"Very well then," exhaled the doctor, taking Numier at his word. "Can you tell me a bit about Mr. Goodwin . . . His hobbies, his profession, anything that might help us understand what led to his condition?"

"Don is a Theology instructor at Sierra High School," answered Numier. "He is well read and well versed in religion and is somewhat of an expert in the Testaments, Old and New, as well as many books relating to, but not included in, the Bible. Along with his many academic accomplishments, he has studied abroad extensively, including participating in several anthropological digs in the Middle East. And although his passion has taken him to far away lands, his home and his heart are in the foothills of Central California. His only hobby is his work, and until today, he was in pretty good health."

"Thank you for that," said Doctor Packer. "The test results reveal something very peculiar and rather astonishing in regards to your friend's injury."

"Like what?" interrupted Amena.

"Well, I'll try to explain . . . The human brain only utilizes approximately ten percent of its mass for cognitive thought. Somehow, Mr. Goodwin's injury has stimulated the remaining ninety percent. And it appears that in laymen's terms . . . his electrical impulses are firing on all cylinders!" excitedly stated the doctor.

"Is this a good thing?" cautiously asked Amena.

"I don't know . . . It might help explain how he survived the accident," he answered, "but beyond that . . ."

"I don't understand," interrupted Numier.

"Well it's rather fascinating," continued the Doctor. "You see . . . the human brain, when injured, swells as it bleeds internally. It seems that the functional portion of the brain floods first, causing pressure and restricting the flow of oxygen, resulting in irreparable damage to the sensitive tissues. But in this case, the entire brain is functioning at an alarming rate, thus minimizing bleeding and swelling by utilizing the increased blood flow."

"So to be clear, you're saying that the severity of the injury actually minimized the resulting brain damage?" said Numier trying to put a handle on the doctor's diagnosis.

"Yes . . . That is my hypothesis," replied the doctor.

"So is he going to be alright?" persisted Amena, pushing for some good news.

"Well, normally, whenever we see this kind of head trauma, we contact the family and begin discussing organ donation," the doctor stated insensitively.

"Oh my God!" she said.

"But in this case, we're all in uncharted territory. Again, this is my hypothesis, which we've not yet proven, but for now, your friend seems to be hanging on thanks to this very odd and very rare phenomenon of heightened brain activity, which could also explain the hallucinations," adds the doctor.

"Hallucinations?" said Numier. "The emergency crew on the ground told me he was found unconscious, several hundred yards from the crash site."

"Well . . . All I know is what I was told by the witness from the scene of the accident," replied the doctor. "Perhaps you should speak to the truck driver."

"What truck driver?" pressed Numier.

"The truck driver involved in the accident. He and his daughter are in the next room waiting to hear of your friend's condition," answered the doctor.

Amena and Numier immediately turned their attention to the waiting room just outside the glass wall of the I.C.U. There sat a rugged man, also in his early fifties, heavy set with a full beard. He wore a thick, red Pendleton shirt, faded blue jeans, and a baseball cap that read BULLS across the front. His boots were layered with mud, and his hands were large and darkened from the grime of engine work.

His eyes were deep-set and saddened, apparently by years of hard work and hardship. It was clear that he'd had a less than fortunate life intensified by the crawling pace of an existence measured in minutes. He was darkly tanned by years of working outdoors with the scars of a rough life displayed prominently in the crow's feet of his eyes.

He looked like a logging man, but something seemed out of place to Amena. Rather than a rough

and tough mountain of a man, the two found a man
visibly shaken and broken.

Amena and Numier entered the waiting room, and
upon doing so, the driver quickly stood and politely
removed his hat.

He stood at least six-feet, four-inches tall, and
every bit of three hundred pounds. A large man
by anyone's standards equaled only by his humble
posture.

Behind him stood a young girl. No more than
thirteen years old, she was small for her age and very
thin. She had long black hair that covered her face,
and her eyes, barely visible, were painted with black
makeup to match her lipstick.

She was facing the ground, uninterested in making
or participating in introductions. Her clothes were
ragged . . . She wore a torn black sweater over a
white lace long-sleeve shirt that puffed out at the
ends covering her hands but revealing short black
fingernails.

Being a teacher, Numier had seen Goth before and
wasn't remotely alarmed or impressed. Nor did her
demeanor seem uncommon for her age.

"Sir . . . My name is Numier, and this is Amena,"
extending his hand to shake.

"Please don't get up!" Amena said to the man.

Saying nothing, the driver shook both Numier and Amena's hands, then slowly sat back down while looking at his boots and fidgeting with his hat.

The girl took a few steps back and shuffled herself into the corner of the room. With her back to the wall she faced them all but kept her eyes on the floor. Her head tilted to one side parting her hair slightly exposing only a fraction of her face.

"Sir, we are friends of Professor Goodwin . . . We understand that you've been through a lot tonight . . . But if you wouldn't mind . . . Is there anything you can tell us about the accident that might help the doctors diagnose his condition?" Numier respectfully asked.

"I don't think so . . . I mean, I di'tn see 'em. I mean, I reached down to pick up a cassette tape from under my brake pedal, and the next thing I knew, I was jackknifed in the middle 'uh the road. Then I heard a loud crash, and saw a man lyen in the stream next to a small car wrapped around a tree," he said sheepishly.

"Wait a minute . . . Did you say he was lying next to the car?" interrupted Numier.

"Well, yeh, I mean, at first he was. But by the time I jumped down off my rig to see if he was alive . . . he was already half way down the stream, runnen like a madman."

"Running . . . Why was he running?" asked Numier, now somewhat suspicious.

"I don't know, I mean, I di'tn yell at 'em or anything, I mean, I di'tn do anything to scare 'em like that!" he answered somewhat defensively.

"What made you think he was scared?" asked Amena.

"Well, when I reached the stream he was already runnen. That's when he looked back, not at me . . . but past me. Kinda like thru me . . . like I wuden even there. Somethen musta spooked-'em real bad in that stream, I mean . . . I never saw fear like that-n-a man's eyes before!" he answered.

"Did he say anything?" asked Numier.

"No sir, not a word. I went to chase after 'em to see if I could help 'em, you know . . . to calm-eem down or somethin. But as soon as I got close to the white waters, he was gone . . . To tell ya the truth, I di'tn think he'd make it down the rapids with-em bleeden like that-n-all," he replied.

"Go on," said Amena sensing more.

"Well that's about it. I looked around and di'tn see any sight of 'em, so I ran back to my rig to radio for help, but I guess some bicyclers already called it in. And just like that, the helicopter was cummen to get 'em," said the driver.

The trucker seemed agitated and nervous when the physician walked into the room with possible news of the Professor's condition. Suddenly the girl stepped forward and stood directly behind the trucker as Amena sensed the change in the man's demeanor.

"Is there something you aren't telling us?" Amena suspiciously asked.

"Who me?" answered the trucker.

"Yes you . . . Come on, if there's something else, now's the time," urged Amena.

The young girl slowly lifted her head and as her hair parted she looked at Amena with one blue eye.

The driver looked down, trying to summon strength from within, and reluctantly said:

"O.K, well . . . I know this is gonna sound a bit weird . . . but it's like somethen strange happened in that there stream."

"Go on," she said as both Numier and the doctor turned to listen.

"Well . . . , when I reached the stream, and saw your friend looking back like that, I turned to see what'n the world he was runnin from, cause I ain't never been ascared a nothin in my whole life . . . , and that's when it happened," he said, noticeably shaken with moisture welling up in his eyes.

"That's when what happened?" pushed Numier.

"Well . . . It's like all the anger, hate, and ugliness in the whole world passed right through me. It hit me in the chest and knocked me down in the stream, and for the first time in my life, I felt ascared . . . I ain't never felt nothin like it!" he said as his eyes overflowed with tears.

"So is that when you left the stream?" asked Amena.

"Yes Mam . . . I'm sorry I lied . . . I'm ashamed to tell ya I never went as far as the rapids to help your friend. When I felt, what I felt, I ran directly to my truck to . . . Well . . . I guess, to run away. On the way to my truck, I looked back to see where he was headed, but he was gone," said the driver while beginning to whimper into the white, cotton handkerchief he pulled out of his back left pant's pocket.

"I believe you sir," said Amena, trying to calm and reassure the man. "And thank you for being so candid with us. I'm sure it wasn't easy."

Amena then took a step toward the girl . . . "You have beautiful eyes," she said as the young girl lowered her head again veiling her face.

"What's your name?" said Amena but there was no response.

"Its OK, you're not in any trouble . . . no one's gonna hurt you."

Then after a long pause the girl slowly lifted her head . . . "Clair," she answered in a soft raspy voice.

"What a beautiful name Clair . . . My name is Amena."

Both the physician and Numier were all but ready to dismiss the testimony of the driver, as his credibility was understandably in question. But as they turned their backs on him to quietly discuss the Professor's condition, the driver, turned to Amena and said:

"Excuse me Mam . . . I know it sounds crazy, and I swear I ain't been drinkin . . . but there was somethin in that stream with your friend . . . somethin real bad, and something I ain't never gonna forget!"

All three almost instinctively and simultaneously took deep breaths, while looking at one another.

"Well . . . What are we going to do with that?" Numier asked sarcastically.

Amena, feeling a great deal of compassion, kept her eyes on the trucker as he exited the waiting room, hunched forward with his head hung low and still fiddling with his hat.

"Wait!" said Amena. "Aren't you forgetting something?"

"I swear I told you everthing I know," he said from just outside the double doors.

"Your daughter," Amena added with lifted brow.

"Who her?" he said looking at the back of Clair. "She aint mine . . ."

"She's not with you?" asked Dr. Packer.

"No Sir," said the trucker. "I aint got no kids."

Amena and Numier both looked at Dr. Packer.

"The E.M.T.'s said they found her at the crash site . . . I just assumed . . ." said Dr. Packer.

"Clair honey . . . do you know this man?" asked Amena pointing suspiciously to the driver.

Clair just shook her head.

"Did you see the accident?" insensitively asked Numier.

Clair didn't respond.

"Maybe she was hitchhiking or something." Numier said to Dr. Packer.

Amena smirked at Numier as she softly moved the girls thin black hair and gently tucked it behind her right ear.

"Sweetie did you see the accident?" asked Amena and after a brief pause but without looking up, Clair answered:

"I was sitting behind the tree that your friend ran into."

"Oh my God!" said Amena. "Are you alright?"

But as Dr. Packer moved in to examine the girl, she pushed past the driver and ran down the hall.

"Clair!" yelled Amena.

"Let her go," said Numier. "We don't need the drama."

Amena just sneered at Numier with disgust as she craned her head out the double doors searching for Clair.

"Thank you for your time Sir . . . You're not obligated to stay here," said Dr. Packer to the trucker. And as the driver walked slowly down the hall, Dr. Packer turned to Amena and Numier:

"Obviously, the man has been affected by the trauma of the accident," said Doctor Packer. "He's feeling guilt over the Professor's injuries and wants desperately to find another party responsible. We see it all the time; he'll be himself in a day or two, and then maybe we'll get the full story," he confidently added.

"But what about the girl?" said Amena, concerned about her unhealthy appearance.

"Probably a foothill kid," said Dr. Packer. "Bored, with nothing better to do than hitch a ride with the E.M.T's . . . This is probably the most excitement she's had in a long time."

"Yea . . . I guess you're probably right," sighed Amena.

Numier and Amena accepted the plausibility of the doctor's assessment and headed back for the I.C.U.

As Numier returned through the glass doors of the I.C.U., his attention was diverted to the television set of an adjoining room. The set was wall mounted, approximately seven feet off the ground and positioned perfectly for Numier to see from the Professor's doorway. He couldn't help but notice the 'Breaking News' banner that rolled across the bottom of the screen. Stopping to watch, he saw a continuation of the alarming news he'd heard briefly in the car on the way to the hospital.

It was a local news feed from a major network affiliate. A young anchorwoman was delivering the story. Without any additional news to report, she reiterated the facts Numier heard earlier with the exception of the follow-up story on the mounting tension between the countries in the China region. She ended by stating that the President of the United States would be addressing the Nation in anticipation of a possible nuclear conflict.

Upon returning to the I.C.U., Amena approached the Professor and held his limp hand in hers while looking at him with heartfelt concern. Though heavily bandaged, she managed to carefully wipe the dried blood from his forehead with a damp cloth. She was still a bit shocked by the trucker's odd story and was saddened by his assertion that Don was afraid in the stream.

"You seem very familiar with him . . . Are you a student?" muttered Numier, as he entered the room, somewhat taken aback by the irregularity of such a show of affection by a student toward her teacher.

"No, not quite . . . Tonight was our first date," she answered softly. "We were to meet at the football game then out for a bite to eat."

"Forgive me; I didn't know. It seems that Don has kept you a secret . . . even from me." Numier replied.

"We were only just reacquainted today after close to six years," she said.

The doctor reentered the room, and while thumbing through the Professor's chart said:

"I've given him a sedative that will temporarily slow down his brain activity to a manageable rate. It's not a permanent fix, as we have no idea when or if his brain activity will stabilize."

"You mean slow down the other ninety percent?" asked Numier.

"Well, actually, all of it, given that the medication doesn't discriminate. I believe his brain has done a good job of protecting itself against the body's reaction to the injury, and I think the danger of further swelling is minimal," said the doctor.

"Will the sedative help him recover?" asked Amena.

"That I can't say with any degree of confidence. But I do believe that when or if he does regain consciousness, the medication will impede any further hallucinations, or at least until we can understand more about this rare phenomena," stated the doctor. "But until his brain activity finds its own equilibrium, it's very important that he not miss his medication. And be sure he takes it as directed. Too much could render him virtually comatose."

"Yes, absolutely . . ." concurred Numier.

And as the doctor made his rounds through the dimly-lit halls of the scarcely-staffed hospital, Numier and Amena settled in for what would prove to be the longest night of their lives.

CHAPTER IV
THE AWAKENING
❧

The hospital was dark; it was three o'clock in the
morning, and the skeleton crew tirelessly roamed
the antiseptic corridors. The I.C.U was dim and
quiet with only the sounds of machinery beeping,
calibrating, and robotically monitoring the
Professor's every breath.

Amena was calmly sleeping, curled up in a fetal
position on a soft chair in the corner of the room.
Her hair flowed gently over her peacefully sleeping
face, as her beauty would transcend even the coldest
and darkest of hospital rooms.

Numier leaned over the Professor and began to
turn the volume down on the machine monitoring
the Professor's heart rate. Just as he touched it, the
Professor's heart beat quickened and a loud beep
emanated from the machine alerting the nurse to
a problem. A startled Numier looked down at the
Professor. In a state of heightened consciousness,
the Professor's eyes were wide open, fixed, and
dilated. His eyes gazed through Numier with terror
and panic. Numier grabbed him firmly by both
shoulders, and being careful not to shake him said:

"Don . . . Hey Goodwin . . . It's me Numier! Its
O.K . . . You're going to be alright . . ."

With an elevated heart rate, and panic in his eyes, the Professor slowly began to focus on Numier.

The I.C.U. nurse rushed to the Professor's bedside quickly removing his breathing apparatus as he coughed and struggled to speak.

"Did you see it . . .?!" He whispered loudly with a raspy, cracking voice.

"See what?" said Numier.

"The beast! Did you see it?!" he shouted while grimacing and clearing his scratchy throat.

"No . . . There aren't any beasts here, Don . . . You're safe. There's no one here but us. You've been in an accident, and you've been hallucinating," said Numier, trying to reassure the Professor though also rather shaken by the condition of his friend.

The Professor looked around the room, franticly studying it for signs of danger. Amena, now on her feet and at the Professor's bedside, was hesitant, visibly unsure of his reaction to her presence. Upon seeing her, he reached for her hand. And while still catching his breath, he struggled to speak:

"I'm glad you're here . . . I'm so sorry about our date."

Relieved that she wasn't overstepping her bounds and that he remembered her at all, her spirits were given a boost as she tried in earnest to disguise her underlying concerns regarding his injuries.

"Well, it's nothing a little groveling wouldn't cure," she softly said with a smile.

"You've been in an accident, and you've suffered a pretty nasty head injury," said Numier. "The doctors weren't sure if you were going to make it, but it looks like you're going to be O.K."

"Keep talking to him; it's calming him down," said the nurse studying the heart monitor.

The doctor entered the room slightly out of breath as he was on the other side of the ward when the heart monitor sounded. The room was clearly his with his arrival interrupting everyone:

"Well, Well . . . It appears that our sleepy head has decided to join us after all," he said in a doctoral attempt at humor. "You've experienced significant head trauma Mr. Goodwin. Apparently you drove head on into an enormous tree, and until just recently, I feared the oak the victor," he added as he studied the readings printing off the monitors.

"Don . . . Do you remember anything?" asked Numier.

The Professor closed his eyes, paused, and took a deep breath.

"It's O.K. if you don't." reassured the doctor. "It's perfectly normal to experience some degree of amnesia after such an event."

"No," interrupted the Professor. "I remember everything. In fact, I can even picture specific details from my infancy, things I in no way remembered before," he said breathing deeply.

"Just keep breathing . . . We need to get your heart rate down," said the doctor.

"Was anyone else hurt?" asked the Professor.

"No. The only other person involved was a truck driver," answered Numier.

"Yes. I remember him. If I'm not mistaken, he was still fumbling around the floorboard of his truck when I was flying through the air," added the Professor.

"Was there a girl with him?" asked Amena.

"No, he was alone."

The doctor momentarily took his eyes off the charts and turned his attention to his patient. Inquisitive of his acute recollection and encouraged by his apparent progress, he instructed the nurse to remove the ventilator from the room.

"Wow . . . I'm impressed. Not too many people have recall this soon after a head trauma," said Dr. Packer. "And not near as accurate."

"Has anyone spoken to him?" eagerly asked the Professor.

"Yes. Actually, he was here for quite a while waiting to hear of your condition," answered Amena.

"Did HE see it?" desperately asked the Professor.

Numier looked at Amena, the nurse, then back to the Professor with empathy:

"No Don. No one saw anything. The truck driver said you were alone. The doctor gave you a sedative designed to slow down your brain activity. You see, the doctor diagnosed you as having sustained a rare form of brain injury that heightens the level of brain activity. The rarity of your type of injury is that it causes your brain to function at or near full capacity, rather than the normal ten percent. He believes that a by-product of your injury may be hallucinations."

The doctor went on to explain the Professor's injuries in more clinical detail. He told the Professor that the medication administered was only temporary. He urged that the Professor take the medication at the exact time indicated, as the effects begin and end rather suddenly. He assured the Professor that he was in good hands, and after a few more tests, they should be closer to a more permanent treatment regarding this unique phenomenon. The Professor put his hands over his face and closed his eyes in deep thought and concentration.

"Do you think Amena and I could have a word with our friend alone, Doc.?" requested Numier.

The doctor and nurse both obligingly left the room, urging them to push the call button if the Professor's condition should change in any way.

"I don't blame you for sending them out," said the Professor. "It just seemed so real . . . I feel like I've lost my mind."

"You're among friends now son. There's nothing here that can harm you," calmly stated Numier.

"I feel a bit loopy . . . not quite myself," said the Professor. "I can't seem to get the images out of my mind."

"I'll tell you what . . . Why don't you tell us what you think you saw. I'll take notes, then later when you review them, you'll have less anxiety, and your hallucinations will seem more like distant memories, like bedtime stories read to you as a child, or an article in a magazine you picked up at the airport," suggested Numier.

"I see you've been dabbling in psychiatry in your spare time, hey Numier . . . Am I your next lab rat?"

asked the Professor, as he squirmed uncomfortably in the bed.

Amena smiled and squeezed the Professor's hand with encouragement.

"I see you haven't lost your sense of humor my good man," laughed Numier.

The Professor took in a deep breath and began with the accident, explaining and describing everything down to the smallest detail. As his story unfurled, Amena and Numier sat by his side. And while Amena held his hand, the Professor went into a sort of story-telling trance.

He recalled the beasts even more clearly than when he experienced them. He was able to pick a scene from the battle at will, and study it and all of its surroundings that may have gone completely unnoticed at the time of his encounter. He was able to describe plants growing between far off rocks in the background of a battle scene with haunting accuracy, down to their genus, species, and continental origin.

He then went on to describe the Cherubim with their many different facades and their Roman-battle gear, down to the smallest details of their armament. He and Numier agreed that the Cherubim were figures from the Bible and more than likely a figment of his long-term memory.

But upon studying the pictures in his minds eye, he noticed hundreds of Seraphim camouflaged within sycamores randomly scattered throughout the foothills. He also recalled Seraphim flying along side Cherubim as they descended onto the stream, but then pulling up just short of engagement only to circle high above the encounter.

The beasts were still a bit of a mystery. He described their horrifying morbidity in vivid detail. Their bodies were as he remembered them, but his enhanced recall illuminated their varying horn styles. Some brandished the horns of bulls while many possessed the downward turned horns of the Cape buffalo. The Professor stated unequivocally that he'd never before seen such beasts, and since he was eerily able to recall everything he'd ever seen, heard or read, even from as early as his infancy, his testimony seemed credible.

The Professor went on for a little over an hour before finally falling back into a deep sleep. Amena was exhausted but still offered to stay and let Numier go home to freshen up and get some sleep.

"I think I'll take you up on your offer my dear." Numier said with a measure of resolve in his eyes. "There is something about this story that calls to me . . . I'll need to get to my computer." And without another word, Numier hurried home.

Amena pulled the soft corner chair closer to the Professor's side, curled up like a small kitten, and fell fast asleep.

CHAPTER V

THE VISITOR

Several hours later, Amena was awakened by the sounds of monitors beeping loudly. She jerked upright in her seat to see the Professor's empty bed and staff members rushing into the room. She then looked over her shoulder and was surprised by the sight of the Professor standing at the window staring out at the flatlands of the San Joaquin Valley. He had apparently woken up in a panic and rushed to the window with wires and saline bags dragging behind him. He was oblivious to the nurse's mumblings as she methodically disconnected him from his many accoutrements.

It was just before dawn, and as the sun rose slowly over the Sierra Nevadas, the overcast sky swirled with the colors of pale violet and lilac, which cast a dullish grey hue across the room.

The ICU was situated on the fourth floor, over one hundred feet off the ground. This elevation, in an otherwise level valley floor, afforded the Professor a view of nearly twenty miles in any direction. He scanned over miles of farmlands, lush with almond trees, pistachio orchards, and grape vineyards as well as several valley cities that popped out of the flatlands like stalagmites. As he inquisitively searched for anything out of the norm, he couldn't help but wonder if the battle he had witnessed could also have been taking place in the cities and countryside below, or for that matter . . . worldwide.

"Could there be beasts and Angels fighting right outside these walls?" he thought as he peered straight down at the hospital's parking lot.

He squinted his eyes tightly and mumbled:

"My God . . . What am I thinking? I must be going crazy."

Although the medication slowed the hyperactive function of his brain, the Professor still received added benefits from his newfound abilities. He was able to remember deep into his past . . . and on up to the present.

He recalled a time in his early childhood, when he was not much more than a toddler. It was near the beginning of autumn, and his older brother had gone off to begin the school year, leaving him home alone with his mother. He and she would sit quietly in the maple and loquat tree-lined backyard and peacefully watch as the leaves changed color with the changing of the season.

They could see the vibrant colors of yellow and gold as the leaves from pomegranate trees began to fall. The trees took on a dormant, almost lifeless, appearance leaving behind their beautiful pink and maroon-colored fruit, engorged with juice from the first autumn rains. He remembered the stories his mother would make up about the neighborhood animals that had come to call on them in their yard. Birds and squirrels became characters in a play as they visited from miles around to enjoy the ruby red fruit that spilled out nutrients from skins that could no longer contain them.

His vivid recall of the blood-red viscera of the pomegranate fruit quickly turned to visions of gore and violence he'd witnessed just hours before. But before his mind could drag him unwillingly back to the horror, a voice pleasantly interrupted:

"How long have you been awake?" softly asked Amena.

The Professor was hardly able to entertain anything other than the images he was so intensely pondering:

"It just seemed too real to have been a hallucination," he said.

"The mind is a powerful thing Don," she replied while stretching and yawning in her chair. "Besides, as far as I know, no one has reported any ten-foot tall, hell beasts roaming the foothills of the Sierras."

The Professor didn't laugh. He just faced the window with a far away look in his eyes. Finally realizing that there was someone in the room who actually cared about him and his condition, he turned to her and said with half a smile:

"Some first date, hey Benjamin?"

"I don't like football anyway," she yawned and replied with a smile.

He paused, suddenly realizing just how very genuine she was and how lucky he was to have been reunited with her after all these years. And for a moment, he felt courageous. It was as if he'd somehow changed in that brief moment in the stream, no longer afraid to live:

"My God you're beautiful!" he said while studying her face. "You may be the most beautiful thing I've ever seen."

As she heard and watched the words roll off of his lips, she felt the tingling excitement of a child. But rather than reveal the depth of her emotions, she remained acutely aware of their hospital surroundings, as she struggled to speak through the lump in her throat:

"You're a sweet guy Goodwin, but after ten hours in a hospital chair, I'm not exactly at my best . . . Come on now; let's get you cleaned up a little."

Amena then took the Professor's arm and began leading him slowly to the bathroom when Numier entered the room in a rush. His eyes were bloodshot with dark bags under them:

"I've been up all night racking my brain trying to remember where I'd seen your monsters before, Goodwin. It's times like these when I could use that super-brain of yours," he said plunking himself down on Amena's chair.

"Why didn't you tell me you recognized them?" asked the Professor.

"Well, I wasn't sure that I had, but while driving home . . . I remembered. Years ago, I read parts of a book about Angels and monsters battling over the plight of Mankind. At the time, it seemed too far-fetched to commit to memory. But after hearing the details and reviewing my notes of your hallucination, I was sure it was the same," said Numier.

"Where is it? I mean, do you have it?" excitedly asked the Professor.

"No, No. I couldn't remember where I saw it, or even its name, but after several hours on the Internet, I did manage to locate a book that tells a story of Angels and beasts matching your descriptions in the Library of Ancient books in Sacramento," replied Numier. "It must be the same book."

"Well what's the name of it man?" yelled the Professor.

"'THE CHERUBIM FIELDS'," answered Numier studying the Professor's face for a visible response.

"I've never heard of it . . ." he said, looking down in disappointment.

"I thought for sure that hearing the title would help jog your memory, Don."

"I agree that it should have, but nothing," replied the Professor, closing his eyes and straining to remember.

"Do you think that maybe actually seeing this book might help you?" asked Amena.

"How could it hurt . . .? Maybe I'll recognize something that will rouse my memory. I mean, I must have seen this book someplace before, and I'm somehow blocking it out. Seeing it again might help me make some sense of it all," replied the Professor as he quickly put his jacket on over his hospital gown.

Numier, unsure of the Professor's condition asked:

"Are you feeling alright Don?"

And with a look of determination in his eyes, the Professor replied:

"I've never felt better."

"Shouldn't we wait for the Doctor; I mean is he O.K. to leave?" anxiously asked Amena.

"Nothing can stop him now . . . You might as well let him go." said Numier.

"Well, he's not going anywhere without me!" replied Amena, grabbing her bag and his things while hurrying to catch up.

"We can take my car, but someone else has to drive so that I can sleep," said Numier as he led them down the hall to the elevators.

Just about half way down the corridor; the Professor and Amena were separated from Numier by a triage of nurses and doctors as they hurried to a room on the other side of the hall.

It was a maternity room in the I.C.U ward for high-risk deliveries. As several nurses and doctors converged around an incubator, a new mother could clearly be seen through the gurney-sized door opening to her room. She and her baby had been diagnosed with toxemia. A rare condition where the mother's body is unable to filter the toxins created during pregnancy resulting in the inevitable poisoning of both she and her fetus.

Nine weeks premature and very ill, the baby had to be delivered. The young mother was still birthing the placenta when a loud buzzer began to sound.

Amena and the Professor were trapped between oncoming personnel and an army of machinery that was hurriedly being rolled into the room. One of the attending Physicians shouted:

"Code Blue . . . we're losing her!"

Up to this point, the young mother didn't even know her baby's gender.

Her panic set in like a frantic gazelle when the lions come for her fawn.

"Noooo!" she screamed. "My baby! What's happening to my baby?`!"

Her screams sent chills down the Professor's spine as tears of sadness and horror began to stream down the face of Amena. She grabbed the Professor's arm and squeezed it for strength while they watched in shock knowing that the trauma of this young woman, a complete stranger to them, had now become part of their journey.

Amena and the Professor remained frozen in the hall just outside the room, as the young mother excruciatingly struggled against her instincts to keep quiet at the urging of the medical staff.

The two looked agonizingly upon the silent intensity of doctors, nurses, and machinery all working together in organized chaos like a well-designed, cohesive unit.

Although his first instincts were to look away, something compelled the Professor to keep his focus on the scene. He curiously noticed a man standing between the lead nurse and Doctor Packer. He caught the Professor's eye particularly because he wasn't wearing the typical hospital attire.

He was extremely tall and slender, resembling a professional athlete. He was dressed in a solid white suit with a white satin tie. He was looking at the baby with the sincerity and familiarity of a close member of the immediate family. And as he gazed at the infant with profound compassion, the baby just barely able to see, reached up, and with a tiny hand, tenderly grabbed the big man's index finger and held it tightly.

The Professor looked upon the man with unusual interest, which initially caught the tall man off guard. And then, without taking his attention away from the baby for even a second, the lofty gentleman lifted his face toward the Professor and addressed him in a soft, whispering voice, calmly asking:

"Can you see me?"

Just then Numier shouted from the open doorway of the elevator oblivious to their situation:

"Are you guys coming or not!?"

And in the brief second it took for the Professor to look at Numier and then quickly look back . . . the tall man was gone. And the baby lay lifeless on the table. Suddenly, a deafening silence filled the air only to be interrupted by the sounds of pain.

"Noooo!" Screamed the mother; intuitively sensing her baby had died.

In an instant, the hopes and dreams of an entire family were crushed. With the young mother's screams of grief ushering in the sadness, a measurable heaviness pressed down upon the hospital.

And as the doctors and nurses tried franticly to revive their tiny patient, chests tightened and lungs filled with the sweet smelling pheromones of sorrow that wafted cruelly and indiscriminately throughout the hospital corridors.

Not able to endure another second, Amena pushed the Professor past the congested hallway and on toward the elevator. The Professor's compassion and concern for the young mother was clouded by his puzzlement concerning the tall man's disappearance at the exact instant that the baby had died.

Could the tall man have been another hallucination of some kind? But the medication was supposed to have been working, so why would he be seeing things? His confusion was apparent to the others, but after explaining the particulars of his sighting, they were not at all surprised. They collectively deduced that his brain was playing tricks on him while still stabilizing to the medication.

Deeply distressed and extremely moved by the scene she'd just witnessed, Amena couldn't help but wonder if she would ever have children of her own? And if she did, would her baby fall victim to the same fate as the young mother's in the ICU. She wondered if she would have the strength to live after suffering such a catastrophic loss . . .

And without saying another word, the three of them hurried to the car and embarked on a journey to find the answers to so many questions.

CHAPTER VI
ANCIENT BOOKS

It was roughly a three-hour drive that took closer to four given that Amena refused to travel any faster than the posted speed limit. With her hands, white-knuckled, grasping the wheel firmly at the ten and two position, it was evident that she wasn't about to speed up, let alone change lanes. Despite being a lengthy drive, the time passed by quickly with the three bouncing back and forth from discussing the Professor's hallucinations, to listening intently to the coverage of the building China conflict.

"Do you think China will actually make good on their threats . . . Do you think they'll actually start a war?" Amena asked naively.

"Why shouldn't they . . ." Numier replied. "Virtually every country in the world has, as soon as they were militarily able, destroyed their neighbor in the interest of increasing their boundaries. Some have even gone so far as to suggest that the inevitable occupation of their neighbor was in an effort to civilize a more savage race of people. It's only natural."

"It's only ridiculous!" barked Amena. "I mean, just because some poor country is without significant resources possibly due to their geographic or environmental limitations, and falls behind, doesn't mean that a super power should just roll in and occupy them, selling to the world that it's for their own good. It's nothing short of barbaric!"

"I didn't say it was right, only that it's human nature," huffed Numier.

"Please . . ." interrupted the Professor. Something tells me the two of you shouldn't discuss politics, that is, at least not in a confined space."

"Oh, come on Don. Political debate is healthy now and then, not to mention invigorating. And more times than not, you'll find that opposing viewpoints aren't always as polar as they seem. Sometimes people tend to say the same thing but in different ways."

Amena laughed at herself and returned her concentration to the road. She noticed the red light illuminating the 'E' on her gas gage.

"We'd better stop for gas soon . . . we're on empty," she said as she slowed down for the next off ramp.

"I got this," said Numier reaching for his wallet as they rolled to a stop.

While Numier pumped, Amena and the Professor got out and went to the rear of the car to stretch their legs. Amena leaned against the trunk of the car. She stood with her head tilted to one side as her hair spilled over her shoulder like a super model posing for a magazine cover. The Professor just stood in awe of her beauty.

"You missed your calling," he said. "You really should have been a model."

He'd hoped for a positive response to his attempt at a compliment, but there was no answer.

She wasn't posing, but listening, with her head cocked to one side.

"Did you hear that?" she asked.

"Hear what?" said Goodwin, relieved that it wasn't his compliment she was ignoring.

"Don, pop the trunk!" she yelled.

Goodwin rushed to the driver's side and pulled the lever with the open trunk lid diagram on it.

"Oh my God! shrilled Amena, as the trunk lid opened.

Curled up between the spare tire and an old toolbox was a young girl.

"It's Clair! shouted Amena reaching into the trunk. She carefully helped the frail child out of the cramped compartment that she'd been laying in for hours.

"Great, this is all we need!" shouted Numier as he rammed the nozzle back into the pump.

Clair squealed loudly as she pushed to straighten her legs while rolling her head back and forth to loosen it.

"What are you doing here?" asked Amena holding Clair's face in her hands.

Clair just looked down.

"Now's not the time to be quiet Sweetie," Amena said slowing down a bit. "Now . . .what are you doing here?"

"I want to stay with you," she answered softly.

"Do you know what trouble you're in young lady?" shouted Numier. "Your parents must be worried sick."

"He's right Clair," said the Professor. "We need to call your parents."

"No . . ." said Clair.

"Her parents have probably already called the police," said Numier.

"I don't have parents," interrupted Clair.

"Everyone has parents sweetie," said Amena.

"They're dead," said Clair.

"Oh honey . . . said Amena as she hugged Clair.

Numier just smirked at the Professor, suspicious of her story.

"Where do you live Clair?" asked the Professor.

"Near the tree you hit," she said still clinging onto Amena.

"With who Clair?" he asked.

"No one," she said.

"Well there must be someone looking for her," yelled Numier. "They'll say we kidnapped her like that trucker probably did."

"Easy Gene," said the Professor. "No one's gonna say we kidnapped her."

"Let her stay here at the gas station then," said Numier.

"Oh please . . ." said Amena. "Have you lost your mind?"

"Listen . . . we're almost to Sacramento . . . let's just find the book and get her back to the hospital . . ." said the Professor. "Someone there should be able to help her."

"Keeping her with us is a bad idea," growled Numier as Amena got in the back seat with Clair.

After a few short turns off the highway, they found themselves in the heart of Sacramento's Civic Center and the Capital of California. As they searched for the entrance to the Capital Library, lawyers and politicians hustled about completely unaware of the quest that was commencing before them.

The Sacramento Civic Center was striking with its plethora of sculpted topiary gardens and hedge-lined pathways that meandered through a myriad of formal-looking buildings. And even though the Professor and Numier had traveled extensively, they were still impressed by the grand marble and bronze structures that surrounded the capital. Each building was toothed with large, silver-veined, white-marble columns that likened themselves to smaller versions of the Capital buildings in Washington D.C.

Despite being clueless as to the exact location of the library, Numier and the Professor refused to ask for directions while moving quickly from building to building inspecting each individual directory. Amena, however, possessing a more reasonable ego, waved down a passing, would-be politician, and politely asked for assistance.

Once in the library, Numier knew right where to go. It was one of the only libraries in the country that had an ancient books section, that is, original books written over five hundred years ago. And although many of them were displayed behind the protection of Plexiglas, simply being in the presence of such literary classics was exhilarating to say the least.

While they searched the shelves for the illusive text, they spoke giddily, like children on Easter morning, each proclaiming their find:

"Dante's Inferno!" the Professor whispered loudly.

"I've got 'The Iliad' over here!" softly exclaimed Amena.

"Yes, Yes, I have it at home," replied Numier.

"No . . . I mean the original," she replied.

After an extensive search by all three . . . they had all but given up.

"I don't think its here Gene," said Goodwin moving toward the exit. "Let's just go."

"I could have sworn it was here," disappointedly murmured Numier.

"Come on Clair," said Amena from the end of the isle. But Clair didn't move.

"Clair honey . . . lets go," said Amena as she approached to help guide Clair out.

"Wait!" said Amena. "There it is."

Directly in front of Clair, in the back of the section, covered in dust and spider webs, was the only copy of THE CHERUBIM FIELDS in the entire Western World. It was a book that, although brilliantly written in Aramaic, was banned by the Vatican many centuries ago. And it, like so many things of its time, was not easily understood or at all politically accepted.

During the crusades, exposing New Testament theology and challenging the teachings of the Catholic Church was considered heresy and not tolerated. It was determined to have been the work of religious radicals, and all copies ordered burned by the Vatican.

A private collector managed to locate and protect the book, saving the original from sure destruction. A few copies of the original were meticulously duplicated only to fall into the tyrannical hands of Eastern European Governments. In the early nineteen-fifties, one of the four-hundred year old copies was translated into the Queen's English and buried in an underground bunker in the remote German countryside. After the fall of the Berlin Wall, the antique copy and its translation were discovered and sent to Geneva for safekeeping along with dozens of other manuscripts previously thought lost or destroyed.

Sacramento, being the Capital of California and residence to many influential, political, and religious figure-heads, applied for the copy. Due to the

City Library's location being in the heart of the Capital Building, along with its depth of references, combined with its twenty-four hour, on-site security and two-foot-thick fire-proof walls, it became the only library in the Western World to host such an impressive collection of rare and ancient books.

"Good girl Clair," said Goodwin as he gently pulled the book from it's dusty shelf and handed it to Numier.

Numier had convinced the librarian that because of his many academic credentials, he could be trusted to safely handle the book. Appreciating its rarity and possible relevance to the Professor's recovery, Numier handled it with the utmost of care, cautiously opening each page only two-thirds of the way, attempting painstakingly not to damage the spine of the historical object.

As they began to peruse the frail sheepskin pages of the ancient artifact, it became evident that the Professor must have seen it before. The book was filled with illustrations, hand drawn in child-like simplicity. The beasts, the Cherubim, the Seraphim, and the foothills were all exactly as the Professor had described them. It was as though he was seeing a version of his own story from someone else's vantage.

"My God," whispered Amena. "Is this similar to what you saw?"

"This is exactly what I saw!" replied the Professor.

Numier then placed the translation along side the illustrated Aramaic copy, and after synchronizing the two, began to read aloud as the tale unfolded:

"And there was war in heaven. Michael and his angels fought against the dragon, and the dragon and his angels fought back. But he was not strong enough, and they lost their place in heaven. The great dragon was hurled down– that ancient serpent called the Devil, or Satan, who leads the whole world astray. He was hurled to the earth, and his angels with him."[8]

"That's Revelations." Amena said.

"Yes it is . . ." replied the Professor.

At first, Numier thought the book to be some sort of radical interpretation of the Bible as it quoted the Bible in many areas. But upon further reading, it became clear to them, that this was something completely different. It was a fictional story based on Biblical principals. And though many of the players were of Biblical origin, they were engaged in a struggle unfamiliar to even the most learned of theologians.

The author of the book made numerous attempts, both expressed and implied, to avoid the reader's misinterpretation as to what was Biblical and what was fictional, as well as avoiding any attempt at rewriting, adding to, or insinuating anything contrary to the Bible's teachings.

The book went on to explain its events in salient detail:

At the moment of Satan's outcast from Heaven, there began a war on earth. The war was not one to overthrow God; the Devil had already lost that war. Instead it was a battle to physically join and overcome Mankind. Satan was not satisfied with living in the dark corners of Man's will, providing an alternative to good. He wanted to walk the earth and rule over Mankind as the Supreme Being second to none.

The Bible speaks of the Devil's earthly walk in Revelations, but only after a series of events in accordance with the Scriptures. But in pure Satanic fashion, this just wasn't good enough. For thousands of years, Satan attempted to march the earth, free to wield his dark sword of despair, only to be held back by the Angelic forces of God . . . Forces that consist of hosts of Angels created solely for the purpose of battling evil.

The book went on to explain that although the war is fought on earth, Man is incapable of seeing or participating in it, as it exists in an alternate dimension . . . A dimension in which Mankind is not intended to unite, view, or even be aware of, at least not until the end of days. . . A celestial dimension called, 'The Cherubim Fields.'

It is a dimensional battleground where Satan along with his army of Dark Angels and conjured beasts fight for the very future of Mankind. The book goes on to explain that Satan must rid The Cherubim Fields of each and every Angel before he is able to cross dimensions. And with the fall of the last Cherub, they will set in motion an unchangeable sequence of events the Bible refers to as Revelations.

As Numier continued reading the ancient book, he arrived at the main body of the text, which focused heavily on the Archangel of the Lord, Gabriel. He read to the Professor and Amena that Gabriel was encapsulated in a hellish tomb. He was trapped there almost two thousand years ago by Satan who swore revenge upon Gabriel for escorting him to hell on a lightning bolt in the very beginning. Hastened into the earth's atmosphere, the serpent was burned beyond recognition and stripped of his Angelic beauty by Gabriel as they fell. Gabriel, on the other hand, prepared by God for the descent, was tempered by the extreme heat created upon re-entering the earth's atmosphere and made all but invincible.

The tomb was a vast cave forged of granite and metals stronger than any created by Man. It was impenetrable, and there were no escape routes. The only hope for Gabriel's release would be from the Hand of God or by a single, large, cast-iron skeleton key; an irreplicable original, fashioned at the time of the tomb's creation and under the constant protection of Satan.

Gabriel, held captive in darkness, had been slaying beasts, sent by Satan for one thousand years never tiring and never stopping. Satan, in an effort to defeat him, created beasts one hundred times stronger than the ones before, but his efforts were always unsuccessful. He even stooped to employ surprise tactics in an effort to destroy Gabriel.

There was a time early on in Gabriel's confinement when, for two hundred years, Satan attempted to drive Gabriel mad with anticipation. The Devil sent no beasts, nothing at all . . . just emptiness. Gabriel stood without flinching or blinking for two hundred years when suddenly, out of the abyss, came a small earthworm-size serpent. It was traveling at the speed of light, and heading straight for Gabriel's heart. Gabriel reacted with a speed not visible to the human eye, and with one swipe, destroyed the tiny beast in flight. He then, while clinching the dead creature in his fist, screamed into the abyss:

"Come On . . .! Is that all you've got . . .! Bring me your best!!!"

Since that day, Satan has thrown everything in his arsenal at Gabriel, hoping for a mistake or a miniscule lapse of concentration that would afford him the opportunity to deliver a fateful blow to the Mighty Angel.

As the three read silently together, they come across a conversation between Gabriel and Satan. It was in the order of 1,000 A.D. At such time, Satan paid

Gabriel a visit in his tomb, which he made a point of doing every half-century or so.

As Satan approached Gabriel in the tomb, Gabriel was engaged in a fierce battle with several fire-breathing dragons. One thousand years of incarceration had all but maddened the Mighty Angel as he laughed crazily while chopping wildly at the creatures. Seemingly unaffected by the beasts fiery discharge, Gabriel dove straight into the flames and plunged his sword deep into the mouth of the largest dragon, laughing loudly in palpable distain for its creator.

Gabriel is an Archangel, one of an elite few. Although capable of many things, these Angels were created with a singular purpose . . . to fight evil. And though not as large as Michael, Gabriel is a stunning Manlike creature. He stands twelve-feet tall with the sculpted body of Michael Angelo's statue of David and the face of an ancient Greek warrior. His hair is golden brown, and his eyes are as blue as an early morning summer sky. His wings are of forged titanium and span some thirty-feet when fully expanded. When not in use, they retract back into his shoulder blades and disappear completely as not to hinder his abilities on foot. He is the perfect fighting machine, a threat from both sky and land.

As Gabriel stood peering into vast darkness awaiting his next foe, a soft but none-the-less evil voice was heard from behind him. It was a low hissing sound, barely audible to the human ear but powerfully piercing and ringing in the brain of the Archangel:

"You know you will never leave this place Gabriel . . ." hissed Satan while crouching behind two ten-foot tall beasts.

Upon hearing the voice of death, Gabriel knew he was about to be lead into the same conversation he'd had dozens of times for nearly a thousand years. And although the conversation was quintessentially futile in nature, he welcomed the opportunity to refute and vex his fallen brother.

Without looking back, he instinctively thrusted his sword rearward, mortally wounding one of the sacrificial beasts he knew would be shielding the serpent. Without ever taking his eyes off the abyss, he turned to face his adversary. Standing less than a stone's throw away, and cowering behind several massive, scaly-beasts, was a small, burned out relic of the once mighty Angel of the Lord.

It was at this point in the story that Amena was nearing her darkness threshold. Early on in her childhood, she'd create a mental and emotional barrier, protecting her from thoughts and images that were too frightening to entertain. But bravely and out of loyalty to the Professor, she remained engaged, but no longer willing to read along, she sat back and let the men continue.

Clair, wanting nothing to do with the book, quietly moved and sat a table away with her back to the trio.

Numier and the Professor, on the other hand, were extremely interested in the depictions of the bad as well as the good. Nevertheless, the Professor in seeing the disturbed look on Amena's face, stopped reading and sat beside her, as Numier continued reading aloud:

Satan is darkened by soot from head to toe. He is an emaciated vestige with virtually no significant physical power. He stands in a hunched posture, stiff and rigid from burn scarring throughout his entire body. No longer retractable, his wings droop down from his shoulder blades to the center of his back. They were singed off in the fall, leaving only diminutive skeletal scaffolds that weep blood serum incessantly from their ends. He has deep-set, black, pupilless eyes that rake hatefully at Gabriel. And although his face has flawless bone structure, he is bald with no facial hair and fused stubs that were once ears. Embarrassed and ashamed by his appalling and putrid appearance, and the constant reminder of the events that lead to such disfigurement, the Devil cloaks himself in darkness.

"Well, well . . . To what do I credit THIS visit . . . Oh unholy one? Are you here to mock me again . . . or to surrender?" asked Gabriel, crazy-eyed with laughter.

"I've come to check on my beast's progress, and to extinguish any hope you may have of ever breathing the sweet smell of air again!" Satan said, while simultaneously reviving the fallen beast with a wave of his hand.

In an effort to avoid another pass of Gabriel's sword, Satan stepped back and once again pulled the revitalized beast in front of him, only to witness another swift death as the unstoppable blade of Gabriel's broadsword beheaded the massive creature.

"Do you really believe you can beat me . . . my brother!" Satan shouted, frustrated by his beasts' performance.

Now serious and breathing heavily, Gabriel looked at him through sweaty brow.

"When the Son of God returns, you will be under my knife!" said the Mighty Angel while pointing his sword at Satan.

"The Son of God? Do you really think he cares for you?

Lowering Himself to the level of man, walking among them, and after what they did to Him!" Satan said.

"You mean what HE did for them!" Gabriel replied. "For it was you . . . who he carried to the cross."

Satan growled through pursed lips and said:

"Yes, I cannot deny my role in that tragedy."

"He will return to deliver Man to the Father, and then your fate will be sealed!" confidently stated Gabriel.

"You are a fool, Gabriel. If you would have joined forces with me in the beginning, we could have defeated Him!" said Satan.

"Your pride and arrogance have always been your downfall brother. You cannot defeat Him. All the Angels in Heaven and hell together couldn't even cast a shadow upon Him. You and I are created beings . . . creatures no more able to defeat Him than a single grain of sand could defeat the highest mountain," Gabriel said smiling confidently.

"Your words have no meaning to me . . .!" Satan said, while turning his back in frustration.

And as Gabriel continued to speak the truth, Satan's frustration grew. His frustration manifested itself into dozens of fiery beasts each stronger than the other. Gabriel, with renewed energy from the conversation, began slaying beasts with ferocity.

"It is you who are the fool my smoldering brother. You've chosen your destiny . . . you fought, you lost, and now you are here . . . relegated to exist in the dark, empty corners of Man's transgression. You are the great deceiver Satan . . . a garbage collector, here to feed on the souls of Men who chose to live in the absence of God. That and that alone is your purpose!" he said through the blood and entrails of beasts as they fell.

"Yes, you speak the truth . . . This is my domain . . . This world belongs to me! Join me, and I will release you. Together we will rule the world of Man . . . in total domination; you may sit at my right hand, my brother!"

"Never! I will rot here for an eternity, killing as many beasts as you bring me, before I will ever entertain the thought!"

Gabriel grew tired of the conversation and recognized that Satan's coy banter had again turned into a futile attempt at recruitment.

"You are no more than a snake . . . a glorified worm. Your power died on the Cross a long-long, time ago when the Son of Man provided forgiveness to the world. It was then that your powers were hobbled . . . The sound alone of the Lord's name will rebuke you, and in the end, Man will look narrowly upon you and realize his folly in following you." Gabriel knew that the power to end the conversation was his.

The Devil, now in a panicked rage, crouched forward with the beasts behind him shuffling nervously with no direction. Satan began shouting obscenities in every language imaginable, simultaneously spitting insults and blasphemy, filling the tomb with hate and rage. Gabriel, though busy with the slaying of beasts that fell at his feet tired of the conversation, and proceeded to remove Satan from the tomb.

He pointed his broadsword directly at Satan and said:

"Satan! In the name of Jesus . . . I rebuke you!"

In an instant, the Devil was blasted backward into the granite cave side and vanished into it, along with the beasts that accompanied him. He emerged on the other side of the foothill, quickly leaving behind his less fortunate minions, who were trapped half in and half out of the hill, clawing to be birthed from the rock with which they were now fused. Screaming in a tantrum, Satan scurried like a wounded field rat into the smoky, burned out oaks, with beasts and minions whimpering to greet him. His sniveling was short-lived as he beheaded two large beasts who awaited him.

The Professor, Numier, and Amena, were all astonished by the books vivid descriptions of the Devil and were equally saddened to learn of Gabriel's fate. Amena seemed the most deeply troubled, as she'd surrounded herself and her beliefs with images of positive and uplifting celestial figures. At no point did she desire or allow herself to imagine the Devil, his appearance, or anything else about him. But with her trust securely with Jesus, she felt confident that she would never have to come face to face with anything as disgusting as Satan.

Upon seeing the horror and sadness on the faces of Amena and the Professor, and before they all became too disheartened, Numier quickly exclaimed:

"Hey, Hey . . . this is fiction. Sure the characters are familiar, but none of this is real! Come on; let's get out of here; I think we've read enough."

Although the Professor wished nothing more than to read on and carefully inspect each page and illustration, he welcomed the break and agreed with Numier.

Once safely back in the car, Amena reminded the Professor to fasten his seatbelt, as it was Numier's turn to drive.

Clair seemed content to lean her forehead against the window and watch the scenery pass by.

"So now do you remember the book?" Numier asked the Professor.

"I've tried and tried, but no . . . I don't remember ever reading or even seeing it before," answered the Professor.

"The subconscious mind is a powerful thing Don. It's possible that you may have read it some time ago, and although you seem to remember everything else, that particular item, for whatever reason, is being suppressed, possibly due to the trauma of the accident," callously stated Numier.

Amena, annoyed by Numier's insistence on supporting any version of reality contrary to the Professor's, sounded off:

"Are you a skeptic about everything or just matters of faith?"

"I suppose you choose to believe all this nonsense about Angels battling Satan to stay Mankind from Armageddon," jousted Numier in a huff.

"Hey, hey you two. Arguing about it isn't going to get us anywhere," said the Professor.

Amena, being the strong-willed woman that she was, couldn't tolerate Numier's closed mindedness any longer:

"Has it ever occurred to you that maybe it wasn't a hallucination . . . and that maybe he really did see these things. That maybe when his mind is in its heightened state, he can see things that we can't!" she argued. "It says in the Bible that God sent a messenger Angel to Daniel to answer his prayer but the Angel was held back by an evil demon for twenty-one days.[9] So if Angels were caught up in spiritual warfare back then . . . why not now?"

"Oh . . . I believe he's seeing warfare all right!" barked Numier. "But I think he's seeing it in his head . . . not in the foothills. Besides, when did I get on your bad side? I mean, if it's any consolation . . . I'm here aren't I. That is, I'm as eager to sort this whole thing out as you are. I'm just not ready to draw any conclusions."

And with that hint of an apology, so cleverly disguised as an explanation, Amena decided to cut Numier a little slack. Despite her heart's willingness to believe the Professor, her mind knew that Numier had a point. She reached for Clair and pulled her close as the young girl leaned her head against Amena's shoulder.

Time passed quickly as they listened intently to the news reporting the brewing conflict in the Far East. The coverage of the tension was uninterrupted. As the broadcast pointed increasingly toward the inevitability of a nuclear conflict, rioting and looting began to break out in virtually every major city throughout the United States. Despite the hording and stocking-up on supplies, people were being urged to stay home and remain calm.

They were about twenty minutes from the crash site when Amena, after assuming that the Professor had been sleeping, looked back and noticed that same far-away look in his eyes.

"Hey, what are you conspiring about back there?" she asked softly with a smile.

And while intensely studying the foothills as they passed, the Professor shouted out:

"Numier, turn right, just up ahead . . . on Sample Road!"

"What's going on Don?" asked Numier.

"There's only one-way to know for sure, besides . . . it's almost time!" said the Professor.

"Time for what?" asked Numier.

"When are you supposed to take your medicine?" suspiciously asked Amena.

"In about twenty minutes . . . Make another right, just up ahead!" yelled the Professor.

Clair began to squirm in her seat.

"Would you mind filling us in on your plan, mister?" asked Numier.

The Professor explained that the only way to even begin to understand what was happening to him was to allow his brain to revert back to its heightened state. Maybe then he would be able to sort out the hallucinations or lack thereof.

He instructed Numier to slow down as they negotiated their way through winding sycamore-lined roads and narrow steel-grate cattle guards.

"O.K . . . Pull over right here!" shouted the Professor while craning his head out the window to get a better look at the foothills.

He had chosen a spot on Tollhouse Road, some ten miles down stream from his initial encounter, or in terms of the alternate dimension, well behind Cherubim lines. Realizing that he must make every effort to conceal himself, the Professor selected a dry ditch between two rolling fields. It was a dry creek bed that only fed the stream during heavy rains and was referred to as 'Dry Creek'.

Clair began to moan and slowly sway her head from side to side.

"What's wrong with her?" insensitively barked Numier.

"The way you drive she's probably car sick," said Amena.

"Don't let her puke in my car!" yelled Numier.

"Here's the idea . . ." said the Professor. The doctor said that without the medication, my condition would almost certainly revert immediately. So I have to position myself within the next ten minutes. I'll stand inside Dry Creek where I won't easily be seen. Then I will quietly observe as my hallucinations unfold. As soon as I've seen enough, I'll take the Medication and walk back."

"And if you don't see anything?" asked Numier.

"Let's hope that's the case," the Professor replied as he got out and looked across the hillside.

"I don't like this plan at all . . . Can't we wait a few days until maybe you've healed a little more, or maybe you've had a little more sleep?" asked Amena.

But the Professor didn't respond. Realizing that his mind was set on trying, and not wanting to interfere any further with his concentration, Amena exited the car and stood silently on the shoulder of the road.

Clair stayed in the car and continued to moan as Numier pulled slowly into the tall weeds on the side of the road.

The Professor took a deep breath, faced the rolling hills and said:

"O.K. . . . I'm off . . . Wish me luck!"

He walked a few steps towards the foothills, and just before crossing the stream, he turned back to look at Amena. She was standing on the side of the road with her elbows to her sides and her shoulders shrugged as the cool evening winds began to blow. Her beauty was breathtaking, as her hair swayed softly in the gentle breeze. She was still wearing the sundress she had on when she first heard of the accident.

She had stopped at the 'Oak Hill Nursery' on her way home and picked up some Asters and Vincas that were blooming so beautifully this time of year.

Amena had always been blessed with the ability to see beauty in things where others could not. And even though it was a damp and foggy day in the valley and lower foothills, she was staying with a girlfriend who lived in Auberry, a small foothill town well above the fog-line. She knew there would be a ray of sunshine somewhere in her garden that would welcome her blooming additions.

Her sundress was an odd choice on such a cool autumn day, but changing into it and planting flowers was the only thing she could do with all the joy and anticipation she was experiencing as a result of her re-acquaintance with the Professor earlier that day.

She had just finished telling her girlfriend, Sarah, how excited she was to be going out on a date with the Professor later that evening when an announcement came over the local broadcast. When she heard that there had been an accident involving a Sierra High School teacher, she knew instantly in her heart that it was Don. Without taking the time to change, she grabbed her coat and bag and headed directly to the scene of the accident.

Standing on the soft shoulder of Tollhouse Road, the Professor stood in awe of her undeniable beauty. A cool, gentle breeze was blowing her thin, cotton, spaghetti-strap dress snuggly against her body, revealing her perfect, statuesque frame. He couldn't help thinking that he'd never seen anything so beautiful in all his life. And no matter what happened next, he felt very fortunate to have had this special time with her. He then slowly walked back to her he said:

"Am I a fool for going back?" with tears of fear welling up in his eyes.

Softly, and calmly she replied:

"No . . . You're the bravest man I've ever known."

Upon hearing that, the Professor gently held the back of her neck and softly kissed her for the first, and very possibly . . . the last time.

CHAPTER VII
TRENCH WAR
✣

The Professor walked silent and alone through a long crevasse between two rolling hills. He positioned himself inside Dry Creek, just beyond a small ravine. A hundred or so yards from the car, he was situated well out of view from Numier and Amena as well as passing motorists. Standing below ground level, the Professor was hidden from the dangers that might encircle him, but as the terrain sloped, the hillside and foothills surrounding the creek bed became visible.

It was a typical Central California foothill, heavily dotted with live oaks, sycamores, and dense underbrush that provided shelter for prey animals of all kinds. Ground squirrels and cottontail rabbits scurried through the tall, emerald-green grass that waived gently in the crisp, autumn breeze.

There was a solitary calm that surrounded him. In an effort to remain undetected by what he might encounter, the Professor stood utterly motionless. He waited patiently while the minutes passed by like hours. Standing in the fresh breeze, he enjoyed the sweet bouquet of ragweed and wild sage so prevalent in the foothills.

He was startled by a covey of valley quail that flew low and fast, hurriedly past his location while making their way towards the lush feeding grounds near Granite Creek. Seeing their flight and feeling the purr of their wings brought back familiar feelings of childhood fear and loneliness. He fought to suppress the unwelcome memories with little success as they flowed uninhibited past his well-established, defense mechanisms.

❦

He recalled hunting dove in the foothills with his father, older brother, and a half dozen or so hardened farmers and their sons. Their intentions were two-fold: to shoot as many birds as they could; and to make men out of the small boys who accompanied them . . .

No more than twelve-years old, he stood alone, holding a gun that was much larger than he was. He patiently and nervously waited, while watching the sun rise slowly over the Sierra Nevadas. Gradually, the over-cast skies above lit up in a burst of vibrant-pink and orange, illuminating the silhouettes of doves as they flew peacefully toward their feeding grounds. Even at a young age, he was able to appreciate the beauty of the scenery that surrounded him.

The peace and aromatic tranquility of the countryside was abruptly interrupted by the sounds of gunshots and boisterous hollering, as birds fell helplessly from the skies. Tufts of feathers still hung in the air, like bursts of fireworks eerily marking the exact location where tiny lives had been lost. The lead and gun smoke that filled the air was immediately followed by the sounds of little boots trudging excitedly through the foxtail-covered fields to gather the men's dead and wounded victims.

After all this time, he was still able to remember vividly the pain and confusion he felt as he witnessed the massacre of innocence . . . At first, his heart broke as he thought of ways to gather the birds and nurse their broken bodies back to life. But then in time, he learned to suppress his compassion and join the hunters, hoping to fit in and be accepted . . . And now, close to thirty years later, powerless to his enhanced recall, he couldn't help thinking that some memories were better left in the past.

For a moment, he considered that the doctor may have inaccurately timed his medication, or that maybe the entire experience was in fact nothing more than one very real-feeling hallucination. But just as he was about to turn back to the car, his head began to tingle. It was a flushing feeling, similar to a chemically induced dizziness or mild drunkenness. The sensation was accompanied by severe pain with his fresh head injury throbbing with every beat of his heart. He was concentrating on the pain when he began to hear the faint sounds of voices. The voices turned into sounds of screaming and roaring that grew louder with each passing second. The noise reverberated into a deafening thunder as images began to appear.

Slowly, but steadily, the Professor was able to make out shapes and figures moving swiftly about the trench-like creek bed. With the images growing clearer, he could faintly see Cherubim Angels hustling throughout the enlarged creek bed, methodically preparing for battle. The Professor stood quietly in the trench and observed the silhouettes of Angels lining its inner walls with crossbows, swords, and an array of ancient weaponry.

As the scene fully materialized, he saw foot soldiers running in all directions while squadrons of Angels descended from above. He now realized that he was standing in the midst of the Cherubim Army, on the outer edge of a battalion. There were thousands of Cherubim inside the trench, all in various phases of battle readiness. Some were loading weapons; many were carrying ammunition, while others were tending to their wounded.

The trench provided much needed cover from the flying rocks, spears, flames, and a sundry of debris. Once battle ready, the Cherubim would employ their art, taking to the skies in groups of three with swords and bows drawn.

The Professor continued to survey his strange new surroundings. He credited his newfound abilities with being able to see miles away with amazing accuracy. He looked down the line of the trench, past the multitude of soldiers, and saw on his left, hordes of Satan's beasts advancing towards the front. They plodded, pounded, and butchered every living creature in their path as they ferociously approached the front lines. They carried and hurled everything they could get their hands on, and due to their incredible strength, anything being heaved by them became a lethal weapon. They were also very dangerous with their bare hands, as their six-inch, razor-sharp claws made carrying a weapon unnecessary.

They were a marching conflagration with beasts pounding pine-sap torches, engulfing everything that stood in their path. The sycamores and oaks so beautiful in their majesty became little more than flaming bonfires emitting plumes of smoke, like veins of mercury merging into a bruised, crimson, and violet sky.

As the skies above cast a hellish blood-red tangerine hue over virtually everything in The Fields, the death bearers spared nothing from the carnage they brought.

Marching behind the minions were hundreds of Dark Angels. These were Angels who in the beginning, were deceived by Satan into rebelling against God. And now, with no recourse, they were sentenced to fight along the side of despair. They were gaunt and pale, soiled by thousands of years of being in the presence of evil. Their wings were

singed to charcoal nubs that drooped down from
their shoulder blades. They wore black, Roman
Gladiator style, heavy-battle armor designed to
protect them against the blades and arrows of
Cherubim. They were equipped with an arsenal of
weaponry and seemed to be proficient swordsmen
among other things.

The Dark Angels all had an ill appearance, each
suffering some sort of limp or ailment. Their
bodies were, although capable of inflicting much
destruction, mere shadows of what they once were.
Their faces were twisted and disfigured, as there is no
beauty in Hell.

They were wielding whips of fire that cracked loudly
onto the backs of the massive beasts, herding and
beating them into submission while marching them
toward the front lines.

The Professor's attention was diverted back to the
trench by the shouts of a different kind of Angel.
At first the sounds were jumbled like words spoken
backwards. But then, in a matter of seconds, his
brain caught up with the disjointed mutter and
merged it together into comprehensible speech
patterns.

In the center of the trench line, in the very heart of
the battle, was an Archangel of the Lord. Truly a
glorious sight to behold, he stood more than twelve-
feet tall and was equipped with massive, war-torn
wings that spanned over twenty feet. He was standing

higher than the rest, on the top edge of the trench, shouting out orders and directing fire, seemingly unaffected by the spears, rocks, and burning trees being hurled at him.

They called him Maximus. He appeared to have a noticeable glow about him, as if originating from just beneath the skin. His face resembled that of a seasoned warrior, centered and relentless. He was much larger than the Cherubim and not nearly as fragile. And although his wings were powerful, his size made him a much more effective foot soldier.

His voice could easily be heard over hundreds of yards, and when he shouted out directives, Cherubim sprang into action as though they were his very appendages.

Behind the trench line and to the right of the Professor, were Cherubim reinforcements bringing precious supplies to the line. The hills there were green and lush with wild Lavender, Baby-Blue Eyes, Fiddle-Necks, and a variety of other wild flowers common to the California foothills. And although the hills looked and felt so familiar to the Professor, he knew he was far from home now.

The Cherubim side of the battleground was heavy with foliage that had not yet been defiled by the hordes of advancing beasts. The trees were littered with Seraphs, each with wings unfurled exposing hundreds of eyes wide open and focused on the battlefield. The Professor recalled his Biblical knowledge of Seraphs and how some theologians believed their eyes to be the eyes of God. In this instance, it certainly seemed as though their only purpose here was to observe.

The knoll rose slightly to the base of a steep butte. The Professor noticed a black cliff at the bottom of the hillside that appeared to have a very large black door embedded into its front. It seemed a bit odd, as nothing on the battlefield appeared to be of any sophistication at all. It was as if they were fighting with ten-thousand-year-old technology.

There were catapults on both sides of the lines. Cherubim labored arduously to pack the massive slings, while Dark Angels, more efficient with their reloading, utilized Beasts that heaved massive boulders onto the ancient devices. Cherubim used bows and arrows, crossbows, and the standard-issue-elongated sica. The Archangels were wielding massive broadswords as their size afforded them the ability to do so. Some beasts appeared to be brandishing large war hammers and heavy clubs with round, spiked, metal heads, similar to the mace of medieval times.

The Cherubim were in control of the battlefield systematically bringing down beast after beast. Their technique was flawless and unrelenting. The Cherubim would attack two strong at the beast's front, distracting it with arrows, while a single cherub attacked from behind. While still in flight, he would sever the legs of the beast with one pass of a machete. Rendered immobile and fighting from its stumps, the beast was an easy target for the two frontal Cherubim, who made short work of ending its morbid existence.

The beasts were stupid at best. They seemed to be constructed with the deceased body parts of a combination of mammals. In some instances beasts possessed the legs of large grizzly bears or gorillas enabling them to stand upright and lunge with great strength. Still others were equipped with the legs and lower torso of bison affording them great power to push trees, boulders or virtually any obstacle impeding their attack but limiting their upright stance in battle.

Their upper bodies were a crude combination of human and animal appendages, each designed with a specific purpose. Some possessed the upper torso of very large, giant-size men with the arms of Kodiaks and gigantic claw-like hands, well out of proportion to the rest of their bodies.

It seemed that in an effort to minimize casualties in battle, many beasts were outfitted with the outer hides of rhinoceroses and/or elephants. The thick skins were shoddily sewn or stapled directly onto muscle, in place of their outer epidermis, leaving large gaps of flesh, where blood, pus, and other secretions would constantly seep.

All beasts seemed to have the decaying heads and faces of men, with the exception of their upper-frontal lobe which possessed many different horn styles of animals such as bulls, bison, and cape buffalo to name a few. Satan was able to conjure creatures of great physical strength, but his ability to produce intelligence was hindered by the brain damage caused by the death of the human bodies at hell's disposal.

The Fields were vast . . . They covered the foothills and flowed well into the valley below. Bodies of beasts and Cherubim littered the theater as neither side possessed the means or inclination to gather their dead. Scavenger parties of beasts were formed as they crawled under Cherubim fire to feed on festering corpses.

The Professor struggled to watch, as his natural instincts were to turn away or close his eyes in order to avoid the ghoulish events unfolding on the dark side of The Fields.

After morbidly acquainting himself with the grim battlefield, the Professor noticed a minion scuttling in retreat, toward a clearing beyond the woods, where there was a gathering of beasts. There he could clearly see their leader. He was standing in the middle of a makeshift, mobile campsite surrounded by Dark Angels for protection. They gathered in a location dotted with heavy-rock croppings, jagged and unforgiving. It was a place called Buchanan Hollow.

There, where there was little vegetation, minions and Dark Angels scraped and chafed against the exposed decomposed granite, struggling incessantly to rid themselves of their bothersome, decaying flesh and rotting tissue, but with no reward given that their continuous pains and discomfort were part of their eternal sentence.

Their leader was much smaller than his Angel brethren as his scarred and shriveled body took on an almost elderly appearance. His body was smoking as if he had just been pulled out of an inferno. In an effort to hide his shameful sores and lesions, he wore a black gown, blood-soaked from the open wounds concealed beneath it.

As he moved about the camp, he attracted field mice, snakes and a variety of other rodents that would annoyingly bustle under his gown to feed on his rotting flesh. He was a hideous sight, a living cancer that the Professor was hesitant to even look upon, but after forcing himself to do so, it became frightfully evident that he was looking upon the Devil himself . . . Satan.

The evil permeated the foothills surrounding Buchanan Hollow and flowed down to the trench where the Professor stood. The energy emitting from the ghoulish Sanhedrin gathered at the Hollow caused the Professor extreme physical discomfort. But despite the dizziness and severe nausea, he kept his focus. He felt compelled to guard himself against the evil he was beholding, as the actual sight of it in its purest form pulled hard against his otherwise relatively innocent soul.

He thought of passages in the Bible and visualized placing the shield of Christ on his left forearm, and the sword of truth in his right hand. But despite his faith in Christ, and a lifetime of spiritual preparation, it was still difficult for him to compel his eyes to gaze at Hell's Darkest Angel.

While watching with reluctance, he could clearly see a small pentagonal box that Satan carried with him throughout the camp. It was made of dark-colored hardwood, and though it shined like new, it was clearly as ancient as the Devil himself. He guarded the box with unbridled passion, as it apparently contained material precious and dear to his very essence.

As their voices carried and with the help of newfound lip reading abilities, the Professor was able to eavesdrop on Satan's conversation with his formerly angelic minions. One Dark Angel approached and asked:

"Why do they make their stand here my lord?"

"They protect the tomb of Gabriel!" Satan replied. "They hope to one day free him. They are fools, and their efforts are in vain."

"But what if they do my lord?" the Dark Angel asked.

And with one stroke of his hand, Satan cut off the curious Angel's head and shouted:

"Be silent you cowardly fool! This is simply not possible!! He will never be free! He will rot in his sarcophagus, as it is his wish to do so!"

Satan closed his eyes, and with a pained expression, indignantly recalled a time long ago when he was an Archangel in good standing with the Lord.

"I was an incredible sight to behold," he said with arrogance. "I was the most beautiful of all the Angels ever created by God. Festooned with jewels and emeralds the likes of which this world has never known. I was the Angel of Light . . . 'The Adorned One' . . ."

"Now look at me. Smoldering embers . . . mere ashes of what I once was. Gabriel and his brother Michael, the Lord's henchmen, did this to me!"

"Is this why you hate . . . my lord?" another Dark Angel asked.

"Silence!" Satan shouted as he cut the Dark Angel in two at the hips. "Do not question me!"

Although self-pity was the Devil's strong suit, he favored inflicting it upon others, rather than himself. And before the Dark Angel's body hit the ground, Satan leaped upon the shoulders of a large beast and traversed it onto the top of a large rock. He often rode beasts giving him a better vantage of the carnage, as well as a temporary reprieve from the hungry rodent's constant attacks.

As he watched the battle rage, he sniffed the air incessantly and said:

"I so love the smell of burning Angels!"

He then opened the dark box and poured a portion of its contents onto a jagged rock formation beneath him. It appeared to be a thick, dark-green substance that oozed and sprawled at the feet of Satan. Leaping off the beast and instructing it to wait its turn, he bent down and gathered the thick slime with quivering anticipation like a drug addict awaiting his fix.

He held the substance in one hand while, with the other, he conjured up countless human corpses in different stages of decomposition. Some were relatively fresh, while others were bloated with gaseous fluids. The lifeless rotting carcasses lay in piles of naked meat that blanketed the side of the rock-strewn foothill. He then sucked the ooze into his mouth and sprayed it over the bodies like a shower of contagion that rained down over them.

Suddenly the corpses began to move, creeping and crawling with life as they moaned and groaned in excruciating pain. In their facial expressions, the Professor could see the fear and terror they suffered upon realizing the horror of their reanimation. They all screamed to be released from their gruesome captivity as they cried out for mercy from their captor.

Although unclear to the Professor at this time, he could only deduce, but with relative certainty, that the green slime was a small sample of the multitudes of condemned souls condensed into a thick-green malignancy. Distributed orally by Satan, they were transplanted into the decaying bodies of other nonbelievers.

The Professor was paralyzed with fear while watching the walking dead stagger about the rocks. From across the ravine, a few managed to make eye contact with the Professor. Through his enhanced mental capabilities, a strange and eerie thing occurred. He saw their lives passing before their eyes, as though he was sharing the memory of their mistakes along with them.

Like a tiny cinema, in their eyes were revealed the various reasons for their internment. They seemed to be ordinary people . . . many of whom lived good, moral lives, thinking that this was enough for Salvation. People who for one reason or another, were led astray from a personal relationship with God, only to be welcomed open armed by Satan.

Some had been deceived into believing that tradition and ritual combined with guilt-inspired good works could somehow save them from the hand of Hell.[10] Many of them were simply too rich or too educated to bow down and accept second position to anyone or anything.

Others chose to cling stubbornly to their worship of religious symbols or mortals who had died before them . . . Somehow believing that because these people had passed on, they'd become some sort of Deity, though none of whom ever claimed to have been given authority to offer forgiveness or salvation.[11]

There were even those who preached and prophesied in his name, wrongfully seeking intercession by praying to the dead. They bypassed a personal relationship with Christ, and their prayers went unheard.[12]

And still there were those that, absent any catastrophic tragedy in their lives, simply hadn't felt the need to turn to the Lord. But for whatever their individual reasons . . . there they were . . . absent the protection from Jesus, and firmly within the jowls of Satan.

Tears of sadness and anguish streamed down the Professor's face when he realized just how easy it was for these unfortunate people to have been led astray, and how, were it not for a few key instances in his life, it could have been him.

After giving life to the hosts of chastised souls that wondered aimlessly about the rocks below, Satan slowly and methodically unleashed blood hungry beasts a few at a time, prolonging the feast so that the souls still writhing in the horrors of reanimation, could witness their impending fate.

Truly nothing could have prepared him for what he was witnessing, but morbidly compelled to watch, the Professor saw Satan recollect the lost souls from what was left of the butchered remains. He then carefully placed them back into the box, only to await their next round of eternal damnation.

CHAPTER VIII

TAMERA

The Professor had hoped somehow to prove that the events in which he'd become an unwitting spectator were real and not hallucinations. But after what he'd witnessed, he hoped on behalf of Numier and other nonbelievers, that the opposite was true. He scanned the surrounding horizon, searching for signs or indications that might in any way, point in the direction of hallucination . . . but found nothing.

And with the images of Buchanan Hollow still burning on his corneas . . . he prayed silently to himself:

"God . . . if it is at all within your will, please have mercy on these souls." He prayed this in earnest though believing full well that their chances were slim to none . . .

He remembered the beast in the stream, and knew it was imperative to remain completely still, and despite his inclination to reach for his pills and return to the safety of his world, he knew he had to remain in The Cherubim Fields until he'd gained enough information to somehow make sense of what he was witnessing.

Finally, as the minion that first caught the Professor's eye approached Satan, the minion dropped to one knee and paid homage, as the Devil was deeply engrossed in conversation with one of his generals. The general's name was Huron. He was the leader of all forces of evil . . . second only to the Devil, and Satan's personal consigliore.

Huron was a newly fallen Angel who had been on the side of evil for less than a thousand years. He was an impressive display of darkness exhibiting only mild battle scarring with no apparent disfigurement or ailment. He was outfitted in black, light armor and carried no shield.

He wielded the great sword of doom known as Kismet. It was a large primordial Samurai Sword, blackened through and through with ancient hieroglyphics etched long ways into its shaft. Kismet was designed by Satan and built by Mongolian artisans whose secret methods of turning and forging made its blade all but indestructible. It was an instrument of death that after many millennia of killing, had taken on evil powers of its own, and was nearly invincible in the hands of darkness.

Huron's fall from Grace happened during the Dark Ages when the world of Man was mired deep in the swamp of despondency . . . perfect conditions for the recruitment of evil. There was a fierce battle over the occupation of Buchanan Hollow where Maximus and Huron, his second in command, held back multitudes of evil forces while awaiting reinforcements from the valley below.

Maximus, being the stronger of the two, weathered the brunt of the attack while thousands of beasts lured and isolated Huron. They cornered him by backing him into a dark cavern called Tamera. It was a place where, having been in the control of evil forces for many centuries was all but stripped of any measure of goodness or illumination from above.

As a squadron of Cherubim reinforcements reached Buchanan Hollow, the lead Cherub yelled:

"Maximus! I bring news from the valley. Our forces are weak, but they are holding. Huron is trapped in Tamera. Shall we commit forces to his aid?"

"No! We cannot afford to loose this stand. The Hollow would be a formidable stronghold should it fall into the hands of evil."

"But Maximus . . .!"

No!" he repeated. "Huron is an Archangel of The Lord. He will fight valiantly, and he will find his way back to The Fields," confidently proclaimed Maximus.

And as the fresh squadron of Cherubim began to drive back the wall of beasts that surrounded The Hollow, Maximus stepped back and faced in the direction of Tamera. Worried and concerned for his younger brother, but appreciating the cause far greater than themselves, he hung his head low . . . and prayed.

After a century of slaying multitudes of beasts in Tamera, Huron grew impatient with his isolation in darkness and longed for the light from which he'd been separated for so long. He began to experience thoughts unfamiliar to him, and although his thoughts remained pure, they were selfish in origin as he began to consider his own desires over and above the Will of God. Satan knew that the only time an Archangel is vulnerable . . . is when he wants.

Sensing that the moment was near, Satan reflected a diminutive ray of light from a nearby opening to The Cherubim Fields and cast it onto the end of a narrow canyon corridor where it would be clearly visible to Huron.

Any Angel with a fraction of the experience of Huron would have recognized the trap, but Huron was blinded by his desire to re-join the others . . . to once again feel the Light of God and regain his position next to Maximus.

As Huron made his fateful move down the corridor, the light that he so desperately yearned for suddenly disappeared and was replaced by Kismet, Satan's black-sword-of-doom. Huron knew at the moment the blade pierced his breast plate that he'd been in the company of evil for far too long, and that it was better to die in battle than to succumb to the forces of evil, which had already begun to change him.

And with Satan and a host of Dark Angels looming over him . . . he kneeled down on both knees . . . bowed his head, and died.

Instantly a shadow fell upon The Cherubim Fields. Maximus doubled over with the pain of loss emanating from deep within his core. Beasts jumped for joy and wild flowers drooped in flaccidity. Every Angel knew that they'd lost a Mighty Angel of The Lord.

Seizing the moment and moving quickly, Satan ripped the heart out of the Dark Angel standing nearest him and placed it into the chest cavity of Huron. Within minutes, his corpse had been reanimated. With virtually no brain damage, he slowly began to show signs of life as his body struggled against the abnormal undertaking. Screaming in pain, Huron drew his first breath as a newly created being, entirely contrary to the one he'd been.

With his Angelic soul in Heaven, he was now an empty vessel with all the physical strength and intellect of a Mighty Angel of The Lord but devoid of the love, compassion, honor or anything else that may have remotely resembled an instrument of God.

With the heart of a Dark Angel beating strongly behind his shattered breastplate, and as the murky black blood of hatred and distain surged rapidly through his veins, he slowly and deliberately groaned to a stand.

Possessing virtually all of his God-given physical attributes, he towered over all of his crippled brethren, and with fists clinched; he gripped Kismet tightly in his right hand and swore allegiance to his new creator . . . The Devil.

It was in that moment that it became elatedly clear to Satan that he'd finally assembled the perfect Beast.

CHAPTER IX

DRAGONS

Back in the trench, the Professor curiously but reluctantly watched the messenger-minion finally rise from his knees and address Satan, interrupting his conversation with Huron:

"My Lord . . . There is something strange in the Cherubim camp . . . It appears that a small, wingless, Angel watches the battle from the trench."

Satan leapt off the beast and quickly separated the messenger-minion from his head.

"You fool! There are no wingless Angels!"

And with his eyes closed as if sampling a fine wine, he again sniffed long and hard into the dust and smoke. His nose had been burned off during his descent leaving only holes in the face of his skull. Every beast, minion, and Dark Angel was brought to a momentary standstill while their master was in complete concentration. As he drew the dreadful aroma of death into his face holes, an eerie silence surrounded the battleground. Then, with furrowed brow and a hateful scowl he screamed:

"Man . . .! Man, you idiots!! Man is on the battlefield!!!"

He knew instantly that this was quite an opportunity. For thousands of years, he had survived on the sins of Man a dimension away. Sins, that however diminutive or grand, were barely enough to sustain him, as they were diluted by dimensional boundaries.

Now . . . he was able to drink deep the sin of Man that reeked only a stones-throw away. All the sins that the Professor ever entertained in act or in thought were now on display for the enjoyment and nourishment of Satan.

His greed and lust for victory completely overshadowed his curiosity as to why Man was on the battlefield, or for that matter, how Man had crossed into his dimension at all. Nonetheless, he seized the moment.

"Man is on the battlefield!" he cried. "Drink in his lust . . . consume his hate . . . feast on his fear! Press forward . . . Destroy everything! Let nothing survive!"

At once, Huron flew downward to the valley floor to initiate an all out assault for total control of The Fields.

The beasts all showed renewed strength and fury. Their anger all but unhinged them. They were intoxicated with hate and rage. They began pulling Cherubim from the sky almost at will. Some even took to killing each other in their madness. Countless beasts, wounded in battle, were fighting without limbs, oblivious to their absence. Determined and driven, they pressed forward slaughtering every living thing in their path.

Another Archangel from down the trench line ran towards the lead Archangel, Maximus, with news from the line. And although more than a hundred yards away, his face looked vaguely familiar to the Professor. His name was Steven. He was a relatively young Archangel, created for the special purpose of escorting babies and small children to Heaven. They were babies who had died prior to their contact with the world, either during childbirth or abortion, and young children, naturally pure at heart, possessing souls without sin, most resembling the Soul of Jesus. They were truly blessed in the Eyes of God, and were treated with the utmost tenderness. Steven's face was the first thing they saw upon their journey to Heaven.

His face was childlike, with long blonde hair that flowed like fields of grain in a gentle breeze. His eyes were set in a constant state of compassion either by design to soothe their innocent passengers, or as a result of the sadness he'd seen in the eyes of grieving mothers.

Although much smaller than Maximus, Steven had been equipped by God with the strength of a thousand Angels. His knowledge of battle and war was extensive. Satan would regularly send countless beasts and minions to attempt in vain to intercept and capture his passel of innocent souls, but to no avail. Satan knew that as long as Steven was in possession of even one soul in transport, he was protected by God and invincible to evil.

But today, in service to the Lord, he was here . . . in The Cherubim Fields . . . where he was vulnerable. This being the case, he was under constant fire on the battlefield.

As Steven approached the command post, half a dozen furious beasts greeted him, roaring and foaming at the mouth in their rage. They jumped into the trench separating him from Maximus. It took Steven much longer than usual to slay the platoon of beasts, detaining him just long enough for ghoulish reinforcements to reach his position and continue the assault.

"Maximus!" he shouted over the shoulder of a falling beast. "The beasts grow angry . . . Their fury is like none I've seen . . . Something puts fuel to their rage!"

Maximus stood tall on the edge of the trench. He tilted his head back and breathed deep, the clean air coming from up the ravine on the Cherubim side of the theater. He then turned and looked a hundred yards up the trench line and directly at the Professor like an eagle spotting its prey:

"Man! Man is on the battlefield!!" he cried.

Steven then screamed in response:

"How can this be . . .?! If Satan discovers him, the beasts will be unstoppable . . . They will destroy us all!"

"You can be sure that he already knows of his presence!" shouted Maximus.

The Professor was still standing motionless in the trench. He believed full well that his very survival depended upon his immobility. He remained unaware that both sides of the conflict had detected his presence. He watched with horror as Cherubim began to fall to the relentless power of the forces of evil. Control on the front line seemed to be shifting in favor of the beasts.

Equally as determined as Satan, Maximus concerned himself solely with the battle at hand and disregarded the details pertaining to the Professor's premature visit.

And in vehement pitch he cried:

"Call down the Sparrows!"

A few hundred yards down the trench-line, upon hearing Maximus' directive, Steven yelled:

"Call down the Sparrows!"

And for a moment . . . all eyes were on the clouds above.

High above the battlefield could faintly be seen an army of Angels circling and awaiting their chance to join in the engagement.

Ten thousand strong, these Angels were smaller, faster, and more agile than Cherubim, making them ultimately more vulnerable on the battlefield.

Through the clouds they came . . . dropping like bombs from the belly of a flying fortress. They descended in a free fall on their backs with their wings cupped around them like birds that had been shot from flight. They fell in a circular cluster in groups of thirty-six, on an even plane, like a team of skydivers prior to separation. As they dropped through the clouds they loaded their weapons, like sea otters cracking shells on their stomachs.

While preparing for battle, they listened intently to the lead sparrow as he shouted orders to his squadron:

"Form a straight line as we approach . . .! We will attack in single file . . . Stay low, beneath the Cherubim fire! Remain in your line . . . If you must break ranks, break into the enemy and fight your way back to the squadron. Stay close to the trench . . . crossbows only; there will be time for nothing more!"

The Angels' faces showed complete indifference having done this many times before. As they approached the earth, they instinctively formed a straight line in a large circular chain converging to single file as they fell, increasing in speed like a funnel cloud. One by one they turned to face the ground. Plummeting straight down, they opened their wings in increments, gaining speed as they approached the battlefield.

They gradually leveled off in a single-file line some eight to ten feet above the ground at speeds of close to two hundred miles per hour. They flew through burning trees and blinding smoke, while drafting the lead sparrow and listening intently to their leader:

"Stay low . . .! Weapons ready . . .!"

They raised their bows against the wind with amazing strength and bravery. Their flight was flawless as they strafed two to three feet off the ground at speeds nearing two hundred and fifty miles per hour.

"Hold your positions!" their leader cried.

Nearing the nucleus of the conflict, they passed several beasts that swatted in vain at their speed:

"Fire!" shouted the squadron leader.

They fired at will with perfect delivery, dropping passels of beasts that grappled unsuccessfully at the arrows penetrating them. As the sparrows began their assault, the Cherubim in the trench also released. Firing some ten feet over the sparrows, they created a wall of arrows, confusing and killing the beasts in droves.

One of the larger beasts hoisted a huge boulder over his head and was quickly pelted by Cherubim arrows. But before he fell, he was able to get the rock off, hurling it into the sparrow's flight path. Several sparrows, unable to avoid the stone, impacted it at speeds of two hundred and fifty miles per hour. Their bodies were crushed and dismembered as they tumbled lifelessly through the air.

More sparrows pulled up to avoid the carnage only to be cut down by cherubim fire directly above their position. And like a chain reaction, the train wreck continued with more beasts launching rocks and trees into the sparrow's flight path. Seeing the bloodbath, Maximus shouted to the Cherubim:

"Hold your fire . . . let them clear!"

The sparrow leader then shouted:

"Pull up! Get above the debris field!"

Several sparrows turned into the enemy, shooting and slaying their way through the beasts. The remaining dozen or so pulled up, to avoid the obstacles, while continuing to discharge their weapons with precise accuracy.

"Regroup for another pass!" shouted the sparrow leader while he disengaged his squadron, clearing the way for the next wave of descending sparrows.

Pulling away from the trench and heading back to the clouds, the squadron leader looked back over the battlefield. He then made his observations and reported back to Maximus:

"Maximus . . . We are taking heavy losses . . . Should we pull back?!!" he shouted through the dust and smoke.

"No! No! Do not stop! Rejoin your battalion and prepare for another pass!" Maximus yelled, frustrated and concerned with the sparrows' lack of effectiveness.

He looked up and saw hundreds of battalions circling miles above the earth awaiting their drop. And although it pained him greatly to send them to their deaths, he knew that if they lost this stand, they would lose control of Gabriel's Tomb.

He redirected the Cherubim to fire beneath the sparrows to avoid hitting them as they would now be approaching from above the debris field and out of reach of the beasts.

With the next squadron of sparrows now reaching the front line, Maximus witnessed something he'd never seen before in the eight thousand years he'd been commanding his forces.

Several of the beasts began to morph into three-headed dragons. They stood thirty-feet tall and breathed fire like napalm from the mouth of a Sherman Tank. The Mighty Angels quickly diverted their attention to the dragons. With fervor, they fired at the massive heads that snapped and gnashed wildly at the Cherubim in the trench. Although accurate in their aim, the dragons were unaffected by the Cherubim arrows as they shattered and deflected off their leathery scales.

The Cherubim were relentless in their resolve against the power of the three-headed dragons, but despite their fearless determination, they were no match for the fiery beasts. Cherubim fell in numbers, like flies passing through the flames of a bonfire.

In an instant, Maximus looked up to the formations of sparrows and yelled:

"Send down the joust!!!"

Suddenly, a specially trained squadron of sparrows fell through the clouds on their backs. One was carrying a long stake, three inches in diameter and twenty-feet long, similar to the jousts used in medieval times. He was holding it tightly against his chest as he plummeted to the earth on his back reaching terminal velocity in seconds.

Upon reaching the end of their descent, twelve broke off and joined hands. One by one they turned towards the earth creating a sort of sling with the furthest most sparrow holding the joust. And as each sparrow opened his wings, the adjacent Angel would gain more speed.

Although they were seasoned warriors, there was a rare sense of compassion in their eyes. The joust was an uncommon mission, and the Angels assigned to it knew that it was a suicide drop.

At the apex of the sling, the jousting sparrow, furthest from the center, opened his wings slightly and released from the chain. Shot forward like an arrow, he reached speeds of over three hundred miles per hour. He aimed himself directly at the three-headed dragon, and though the beast saw him, it was not able to react in time.

The joust and sparrow entered the beast, penetrating its heart with lethal accuracy.

The Angel then passed through the dragon's body, exiting through its back, falling to the ground some fifty yards up the foothill. He was covered with flesh and blood of the beast and his wings had been torn off by the dragon's ribcage upon exit. And though the impact was not survivable, the Angel managed to stay conscious just long enough to witness the remainder of his chain reach the beast and finish it off with surgical precision. Acquiring peace by knowing that he'd served the Will of God, he took his last breath and laid his head down on the wildflower-covered hillside.

Maximus watched with waning encouragement as dozens of beasts began to morph in the distance.

They took to the skies like Birds of Prey. No longer in a defensive posture, they hunted down and torched Cherubim by the thousands. It was a scene straight from Hell as Angels of the Lord fell from the skies like burning hail.

Maximus knew that this new development on the battlefield was anything but normal.

As Steven was bringing news of the battle in the valley, a massive dragon came between he and Maximus, pinning Steven against the side of the trench with streams of fire from all three mouths of the beast. Steven held one wing up like a shield, buying precious seconds while Cherubim rushed to his position.

Less than a hundred yards from the command post, Maximus could vaguely see Stevens' face through the flames as he screamed:

"Maximus! It's the man!! He's finishing us!!!"

Maximus with clinched fists threw his head back and screamed in desperation into the sky:

"Gabriel!!!"

From inside the tomb, Gabriel could faintly hear Maximus' cries for help. Frustrated, he turned to the side of the tomb where the screams were emanating while butchering beasts of his own by the thousands. And though the helplessness he felt was all but insufferable, he kept his edge by visualizing the day that he might again rejoin his brothers in The Cherubim Fields . . . But for now, all he could do was answer Maximus' cries of desperation with a single directive:

"Kill Him!"

"Kill Him!!" he screamed, sensing the Professor's presence and hoping Maximus would hear his order.

Through all the screaming, fighting, and dying, the Professor never moved a muscle. He was still standing in the exact place and in the exact same position. His ears were ringing from the battle, and his head was pounding from the blood engulfing his brain. Overwhelmed with trauma, he was in a near complete state of shock and totally unaware of the blood dripping from his nose, eyes, and ears; no doubt a result of the incredible strain and terror of the horrors he was witnessing.[13]

As the battle continued to ramp in the favor of evil, it became alarmingly clear to the Professor that his very survival depended upon leaving The Fields at once.

He quickly fumbled through his pockets searching frantically for his medication. His movement caught the attention of many Cherubim in his vicinity. He located his pills, and quickly swallowed as many as he could while beginning to run back up the trench line.

Now in full retreat, he passed several Cherubim, only to receive looks of confusion. Some even moved out of his way, allowing him to pass, not knowing the significance of his presence. He hoped that the medication would take effect before they figured it out. But the Professor's luck was not to last. Three Cherubim sprang into attack mode and closed in quickly on his location, after having been directed by Maximus to search and destroy the man in the trench.

The three were in close pursuit, running behind him in the trench. But soon it became clear that they were no match for his foot speed, so they took to the air, risking life and limb of their own, dodging flames and debris as they flanked from outside the trench.

The Professor, realizing the gravity of the situation, kicked off his shoes in mid run and sprinted for his very life. He quickly outran the protection of the trench while hurdling over fallen trees and plowing painfully through the thistle that bunched up under the oaks that remained standing. He began to gain ground only to be hindered by the burning bodies of falling Angels as they plummeted to the ground around him.

The trailing Cherubim were each aiming their crossbows directly at the Professor. They were all experienced marksmen and once given their orders, would not miss their target. Knowing this, the Professor ran into a thick patch of oaks on the outer edge of The Fields. He weaved in and out of the trees making it difficult for his pursuers to get a fix on their prey.

And while running with all his strength and speed toward the stream, he couldn't help but make a fascinating observation. The pursuing Cherubim were utilizing skills that had only been hypothesized and theorized about as defensive . . . that is until now. As they flanked him from outside the camouflage of the dense clusters of oaks, they rapidly and methodically changed the angle of their heads, presenting to the Professor their different faces. He quickly deduced, while dodging through the oak obstacle course, that they were trying to confuse him into faltering for even a split second enabling them to get off a clean shot.

At first they presented mostly the face of an eagle, designed to frighten many smaller animals such as rodents or venomous snakes. Then they angled to display the face of an ox whose size would confuse and intimidate many smaller creatures into submission. Finally after realizing the speed and determination of their prey, they all set their faces to the lion, which oddly enough, even though the Professor knew they weren't lions, evoked an instinctively fearful response, which only served to encourage his flight.

The Cherubim flew like helicopters. Their wings flapped rapidly like those of a hummingbird, enabling them to hover and move laterally in any direction. Their bodies pivoted in all directions during flight, moving almost independently of their wings. Frequently they rotated backward, angling for a clear shot, while flying forward to keep up with the Professor. As the Professor neared the creek that separated the battlefield from the road, he knew that leaving the protection of the oaks would render him vulnerable.

While approaching the familiar waters of Granite Creek, he pushed harder and ran faster than he ever thought possible. He ran into the shallow waters of the stream just as the medication took effect. Reaching the center of the creek, three arrows were released. They flew at him with deadly accuracy, but fortunately for the Professor, as the battlefield faded, so did the arrows . . . with the exception of one.

It struck the Professor's left shoulder dropping him at the waters edge just at the base of the road. He lay still in the icy-cold waters of Granite Creek, face down, bleeding and exhausted. He was in a mild state of consciousness with the medication leading him deeper and deeper into a medically induced coma.

As he began to entertain thoughts of his own mortality, images of Amena appeared before him like visions from Heaven. And despite his efforts to remain optimistic, he couldn't help but wonder if he'd ever see her again. He could almost hear her voice soothing and comforting him as he slipped into a total state of unconsciousness.

CHAPTER X

CONFESSIONS

❦

Amena and Numier nervously remained on the side of the road while motorists passed unknowingly by, like migrating wildebeests trotting past lions as they devour their kill just feet off the path.

Amena made regular visits to console the crying child.

"It's o.k." Amena said softly hugging Clair in the back seat of the parked car. "Don't be afraid."

"I'm afraid for him," she said as her tears rolled, leaving black streaks of heavy mascara down her otherwise white face.

"He just went for a walk sweetie . . . He'll be right back."

"You know we can't keep her," said Numier as Amena returned to the side of the road.

"I know," she said looking back at the car. "But something tells me she has nowhere else to go."

They waited beneath an alizarin-crimson sunset that on any other day would have been taken for granted. They took a moment to admire the fucia and orange jet stream that mirrored the blazing, blood-soaked earth of another world. While taking their eyes momentarily off the creek, they didn't notice the Professor sprinting back into view.

Suddenly they were startled by the sound of a loud splash in the water at the edge of the creek . . . The Professor's body was laying face down in the stream with an arrow protruding from his shoulder. Amena and Numier ran franticly to his side, pulling him out of the water with precious seconds to spare.

"Oh my God!" Amena shouted. "He's been shot!"

After checking the Professor's breathing and vital signs, Numier quickly inspected the wound and was sure the arrow had missed major arteries and was well above the lungs. But seeing the amount of blood coming from around the wound, he knew the arrow had to be removed and the bleeding stopped at once.

"There is no time to waste. Help me get him into the car!" he said, knowing there was not enough time to drive to the hospital. "We'll take him to Johnsey's Station; it's just around the corner!"

Johnsey's Station was an old pack station built in the early nineteen-hundreds. In the days of horse and buggy, when mountainous trails became too steep for carriages or early motorcars, supplies and belongings would be transferred onto horseback and pack mules prior to continuing into the rugged mountains.

Midway between the populated valley towns and the high country, it made a perfect rest stop for weary travelers. But later, with the construction of suitable roads and four-lane highways, it inevitably became little more than a small café and snack shop for locals or the occasional bicyclist with a fried-food craving.

Numier knew Johnsey's well. He'd spent part of his High School summer vacations working there as a short-order cook. He knew that being a diner, it would have a first-aid kit on hand.

"What's Johnsey's Station, and why aren't we taking him back to the hospital?" grunted Amena while franticly helping hoist the Professor's dead weight into the car. "Shouldn't we call an ambulance? I mean . . . my God, he's unconscious and losing blood!"

"I know, I know. We'll call from Johnsey's . . . but if we can't get help . . . we may have to remove the arrow ourselves." he said.

"You're kidding me right?" she replied.

"Johnsey's is an old diner just around the corner. They have sharp knives and a stove to boil water. The roads this time of year are very slick and can't be traveled quickly. If we drive him all the way to the hospital, he could bleed to death. We need to stop the bleeding and stabilize his condition before we move him any further."

"I hope you know what you're doing . . . I mean, he's a human being for God's sake and not some dog we found wounded by the roadside. I knew this was a bad idea!" she shouted.

"Easy, Please . . .! You heard the radio. There's looting and rioting everywhere . . . We may very well be on our own. Besides, his vital signs are strong, so as long as we get the bleeding stopped, I think he's got a chance."

Johnsey's, no more than three to four minutes away, was situated on Tollhouse road, nestled into the base of Black Mountain, and just down the street from the high school. It sat on the South side of the road with its back to Granite Creek. A working windmill and year-round Christmas lights added to its foothillish charm.

Night had fallen and the cold mountain mist had set in. The full moon illuminated the thin layer of cloud cover from behind, transforming the skies into an iridescent purple-violet. This, in combination with the heavy drizzle, created an eerie bog-like mood that Amena was not at all comfortable with. They pulled into the parking lot of Johnsey's, and while Amena held pressure to the Professor's wound, Numier ran up to the café.

"Can this get any creepier?" she asked while looking around the parking lot for any sign of humanity.

"Only that the place is deserted!" added Numier realizing that Johnsey's was closed. "I forgot that due to the seasonal drop off in business this time of year, the diner doesn't keep regular hours. Wait here while I look for a key."

It had been almost forty years since Numier's stint at hourly employment, but oddly enough the spare key for employees was still where it had always been.

After successfully carrying the Professor's cataleptic body into the safety of the dimly lit diner, Amena grabbed the phone and with bloody hands dialed 911, only to be greeted by a pre-recorded message:

"All circuits are busy . . . if you have an emergency, please try your call again."

In a mild state of shock and disbelief, she gently set the phone down and looked at Numier.

"O.K.," he said. "We can do this!"

Amena quickly located the hunting and fishing first aid kit, in the kitchen, while Numier prepared an oversized dining table for surgery. Together they positioned the Professor's body on top of the dining table and carefully removed the shirt fabric from around the wound.

"Clair, bring some kindling in from the back porch, we need to get a fire going!" shouted Numier.

Numier had seen old Spaghetti Westerns where arrows were extracted from wounded soldiers by breaking off the arrowheads and pulling the shafts out. Numier's plan was simple. Since the arrowhead was protruding through the front of the Professor's chest, he would push the arrow through the shoulder in the same direction it entered minimizing further damage to the surrounding tissue. He removed the feathers carefully leaving only the smooth cylindrical shaft, took a deep breath and forced the arrow through with one swift push from the heel of his hand.

With the arrow now extracted, the blood flowed instantly from the opening in the Professor's shoulder. Numier haphazardly began sewing at the wound with a crude set of sutures from the first aid kit.

"That won't work!" Amena cried, "You have to stop the bleeding first!"

Seeing Numier's uncertainty, she abruptly snatched the sutures from his hand. She knew intuitively that there was no time to spare as each and every drop of blood counted. Quickly overcoming her fear and nervousness, she somehow impulsively located the punctured vein with her finger and quickly sewed it in swashbuckling fashion.

"Well I think that's got it," she said, with trembling hands, while applying pressure to the freshly sutured wound.

"Where did you learn to do that?" he asked.

"Many years ago when studying to be a veterinarian, we would practice suturing almost daily. To be honest, I'm surprised I remembered any of it . . . but I guess when you do something enough times, the training kind-of takes over," she answered while applying dressings to the Professor's shoulder.

"It's just a good thing he's unconscious, or this would hurt like hell!" added Numier.

"The doctor said that too much of the medication he prescribed could induce a slight coma," said Amena.

Numier quickly searched the Professor's coat pocket and discovered an empty pill container and no lid.

"Well . . . your hunch is accurate . . . either he took half the vial, or he spilled it along the way," said Numier, while inspecting the pill container for clues. "Nevertheless, it looks like he'll be out all night."

The two sat still, staring at the Professor's wound and chest as it expanded and contracted with every breath. Satisfied that he was stable, and with the Professor sleeping soundly, Numier turned to Clair.

She was standing by the fire she'd made in the turn-of-the-century, cast-iron, pot-belly stove designed to add ambiance to customers' dining experience.

"Good job Clair," said Numier while adding another log to the fire.

For the first time Numier really looked at Clair. She was staring at the fire with her hair pulled back revealing the features of her face. Although very thin, her cheeks were still round with baby fat.

"You look better without all that eye makeup," said Numier.

She continued looking straight into the fire and said:

"Making the fire was always my job in the house," she said. "My Pa always said we'd never freeze as long as Clair was around."

"How old are you Clair?" asked Numier while she was in the talking mood.

"I've had thirteen birthdays," she said. "But my Pa always said I seem older."

Amena, worried about the Professor's condition, cleaned the dried blood off his face and neck with a damp cloth. By the light of the fire, she could see the apparent aging of the Professor's formerly youthful-looking face. His hair had new streaks of grey, and the fine wrinkles on his face seemed strangely more pronounced.

"It's as though he's aged many years in a very short time," observed Numier.

"The whole ordeal has taken its toll on him," Amena replied.

"You care for him don't you?" asked Numier watching her pull thistle needles from his shins.

"The first time I saw him . . . I sat in on his lecture as a favor to a friend. She couldn't attend so I went to take notes for her. I sat in her seat in the back of the class, trying to keep a low profile, but when I saw him . . . I felt instantly drawn to him. The sensation began in my stomach, and moved to my chest, like something was tugging at my insides. I know that must sound ridiculous, even more so for those who know me. But as I continued listening to his lecture, I felt increasingly giddy, like a little girl, which was not at all my nature. I tried to hide my embarrassment when he called on me by my friend's name. I thought for sure everyone could see my innermost thoughts and feelings, so I kept my answers brief and my head down."

"Wow. So did you introduce yourself to him? I mean, did he ever know how you felt?" Numier asked with a somewhat surprised look on his face as this was the first he'd heard of such a noteworthy event in Don's otherwise lack-luster love life.

"I was a senior visiting Sierra High from another school and my two weeks were up. I left the next day feeling confused and a bit shocked by my behavior. I convinced myself that it was a schoolgirl crush, and that I should dismiss it at once. After all, he was an instructor. But as the years passed, I found myself longing to see him again. I would even look at his picture in my girlfriend's yearbook, and imagine his wife and kids. Was she pretty? Were they happy? I hoped that they were."

"So what brought you back?" asked Numier.

"Well, when I was informed that I was to intern at a high school to complete my credentials, I applied to Sierra. It would be an understatement to say that I was excited when I learned that I'd been accepted . . . I think my heart skipped a beat at the thought of seeing him again. But my enthusiasm was dampened by the reality that he might very possibly have been spoken for; nonetheless, I took a chance . . . and I'm glad I did."

"So you're in love with him," said Numier.

"Yes . . . And I suppose I always have been," she replied.

Numier stood up, grabbed a poker, and began to stoke the fire. While examining the logs and burning embers he said:

"He's always been a bit of a loner . . . with very few friends to speak of and an unsympathetic family who never really understood his eccentricities or his beliefs: he's always kept to himself.

I met him when he was still in graduate school on a dig site in Egypt. We hit it off right away, both sharing the love for theology and anthropology. And while his studies solidified his Christianity . . . mine only strengthened my atheism."

Amena was startled by Numier's disclosure. She'd been a Christian all her life and grew up in a community of believers not normally hearing the 'A' word. She responded quickly:

"How can you say atheism? I mean . . . I assumed since you were Don's friend . . ."

"It all seems so big . . ." he said. "I mean, the idea that everything we know was created by a Supreme Being . . . a Being that we can't see . . . left to rely on faith alone to believe. My education has taught me to trust in facts, proof, and evidence, none of which had pointed conclusively to the existence of God."

"Before today, I was confident in my disbelief . . . taking comfort in knowing that when I die . . . I would just end. Oh sure, I live a good and honest life, but one without fear of condemnation or hope for anything after," he said.

"To live your life expecting to die and then just end . . . and with all that you've learned? It doesn't make any sense," she said.

"You have a point. One could say that in all my years and all my travels, including thousands of books I've read, and in all the theology on which I've lectured, I've learned nothing of any real significance. That is, until today," he said while holding the arrow in his hand.

"Does this mean you've decided to believe Don?" she said suspiciously.

"Actually no . . . It's the arrow," he replied while thoroughly inspecting the ancient projectile.

"Based on what we know, let's examine this arrow analytically", he said while pacing the room in deep concentration. "A skeptic like me would look for a rational explanation . . . like a child target practicing in the woods or something odd such as: It fell out of an airplane carrying sporting goods. Normally I would try to give teeth to the most probable of explanations."

"Yet, you would close your mind to the most corroborated explanation of all . . . God," she replied.

"Touché . . . And until today, you would have been right on the mark. But there is something about this arrow," he added while gesturing for Amena to take a closer look.

"Look at these markings here," he said while holding the arrow under the lamp. "Note the hieroglyphics written long ways down the length of the shaft."

"They look familiar to me . . . are they Assyrian?" she asked.

"Aramaic, to be precise," he answered.

"Babylonian?" asked Amena.

"Yes . . . I would date this arrow at around eight hundred years B.C., during the Late Dynastic Period in Egypt," added Numier.

"But how can that be . . .? she said. I mean, I don't understand,"

He went on to explain:

"Many years ago, Don and I worked together on a dig in Cairo where there was legend to have been a fierce battle. The locals believed that God became very angry at the Assyrians' paganism and barbarism and sent Angels to annihilate them. Being men of science, we needed proof to corroborate such a claim, and after several months of digging, we found it."

"Hundreds of arrows littered throughout the battlefield and each of them with the exact same inscription, "Holy, Holy, Holy is the Lord". Some human fossils were even found with arrows embedded in their bones."

"And still you didn't believe," she said.

"No . . . many of us dismissed the arrows as belonging to other warring tribes of Assyrians fighting for power and ultimately destroying themselves, and that the hieroglyphics were added to frighten their enemies. But some, like Don, believed the arrows were shot from the bows of Angels," he said.

"And were the inscriptions similar to these?" asked Amena.

"Yes, they were exactly the same . . . "Holy, Holy, Holy is The Lord"," answered Numier.

"So you think the arrow came from Angels?" she asked.

"I don't know . . . All I know, is that he claims to have seen Cherubim, and now here he lays, unconscious and shot with a twenty-eight hundred year-old arrow . . ." he replied with furrowed brow.

"He said he saw Angels warring with beasts, and that one even helped him evade the creatures. He believes in God and has faith in Jesus, so why would Angels try to hurt him?" she asked.

"That's a very good question, and one that only the good Professor can answer, I guess it will have to wait until morning," he replied.

"If you would like to freshen up and get a few hours sleep," he offered. "There is an employee's sleeping quarter in the back."

"Thank you, but I think I'll stay out here with Clair, in case she gets scared . . . and in case Don wakes up," she said.

Numier then brought blankets and pillows and excused himself to the back room for some much needed rest. And as he rounded the corner into the kitchen, Amena said:

"Thank you for being such a good friend to him. I don't know what he would have done without you . . ."

He shrugged his shoulders a bit and said:

"Well, what are friends for? Besides," he said as he started into the kitchen, "maybe he'll start to rub off on me."

Amena smiled genuinely, hoping that the men's friendship was strong enough to weather the differences in their beliefs.

She then fixed some herbal tea, curled up by the fire, and together with Clair, fell into a fitful sleep.

A few hours later, she was awakened by noises coming from the next room. After seeing that the Professor was no longer on the table, she looked to the kitchen and spotted Don. Careful not to wake Clair, she quickly stretched herself upright, wrapped herself in an old, hand-made, patchwork quilt, and briskly shuffled her way to the kitchen not knowing what to expect.

"My goodness!" she said. "Are you alright?"

"I've never felt better." He said while drinking a glass of orange juice out of an old recycled mason jar. "How long was I out?"

"Four or five hours at the most," she said. "Come over here, close to the fire . . . let me change your dressing."

As she unraveled his bandages, she was amazed and perplexed to discover that his wound had completely healed.

"You were shot," she said, "through and through by an ancient arrow!"

"Yes . . . the Cherubim were after me. I barely escaped with my life," he said.

"But why? And how could it have healed so quickly?" she asked.

"I'm not quite sure. Maybe they thought that I was a spy. They seemed to think that I was in league with the enemy," he answered. "And as for the wound, I don't know. Maybe the accelerated brain activity caused the rapid healing."

"You had thistle needles in your shins and your feet were torn up pretty bad . . . And what happened to your shoes?" she curiously asked as she tossed kindling onto the glowing embers.

He stared into the fire as his mind began to drift back to the images of battle. Dancing flames reminded him of fire from the mouths of dragons, while erupting kindling began to resemble the burning bodies of Angels that littered the battlefield. While closing his eyes tightly, he hung his head down, covered his face with both hands, and said:

"It was horrible. I saw Satan . . . You couldn't possibly imagine how foul he is, and the things he was doing to the condemned that he held captive. Even though they were far away, it's like I could see them perfectly. I think I was even able to read their thoughts . . ."

"So many Angels died while I watched, powerless to help them. I feel like my soul has been torn apart."

While staring into the fire, a tear ran down his cheek. Seeing this, Amena leaned forward and kissed his face, drying the tear with her lips. He turned to her and kissed her as the tears began to flow.

"Thank you for being here for me," he said while holding her face in his hands.

"There's no place in the world I'd rather be than right here with you," she said into his eyes.

They spoke a bit more and fell asleep in each other's arms until dawn.

When they awoke, Numier was sitting in the kitchen over a fresh cup of coffee, reading the notes he'd written on the drive back from Sacramento.

"Somehow I figured you would bounce back from your injury," said Numier to the Professor. "How are you feeling?"

"Physically, I feel fine . . . but there are still so many questions . . . so much confusion," he said.

Numier poured them both a cup of coffee and proceeded to offer his observations:

"I can't even pretend to understand what you must have been through. Perhaps, in time and when you're ready, you will tell us. But I will say this; the arrow in your shoulder has raised the stakes entirely. We need more information before you even think of going back." he said.

"How do you suggest we do that?" asked Amena.

"There was a caption at the very end of The Cherubim Fields, written in bold lettering, distinguishing itself from the rest of the book. But unfortunately, it was left untranslated, and my Aramaic is weak at best," said Numier.

"Well, why do you suppose it was left untranslated?" asked the Professor.

"I have no idea, but when I originally researched the whereabouts of the book, I came across the name and address of the man who translated it into English in the early fifties. I think it's worth a try to pay him a visit," said Numier.

"My gosh, do you think he's still alive?" asked the Professor.

"Well, although I wasn't able to find a telephone number or email address, the internet showed that his home address is current. Maybe we'll get lucky," said Numier.

"It's worth a try," said Amena. "But what if it turns out to be nothing . . . ?"

"Well at this point, I think it's our only lead," replied Numier.

"Hey, what's going on in Asia?" asked the Professor. "Last I heard there was some serious tension and posturing. Have things gotten worse?"

"Well . . . there is another development that I've neglected to tell you both. While we were sleeping, China invaded India and South Korea. The President of the United States has made every effort to help negotiate a deal with China, but they're not responding. It appears as though there is nothing that can be done to suppress the determination of the Chinese."

"But why are they invading?" asked Amena "What exactly do they want?"

"No one knows . . ." replied Numier.

"Are they reporting any other skirmishes?" hesitantly asked the Professor.

"As a matter of fact yes. There is an alliance formed between eleven Arab countries, and together they are moving massive numbers of troops throughout the Middle East toward Israel," answered Numier. "Why do you ask?"

"I'm not quite sure, but it feels to me that all of this is interconnected," said the Professor.

"Are you saying that your hallucinations are somehow resulting from the violence breaking out all over the world?" Numier asked, suspecting that the Professor may have completely lost his mind. "But then I suppose it would make sense that your concerns about China may have manifested into hallucinations."

"No . . . Not at all," quickly responded the Professor. "On the contrary; I'm somehow developing a strong intuition that it's just the opposite."

"You mean that maybe the violence you've been witnessing and the violence around the world are somehow interrelated?" said Amena

"Yes," said the Professor.

"There are a lot of assumptions being made here," said Numier. "Maybe we should wait until we are able to make better sense of the book before we draw any conclusions, since it seems thus far that the book is the closest thing we have to understanding what's happening to you."

The kitchen door opened slowly and a groggy Clair came through. She stopped just short of the Professor and squinted her eyes to see him more clearly:

"Are you dead?" she said to him in a whispery voice.

"Would he be standing here if he were dead?" said Numier.

"Hey!" barked Amena. "She isn't even awake yet."

"Clair . . . we're going for a ride honey," said Amena.

"Absolutely not," stated Numier. "It's bad enough that she spent the night with us . . ."

"Why not ask her what SHE wants?" said Goodwin.

"Would you like to come with us Clair?" asked Amena.

"I want to stay with you," said Clair.

"Come-on, she's safe with us . . ." Amena said. "And look," as Clair gulped down the Professor's orange juice and tore into a box of cookies. "She'll probably eat better with us anyway."

"We can call the local authorities and see if there have been any missing persons reports filed," said Goodwin while gathering his things.

"We tried that . . . to get help for you . . . but I suppose we can try again," said Amena.

"Fair enough . . ." growled Numier. "But she's your responsibility, not mine."

They all concurred and immediately set their sights on the home of Mr. San Miguel Liberarte, located deep in the woods of British Columbia on the outskirts of Vancouver

CHAPTER XI
INSPIRED TRAVELS

Numier suggested that in the interest of time they should fly. But the Professor, still unsure of his condition, thought it would be best to drive the long journey to Liberarte's home in Canada. Amena agreed whole-heartedly since she loathed flying. They packed light and wasted no time in setting their sights north.

It was roughly an eighteen-hour drive, but if each driver took a three-hour shift, they could make the journey non-stop. The rotation allowed each a six-hour period of time in which to rest, or in the Professor's case, to reflect.

As they passed through blackberry-lined back roads of Oregon, Numier, while driving, was no longer able to contain himself:

"Well . . . let's hear it . . . what happened? I mean, where did the arrow come from?"

Part of the Professor wished to avoid the uncomfortable conversation with Numier as he'd done for so many years, and still part of him knew that it was inevitable.

"I suppose you deserve an explanation, since you did save my life," said the Professor.

"If you're not comfortable talking about it . . ." interrupted Amena.

"No, No. It's not that . . . It's just . . . Well, if I wasn't there myself, I'm not sure I'd believe it."

The Professor began to describe the trench battle in vivid detail. He described the beasts with their array of horn styles and various combinations of appendages. He described the Cherubim and Archangels with perfect detail. He told of the heroic bravery of the Sparrow's as they fought relentlessly against the mounting forces of evil.

"Clair," Amena said.

Clair lifted her forehead off the window she'd been staring out of for hours, not moving and not talking. Shrouded by black hair concealing her face.

"Is this conversation frightening you?" Amena asked.

Clair paused then slowly shook her head.

"Okay sweetie, you just let us know if it's too much for you okay?" Amena added.

Clair just leaned back against the window and continued to stare at the blacktop.

The battle scenes and characters, though painful to remember, were easy to recall. But when it came to Satan's treatment of the nonbelievers, the Professor paused. He knew that he would be drawing first blood against an old friend, delivering a blow directly into the very fundamental belief system of a man who had always been there for him. Nevertheless:

"Numier . . . I know that you consider yourself an atheist, but what exactly does that mean? Do you believe in the possibility of God at all; are you searching; or are you convinced that we evolved from a single cell organism?" the Professor asked.

"I suppose you could consider me an evolutionist," Numier confidently replied.

"Amena told me that you believe that when you die, you will simply end, like an insect at the end of its life cycle," said the Professor.

"Yes, that is correct," he answered while entering the lush countryside of Washington.

"Well, I have bad news for you my good friend . . ."

The Professor went on to explain in gruesome detail the horrifying events that took place in Satan's camp. He couldn't have painted a bleaker picture of the fate of the condemned souls at the evil hands of Hell.

And as Amena put her hand in front of her mouth, he continued:

"You know that I've never preached to you. I've always respected your beliefs or lack thereof, all the while assuming that one-day, and in your own time, you would find God. But all that has changed after what I've seen. I feel a greater sense of urgency to share with you my findings and to put everything on the table, as it were."

The Professor continued as Numier and Amena listened intently:

"I have to admit Numier, I admire you to a great extent for having conviction in your beliefs and not making excuses for them. However, it's a pity that your ideas and learned attributes are being used for the advancement of evil . . ."

"Now wait a minute," interrupted Numier. "I never said anything about believing in, or trying to advance any evil."

"Forgive me for using such absolute language, but based on what I've seen, in the interests of good and evil, there is no middle ground."

"This may seem like an over-simplification to you, but it's a multifarious equation with a very simple solution. Many claim to be too intelligent or too educated for God, yet they miss the most basic and fundamental element of salvation. Intelligent men try desperately to over-think and over-analyze the meaning of life, when it's really very simple."

"It's pure irony that in such a complex world filled with technological advancements, countless religions, and clearly defined boundaries of moral values designed specifically to facilitate coexisting in an elaborate, civilized society, that there exists just one simple solution," the Professor said, while looking out the window, in an effort to avoid eye contact with Numier.

"We either develop a relationship with our Creator, or we don't."

"Every single thing that brings a soul closer to a relationship with God is inherently good, and ultimately a blessing. Conversely, every single thing that leads a soul away from that relationship is inherently evil, and leads to their damnation."

"Oh. So now you think I'm evil," huffed Numier. "One minute, I'm helping a friend sort out some bizarre hallucinations, and the next . . . I'm the Antichrist!"

"No, that's not at all what I'm saying," said Goodwin. "What I'm saying is that you have a great gift of persuasion. You're a teacher . . . a Professor. You can enter into any religious or spiritual conversation, and by using your intelligence and your life experiences, you can, and do, influence people's beliefs."

"For example, here you are, a successful business man, P.H.D., college professor, and, an atheist. Did it ever occur to you that the impressionable minds to whom you've been entrusted to teach, might actually strive to emulate you?"

"And so what if they do. What's wrong with that?" barked Numier.

"Mankind has inflicted upon itself every heinous crime imaginable, all of which were considered to have been inspired by evil," continued Goodwin.

"When in fact, the only true evil is to relieve a believer of his or her faith, or to add credence to a nonbeliever's delusions of atheism. This is the only true power the Devil has over us. The power to, in any way possible, distract us just long enough that we miss our opportunity for Salvation."

"Consider this as you reflect upon your own individual role in the struggle between good and evil: What a shame it would be if even one of your students, so intently hanging on your every word, were to sadly end up in that black box as a result of one of your lectures."[14]

"So what you are saying. . ." responded Numier "is that I am a tool for the Devil, and that despite my own personal convictions . . . I should keep my mouth shut. And if I am to understand you correctly, anyone and everyone, regardless of how they live their lives and regardless of what their belief system may be, whether born into or chosen, if they aren't a Christian and don't accept Christ as the Son of God and their Savior, they'll be condemned to hell for all eternity?"

"What I'm begging of you is that you strongly consider that what I've experienced are not hallucinations, but are in fact, very real. And after reaching that milestone, and in that very moment, you can save yourself and some of your students, from the horrors I've seen, and the fate that awaits you . . . by simply calling on Jesus." said the Professor.

And as Numier and Amena sat quietly, the Professor continued:

"Accepting Salvation is the easiest, simplest, and yet most important thing we can ever do in this life. And its simplicity is only made possible by the fact that Salvation has already been bought and paid for by the Blood of Jesus Christ two thousand years ago . . . Salvation that none of us deserves . . . but all of us are offered."

"Jesus knocks at your door Numier . . . all you have to do is open it."

Numier felt disturbed at best. After all these years, the Professor finally verbalized his concerns regarding his best friend's atheism. He knew the Christian stance on nonbelievers, but until today hadn't heard it from Don. Being an intelligent man with a keen sense of consideration, Numier realized how very difficult it had to have been for the

Professor to make the leap that would likely change their relationship at its most fundamental level.

Insightfully, he resolved himself to leave it alone and credit the whole conversation to the injury and lack of rest, but as they pushed further toward the home of San Miguel Liberarte, Numier decided to rile the other Christian in the car.

Amena kept silent, intuitively respecting the dynamics of the men's egos as they were at an apparent impasse, but Numier would have none of it.

"Well what about you?" he said looking in the rear view mirror at Amena. "This is an open forum. You won't have many opportunities like this one, at least not with me."

Amena just looked away onto the wild blackberries that garlanded the miles and miles of rusty barbwire fencing that lined the beautiful Northern Washington roadsides.

"Oh come-on now . . . doesn't the Bible call you to witness your faith? Or are you just going to let me burn in hell and be eaten alive by hell-beasts?" said Numier in an effort to bait Amena into a theological debate with a very experienced devil's advocate. "And while I'm on the subject of burning in hell, what kind of God would let me suffer the fate of that little black box anyway. Isn't YOUR God supposed to be a loving God?"

The Professor bit his tongue and sat this one out. His many years of studying the scriptures had prepared him for such a question. But he knew that it was a tough question for a young Christian to field, and so, despite his instincts . . . he remained silent.

The temptation was far too great for Amena to resist, so she cleared her throat, and weighed in on the issue:

"You can play dumb like a fox with me Numier, but I know that you've posed that question to theologians much better read than myself and with much better understanding of the Bible."

"So rather than fall into your tiger's snare, I'll share with you a theory of my own. It's an original concept that you might find more challenging to refute."

The Professor sat up and turned sideways in the passenger chair, giving his full and undivided attention to what could prove to be an even deeper look into the soul of Amena with whom he was already impressed.

"I call it 'God doesn't eat junk food'," she said further clearing her throat hoping to present eloquently her concept to a lion waiting to pounce.

"First of all, love is only one of God's known attributes, wrath is another. The Bible tells us that God sent three Angels to Sodom challenged with the task of finding ten just men, and in doing so, would spare the city from sure annihilation. The Angels, after failing to find even ten just men, instructed Lot to take his family out of the city warning them not to look back while they fled. His wife, not able to resist, looked back on the city as it was being destroyed by God, and as a result, also perished."[15]

"Another example of God's dissatisfaction with Mankind is Noah. God flooded the earth, drowning every man, woman and child with the exception of Noah's family and the animals in the Ark. We routinely gloss over the undeniable cruelty of such a mass extermination. It was an act of Genocide unlike any the world has ever known before or since. We can only imagine the sounds of screaming children and babies trying desperately to cling to their mothers before finally being silenced by the flood waters of God."

"I think it an irrefutable fact, historically proven and well documented in every language on the planet . . . that God has proven to Mankind that He owes us nothing, and that He is fully capable of destroying each and every one of us if and when He wills it."

"Yes, Yes," interjected Numier, in an effort to encourage Amena to get to the point. "We are all aware of the doom and gloom of the Old Testament, but if this is the make-up of the God you believe in, dissatisfied with the choices of Man, routinely destroying Mankind and ultimately owing us nothing, then Heaven must be a rather empty place."

"Well, actually it was. The Bible teaches us that Jesus is the first born of the dead,"[16] she continued. "And it is only through our understanding of God's wrath, that we can fully understand and appreciate the immense importance of Jesus."

"Getting back to 'God doesn't eat junk food'," she said. "Clearly it is difficult and virtually impossible to attain the Kingdom of Heaven on our own, yet we are offered a subterfuge through his Son, Jesus."

"Are you suggesting that we sneak into Heaven?" asked the Professor, hoping to help clarify Amena's proposition.

"No . . . not at all," she replied. "In fact, nothing happens if it weren't the Will of God. What I'm saying is, 'we hide in Christ'."[17]

"It must have been a difficult concept for the disciples during the Last Supper when Jesus told them to, take this bread and eat it, for this is My Body, and take this wine and drink it, for this is My Blood . . ."[18]

"Again, we gloss over these words every Sunday in Church as we receive the offering of Communion; but when you really stop and think about it . . . what a truly odd thing to say."

"But as odd as it may be, Jesus instructs His Church to perform this 'morose' analogy on a regular basis."

"By consuming the Body and Blood of Christ, He becomes one with us as we carry Him throughout our lives. Scripture illustrates that Jesus brings this same concept forward to our souls when we accept Him as our Lord and Savior."

And as the men listened intently, she continued:

"By being spiritually consumed by Christ upon rebirth, we become one with Him, thus entering the Kingdom of Heaven by hiding in Christ. And it is through this process that we take our place in Heaven . . . in the constant company of God forever.[19] But without Jesus' spiritual consumption of us, we couldn't possibly be in the company of God . . . Hence, 'God doesn't eat junk food'"

"O.K. now . . . Let me try to make sense of your theory of hitching a ride to Heaven in the Belly of Jesus," facetiously spouted Numier.

"You're saying that if God were a strict vegan and did not allow junk food in his house, the only way junk food could enter, is that which surges through the Veins of His Son, who happens to love junk food?"

"Well . . . that would be an oversimplification . . . but yes, in a nutshell . . . yes," said Amena confidently owning and standing behind her hypothesis.

Numier upon recognizing that he'd underestimated his sparring partner, tried again to trip up the young Christian.

"Why hell then?" poses Numier, "Why does your faith profess that we cannot just die and end as nonbelievers. Why the condemnation?"

"I prefer to look at condemnation as accountability," she replied. "Both Old and New Testaments speak of original sin. This world has already been given to Satan. We are all born with a one-way ticket to hell. We either choose to take Christ's off-ramp . . . or we don't."

"God raised the stakes when He offered us a way into His Kingdom of Purity. He gave us His one and only Son who died for our sins so that we may be forgiven and obtain the Kingdom of Heaven . . . and with very little effort on our part.[20] And with that colossal offering of love and sacrifice by God, it suddenly became personal." concluded Amena.

And as Numier pulled the car slowly into the Canadian-border crossing, he said:

"But, of course, your entire hypothesis, as good as it may be, hinges entirely on the assumption that there is a God, and that the Bible is in fact the Word of God . . . an assumption that I'm still not willing to make."

Amena curiously peered over the shoulder of the Professor at the upcoming border crossing, relieved that she'd managed to witness, but not at all surprised at Numier's lack of reception to either of their efforts to enlighten him.

CHAPTER XII
THE TRANSLATOR
❧

It seemed as tough they'd been driving for days.
They traveled many miles without so much as a
glimpse of another motorist, which was quite a
change from the bumper-to-bumper traffic of
California. They passed along salmon and rainbow-
trout-filled streams, traversed over century-old,
pine-covered bridges, as well as hardwood-fortified
monoliths, designed to endure the weight of massive
logging trucks that for years have hastily trampled
over them.

The mountains and back roads of Canada were
breathtaking as they negotiated through the
picturesque scenery. The hillsides and creeks were
teeming with vegetation and wildlife. The three
were in awe of nature's splendor as the forests that
surrounded them were in a vibrant state of fall color.
Thick patches of giant trees in lime green and Myers
yellow cascaded gently down toward the road.

Scenic beauty not withstanding, the three felt as
though they would never reach their destination,
when out of nowhere, they approached what
appeared to be the end of the road.

At the very end of a loosely paved, Canadian-mountain
road was a gate. Not just any gate, but an enormous

gate. Amena likened it to the entrance of an old small town; welcoming visitors with the town's name arching over the road.

There were two twenty-foot tall, large, grey-stone columns on either side of the road, onto which two very large gates were hung. On the face of each column were several large copper plaques darkened and jaded by time, but still legible. Through the copper and olive patina could be read inscriptions in many different languages, none of which the three were able to decipher.

The gates were made of cast-iron, several inches thick and seemingly impenetrable. Even the hinges upon which the gigantic black gates were affixed were massive, no doubt custom designed to handle the enormous weight. Adding to the barricade were several very old vines that twisted and meandered tightly throughout the gates.

The vines were several feet thick in some spots, fusing the gates together like one massive amalgamation of wood and iron. There were no locks, as the enormous gates were far too heavy to have been opened by hand, or even pushed by conventional automobile. The three exited the car, seizing the opportunity to stretch their legs while further inspecting the structure.

"I think I see an intercom!" shouted the Professor from the base of one of the columns.

"Push the button . . . let's see if anyone's home!"
Amena shouted eager to find a restroom and freshen
up a bit.

"It's rusted shut!" the Professor said while clearing
the cobwebs for a better look at the device.

As Numier approached with a tire iron to help
encourage the intercom, a voice emanated from a
speaker hidden within the column.

"May I help you . . .?"

"Uh, yes . . . We're here to see Mr. San Miguel
Liberarte," replied the Professor.

After a brief pause, a voice from the column asked:
"Do you have an appointment?"

"Uh . . . no . . . We're here to speak with
Mr. Liberarte about a book he translated many
years ago," said Numier.

"My employer has translated many books . . . To
which are you referring?" asked the voice.

"THE CHERUBIM FIELDS", answered the Professor.

Without another word, loud cracking and screeching
came from the gates as they began to move. Amena
instinctively covered her ears while the enormous
gates slowly began to open. They moaned and

creaked stridently as they tore loose from the labyrinth of ivy and debris that imprisoned them. Huge chunks of wood and iron fell, narrowly missing Numier.

"Hurry . . . Everybody in the car before they close again!" yelled Numier.

And as the four drove past the gates, Amena suspiciously asked:

"Did either of you see a motor on that gate?"

"Come to think of it . . . I didn't see any kind of opening device at all. One would have to employ quite a substantial power source to open a gate of that magnitude," concurred Numier.

"Come on now you two. I thought I was supposed to be the crazy one . . . It could have operated on some sort of underground pulley system," said the Professor. "I know it's been a long drive, but keep it together a little while longer . . . We're almost there."

They drove slowly and cautiously while pondering the mystery surrounding the enchanted entrance to what would appear to be the world's longest driveway.

They drove for miles through majestic oaks and sycamores, not at all indigenous to the Canadian mountains.

"I thought oaks and sycamores were native to California?" suspiciously said Amena.

"Yes they are." replied Numier, "but once transplanted, I see no reason why they wouldn't thrive here as well as any other form of vegetation."

"Yes . . . I suppose you're right," said Amena with one eye squinted and the other brow lifted.

After driving several miles down the dirt and gravel driveway, they came upon a clearing. It was a green-grassy meadow, bordered by Baby-Blue Eyes, Poppies, and Fiddle-Necks, also oddly indigenous to the California foothills. Surrounding the city-block sized meadow were forests of Giant Sequoia Redwoods, the largest known trees on the continent. They stood several hundred feet with diameters in excess of thirty feet.

There were full-grown stags with families of fawns and does prancing carefree across the meadow. Pheasants and quail flew out from in front of their vehicle, as wild geese circled just yards above their heads.

"I've never seen anything like this before in my life," whispered Amena, trying not to frighten the animals or wake Clair.

"This must be some kind of game preserve, like Yellowstone or something," said Numier.

"Not necessarily," replied the Professor, "Canadians don't need game preserves due to the abundance of wildlife combined with their respect for the environment. Besides, they probably all belong to that!" as he pointed up the hillside.

Numier slowed the car down to a crawl as they marveled at what appeared to be an ancient European castle built into the side of the mountain. The fortress appeared to be several hundred feet tall, easily towering over the giant redwoods that surrounded it.

It was enormous in scale, elegant in its splendor, with dark gothic undertones. It was a perfect example of neo-classical architecture. Standing twenty-stories high and built of solid rock, the castle resembled more of a compound than an actual residence. It was a rectangular structure with large round towers at its front corners. The flat roof with scalloped edges added to its gothic, war-like appearance. There was a mysterious and threatening quality to the building which caused them to approach with caution.

As they drove closer, they could clearly see the solid, slate-covered turrets in perfect condition.

"This must be some sort of replica of a French castle," said Numier.

They negotiated their way slowly through English boxwood-lined paths, coming to a stop in the middle of a cobblestone-paved courtyard, with the walls of the giant structure looming over them.

"Wait here . . . I'll see if we're in the right place," Numier said as he slowly walked toward the front door of the castle.

In the center of the courtyard was a huge, solid-stone fountain. Columns of water spouted high into the air from the mouths of three large-winged creatures, which confounded Numier, as he couldn't quite distinguish the animals through the water cascading loudly over them.

Still marveling at the enormous fountain, he stood in front of a twenty-foot tall, solid-mahogany door. It was arc-shaped and wide enough for a locomotive to pass through unobstructed. On the face of the door were two massive iron lion heads. Each head had a huge cast-iron ring in its mouth the size of a car tire. Numier was hesitant to attempt to operate such a large doorbell and prepared to return to the car where Amena and the Professor waited cautiously.

"Ring it!" Amena shouted, eager to get out of the vehicle she'd been sitting in for over seventeen hours.

"Ring it? I can't even reach it!" shouted Numier from the doorway.

Just then the door opened slowly and loudly. Again creaking and cracking as rust and debris fell in

chunks from the hinges. The massive doors had clearly not been opened for quite some time.
And as both doors opened simultaneously and completely, they revealed an elderly man dressed in what appeared to be a century-old tuxedo, sinisterly standing very still.

"My name is Bohramee . . . I have informed my employer of your arrival, and he is awaiting your company in the library . . . come . . . I will be your escort."

The elderly man was apparently some sort of butler. He was very tall and very slight, with thin white hair and an almost opaque complexion. Clearly well into his late eighties or possibly even early nineties, he seemed relatively normal in every way with one obvious exception. His eyes were white, devoid of any color or pupil, and for all intents and purposes, useless.

Exiting the car, Amena turned to the girl:

"Come-on Clair," she said. But there was no answer.

"Clair?" Amena said louder. There was still no response, just a slow shaking of the head.

"Okay then . . . if you change your mind, or if you need anything, we'll be right inside."

Clair just kept quiet with her head slumped over, firmly pressed against the left side passenger window.

CHAPTER XII ½
THE CASTLE

His blindness concerned them initially, but as Bohramee began walking briskly down the main corridor, it became apparent that his severe handicap was inconsequential as he obviously possessed an intimate knowledge of the castle.

While Bohramee confidently guided them through a network of corridors, they were taken by the impressive display of antiquities. There were rooms paneled in solid oak, finely carved by artisans who possessed skills long since extinct. The hallways were lined with century old, neo-classical paintings by artists of the caliber of Rubens, Canaletto, and Monet.

"My Gosh . . . the art in this place alone must be worth a fortune!" said the Professor, as he examined the collection of Monets.

"I don't think I could put a value on the paintings on this wall alone, not to mention the artifacts," Numier replied while gawking at what appeared to be original sketches from Picasso.

As they continued quickly through the massive castle corridors, they were surrounded by statues and displays of battle scenes from ancient times.

They passed through rooms filled with full body-armor, no doubt from actual battles, with their scars of engagement and blood-stained tunics pointing compellingly to their authenticity.

They entered a grand foyer in what appeared to be the center of the castle. At one time, it was likely the entrance to the castle which over time had been engulfed in the interest of expansion. The room was enormous with forty-foot tall ceilings on which were displayed the frescos of Angelic battle scenes of Biblical proportion.

On the walls of the foyer were displayed hundreds of heads of animals of every species. The mounts ranged from creatures as small as tiny, rabbit-sized African antelope, to full body mounts of two Madagascar Lions engaged in battle. They were reared up on their hind legs, standing fifteen feet or more, and were embraced in a mutual death hold with three-inch-long fangs deeply embedded in each other's necks.

As impressive as the lions may have been, the three encountered mummified remains of creatures larger still. They stopped speechless at the feet of a male, African elephant in perfect preserved condition. Its ears were unfurled and displayed completely expanded, protruding outward from the sides of its enormous head in full attack mode. It was flanked by two large male rhinoceros, the smallest of which was taller than Numier.

"Now I know what happened to Noah's ark!" Amena said while snickering with nervous energy.

"Keep in mind that it hasn't been until recently that these animals were protected and illegal to hunt," said Numier while inspecting the authenticity of the rhino's horns.

"Say whatever you want . . . but this guy either has a penchant for killing things, or a fetish for dead things . . . or both!" Amena stated as they continued on into the next room.

They proceeded down a stonewalled corridor, when strong smells of mold and moisture combined to create a fusty, subterranean odor. As they continued, the corridor opened onto what appeared to be the backside of the castle. And as a blanket of cold, misty-evening air hit them, Numier said:

"Excuse me sir, but why are we leaving the castle?"

"We are not," answered Bohramee, somewhat exhilarated by the soggy evening air.

The three stopped cold in their tracks . . . speechless and in awe as they realized that they were not, in fact, exiting the castle, but entering an enormous cave that seemed to hollow out the entire mountain.

"It is the largest room in the castle," said Bohramee as he walked briskly in front of them. "Its five-miles long, two-miles wide and five-hundred-feet high," he added as his voice slowly echoed back.

"This is the most incredible thing I've ever seen," said Numier. "We've uncovered large caves on our digs but nothing as spacious and unobstructed as this . . . it's like a valley with a lid on it!"

"Oh, no sir . . ." responded Bohramee. I can assure you that this is no cave. It was all excavated by hand. And at every quarter mile, to prevent collapse, it has been fortified with stone pillars that as you can see, clearly dwarf the Giant Grizzly Redwood trees that you passed on your way in."

There were openings cut into the stony, cave top, allowing rain, air, and some light to enter. The walls were covered with rocks, soil, and intricate networks of exposed root systems that climbed upward disappearing into a thin but dense layer of moisture that lined the edges of the cave's ceiling.

Hurrying to keep up with the now trotting Bohramee, their obvious gawking at the architecture of the enormous cavern was interrupted by yet another engineering feat.

It was a massive fence that surrounded them. It formed a semi-circular pattern that allowed them to enter the cave but blocked their passage in all directions except back into the corridor from whence they came.

It stood at least eighty-feet tall, with thousands of three-foot-thick pickets, spaced no more than two-feet apart. It was constructed of solid steel and seemingly impenetrable. And as if its mammoth size wasn't enough, there were several large red and white signs positioned every fifty yards or so that read, 'High Voltage!'

"Is this thing designed to keep us out . . . or to keep something else in?" asked Amena clearly alarmed by its size.

The Professor took several steps back toward the safety of the castle. His face took on a distressed expression as the blood departed his head leaving him clammy and pale. He shook his head and fought against the impending panic as he frantically studied the fence and surrounding areas of the cave.

"What's wrong?" Amena asked, quickly walking to his side.

"That smell . . . I remember it from The Fields," answered the Professor in a whisper.

"Yes!" added Numier, "When I was serving in Vietnam, I too have had the misfortune of experiencing the odor of decaying bodies. We called it 'The Smell of Death'." And without another step he shouted, "What is this, some sort of mortuary?"

"I can assure you . . . you will be safe . . . but we must move quickly!" said Bohramee.

And with the three following cautiously behind, Bohramee, stopped dangerously close to the electrified structure and shouted:

"Please go no further!" holding his arms out widely.

The trio stopped, gladly keeping their distance from both the fence and Bohramee as he turned to them and said:

"It is roughly a thirty-minute walk to the library, but in the interest of time and safety, I've arranged for suitable transportation."

And before his echo returned, the ground beneath them began to rumble and quake. Amena held onto the Professor's arm and buried her face into his jacket as Numier stepped in close to their position.

Suddenly a loud buzzer began to sound intermittently as a large portion of the fence began to move. Through the opening it created emerged a very large team of horses. A herd of twelve Clydesdales pulling a large, black coach burst through the breach and skidded to a sudden stop as the enclosure swiftly slammed shut behind them.

The horses were huge. The largest of their kind, hand-picked for their size and speed, they stood ten-feet tall to their withers and weighed several thousand pounds each. They were solid black with the exception of the silver fur that covered their hooves.

The coach's exterior was constructed of black, cast iron. It was very large, similar to the caboose section of a locomotive. Its windows were made of tempered glass at a minimum of three-inches thick. Its wheels were fashioned of solid steel, devoid of any visible rubber.

The three walked quickly to the coach, as the horses respired heavily with steam billowing from their flared nostrils with each exhale.

"Does this guy do anything on a small scale?" Amena nervously asked.

Bohramee, now several paces ahead said:

"I hope you'll find the accommodations suitable," as he opened the door to the coach.

Cautiously entering the carriage, Numier took a deep breath and said:

"Ahh . . . now that's better . . . the smell of fine Italian leather!"

"It's Greek," answered Bohramee while fastening himself securely into the captain's chair located at the front of the coach, positioned rearward facing his guests, "Unborn lamb's leather to be precise . . . the softest in the world."

"That is sooo wrong," said Amena while slowly stroking the smooth seat cushion and rubbing her face against the headrest. "But very, very nice."

As Numier further inspected the coach, he marveled at the fine craftsmanship of the ornate woodwork meticulously carved from solid mahogany. The interior walls of the carriage were lined with deep-purple velvet, silk, and satin, adding to its gothic-boudoir atmosphere.

"This carriage must have set your boss back a fortune," said the Professor.

"It is not for sale!" barked Bohramee while impatiently and insistently instructing them to take their seats.

And as the three found their seats, momentarily suspending their inspection of their strange and inexplicable surroundings, an opening in the fence appeared. The horses slowly trotted inside and stopped completely with the massive doors slamming shut behind them.

"Why have we stopped?" whispered Amena.

Their conversation was abruptly interrupted by the distant sounds of roaring that echoed ferociously and violently through the cave.

"What was that?!" shouted Amena as she sprang up from her seat to look out of the nearest window.

"It sounds like a pride of lions!" said Numier."

And as the men hustled to securely fasten their lap belts, they pulled at Amena encouraging her to return to her seat.

But the roars grew louder as they rapidly approached the coach.

"I didn't come here to get eaten up by some of your freak employer's exotic, wild animals!" franticly screamed Amena. "Take us back!"

"I can assure you, you will be safe inside the coach! Its exterior has been designed to withstand such an attack. Now would you please remain in your seats and fasten your lap belts!" shouted Bohramee.

"Attack?! What do you mean attack?!" screamed Amena while franticly securing herself back into her seat.

And as the deafening sound of the approaching roars, filled and engulfed the cave, the Professor, calm until now shouted:

"Why aren't we moving? Are we to wait here like sitting ducks?"

"The animals see movement, like the ones you are making by panicking about the coach. Remain calm . . . The horses will know exactly when to proceed!" shouted Bohramee.

Just then the coach was struck by a high-speed impact. The four passengers were thrashed about as the capsule rocked violently from side to side with their screams filling the perilous vessel.

Almost instantaneously, the coach burst forward, steadily increasing in velocity towards the dark side of the cave. The three screamed in fear as the sudden G-Force produced by the rapid acceleration of the carriage pressed them all firmly into the back of their seats. But their screams were replaced with sighs of relief when they realized the carriage's thrust seemingly shook loose its violent attackers.

The cave became hauntingly quiet as the carriage reached velocities of over one-hundred-miles per hour. Numier managed to glance briefly out an adjacent window, only to see quarter-mile columns passing by like strobe lights. But shortly after reaching cruising speed, their mystical vessel began to slow to a stop. Screeching and squealing, the wheels of the carriage stopped cold, coming to a standstill even quicker than it had accelerated.

Hurled forward, held back only by the tension in their seatbelts, the three again screamed until they were out of breath, and the coach had finally come to a complete stop.

CHAPTER XIII
THE LIBRARY
⊗

"You may exit safely, as we are once again behind the security of the gates," instructed Bohramee.

And as the three apprehensively exited the coach, and while still catching their breath, Amena noticed something peculiar about the vessel.

"Did either of you see a driver on that thing?" she said.

"There wasn't even a place for one to sit," added the Professor while glancing back at the coach.

The three were then led into a tunnel-like opening at the back end of the cave that passed between a dark mahogany-lined dining room and a commercial-sized kitchen. They followed Bohramee down the damp, dimly-lit corridor, stopping just outside the entrance to what appeared to be yet another wing of the castle.

The light in the room was fainter than the others, which seemed to add to its daunting purpose. It was the armory. On its walls, virtually covering every square inch, were thousands of ancient weapons. Shields and breastplates, from various time periods and practically every imaginable battle, papered the walls from floor to ceiling.

There were swords of all types, from small daggers and knives, to ancient bloodstained broadswords held in the hands of knights posing in full-battle armor. Flint-operated long rifles and dragoons adorned the entrance to the library, which was the last room of the castle and their final destination in their search for Liberarte.

"I'm not sure coming here was such a good idea," Amena said. "I'm worried about Clair."

Goodwin held her close and said: "She'll be alright."

Upon entering the library, they couldn't help noticing the priceless antiques that decorated the massive room. It was a perfect example of gothic craftsmanship. The walls were twenty-feet high, faced from floor to ceiling with dark, hardwood shelving that overflowed with books. On the only blank wall of the room was an enormous fireplace, which itself looked like a large room; hand carved from solid stone and decorated with marble carvings of even more ancient battle scenes. It had what looked like a full-grown and unpruned tree burning in it, and due to the light created from its combustion, there was no need for any additional illumination.

Positioned between the library-shelves and the blazing tree was a large ball and claw, teak-wood desk and an oversized, high-back chair. The chair was on the far side of the desk, facing the fire, with its back to the trio.

"My God," Numier said. "I've never seen such an incredible collection of primeval books and references. This makes the Library of Ancient Books look like a child's bookshelf!"

As the three marveled at the volumes within reaching distance, they heard a voice coming from the fireplace area:

"Who are you . . . and why have you come here?" spoke a deep voice from the large, high-back chair.

"We are here seeking information about a book," tentatively answered Numier. "Would you be Mister San Miguel Liberarte?"

"Yes . . . I would be he. My servant informs me that you have questions concerning a book that I translated long ago . . . THE CHERUBIM FIELDS is it?" said the voice.

"Yes. In the book there is a section that was left untranslated . . . and possibly, if you could help us, we could more fully understand the book's meaning," continued Numier.

"Meaning? The book has no meaning. It is fantasy . . . fiction . . . food for the youth and eccentrics whom hunger for gothic fairy tales!" sternly barked Liberarte.

"If that's the case, then what harm would it do to complete the translation?" asked Numier.

"Very well then," exhaled Liberarte in an annoyed tone. "It says, "Herein is written an imaginary tale of make believe, composed for dreamers and fantasists . . . He who believes in it . . . is a fool"."

"No! That's not what it says," interjected Amena. "Pardon me sir. I mean no disrespect, but my grandparents were Assyrian, and although I haven't spoken the language in many years . . . I'm sure that's not what it says."

The large chair turned slightly, partially illuminating the silhouette of a large man sitting upright with a book open on his lap.

"Very well then . . . educate me. Complete the translation and tell us what it says," he said from his chair.

"It says . . . 'For the world, here is written an imaginary tale of make believe, composed for dreamers and fantasists. But for one man, it is real. For the one man with the gift to cross celestial dimensions, this book is an instruction manual.'"

The Professor and Numier both looked at her with their mouths partially opened clearly impressed by her hidden talents.

"Why didn't you tell us you could read Aramaic?" whispered the Professor.

"I wasn't confident in my translation, especially since it didn't make any sense," she said.

"Very good my Babylonian guest. You seem to have a keen understanding of a language that is all but extinct. Now if that is all, I bid you a good day! Bohramee will escort you out," he said while turning his chair back to the fire.

"No. Wait. We need your help!" pleaded the Professor.

"Your translation is complete!" shouted Liberarte. "The book is fiction . . . pay no attention! There is no need for further conversation. Now if you'd please. Bohramee will show you to . . ."

"It's me!" shouted the Professor. "It's me . . . I'm the one! I've been there . . . I've seen 'The Cherubim Fields'. I've seen the beasts, the Angels, the bloodshed . . . I was there!"

And for a moment . . . time stood still. The Professor had exposed himself and his vulnerability quickly overshadowed his confidence. An eerie silence filled the room as the three bunched together in anticipation of their host's response to the Professor's seemingly unbelievable claim.

Liberarte turned and slowly stood up from his chair. The Professor and Numier quickly stepped back as Amena jumped behind them in fear. Liberarte stood peering at them in ambient silence. He stood at least twelve-feet tall, lean, and powerfully built like a finely trained athlete. Through his snug, white, collarless-shirt could be seen enormously muscular chest and upper arms. His hands were huge, heavily veined and oddly soiled.

His face was tan with olive undertones and glowed as if illuminated by an unusual light source separate from the firelight behind him. With a prominent Roman nose and rectangular chin, his features were weathered and masculine. But although his appearance was hardened, he possessed an almost feminine beauty.

He had shoulder-length, wavy, black hair with streaks of white that flew back as though he was facing into the wind. His eyes were a piercing cobalt blue, deep and mysterious, but with an overriding compassion and sincerity.

He stood erect and self-assured but with a slightly humbled posture. And as he gently pushed his chair back behind him, he faced his guests, and in a deep thundering voice, he spoke:

"Did you see the tomb?"

But there was no response as they were all stunned and utterly confused by the enormous size of their host. Their combined fear of the giant in the room caused them to pause for words.

"The tomb . . . did you see it?!" he repeated loudly.

And as the room shook from the vibration of his voice, the Professor nervously and apprehensively answered:

"I don't know . . . there was so much confusion."

"It would have looked like a large black door in the face of a mountain," said Liberarte.

"Yes, Yes. At the bottom of the cliff. It looked out of place," said the Professor.

"How far behind the front line was it?" asked Liberarte, as the ground shook and books fell from the reverberation of his voice.

"I don't know . . . I mean it's hard to tell. Two hundred yards . . . maybe less," answered the Professor while trying to keep his balance.

Liberarte, in realizing that the Professor could have easily obtained this information from the book, escalated the difficulty of his questioning:

"The book fails to describe a certain object in the possession of one of the Dark Angels. What was the object, and who was carrying it?"

The Professor closed his eyes and painfully recalled the images he so earnestly wished to forget as Amena clung to his arm in fear:

"It was a little black box that Satan carried with him throughout the camp. He turned to it almost vengefully when things weren't going his way. It appeared to contain some sort of dark-greenish, gooey material . . ." And after a brief pause, the Professor sheepishly asked, "should I continue?"

Liberarte glanced downward in deep thought and said:

"He's come a long way . . . my dark brother . . ."

Amena stuck her head out from behind the two men and said:

"O.K. Now this is starting to freak me out . . . I think it's time we should be leaving."

Liberarte, realizing he had frightened them, softly and calmly said:

"Please forgive me . . . I've been rude, and not entirely forthcoming. You see, not only did I translate the book, but I also wrote it."

The room was quiet and the shaking subsided. The three hesitated, trying with all their combined intellect to process the unnatural information.

"But THE CHERUBIM FIELDS was written over a thousand years ago . . . How could you possibly be its original author?" Numier asked though not at all prepared for the answer.

"Allow me to introduce myself . . . I am Michael . . . Archangel of the Lord, and author of the book."

Along with the introduction, from behind his back unfurled a pair of wings that spanned thirty feet from tip to tip. They were brilliant white in color, filling the room as they knocked down lamps and pushed over furniture. They virtually obstructed the firelight radiating from behind, leaving only the silhouette of the Mighty Angel.

Although the introduction warranted a response, the three stood slack-jawed and speechless. Standing wide-eyed, marveling at the Archangel, the Professor's adrenaline increased his blood pressure which worked against his medication. While fighting to stay alert, Amena's breathing became quick and shallow. She found herself in shock and fear at the vision she was beholding. Her face grew pale and clammy as the blood exited her extremities in favor of more vital organs.

The Professor and Amena dropped to their knees with fear and respect in the presence of the Angel. Amena's traditional apostolic upbringing taught her a good deal about Angels, but much of what she'd learned caused her to imagine Angels as chubby little cupid-like babies with wings, brandishing miniature bows and arrows in their tiny little hands. She never imagined that she'd be in the company of such a towering Angel of The Lord.

The Professor was the only one who had seen Angels but had been unsure of his own credibility . . . that is until now.

Numier, on the other hand, a skeptic through and through, took several steps back, but stood his ground. Taking nothing at face value, especially something as significant as this, he diligently inspected every detail of the spectacular being from wingtip to wingtip. He looked for signs of fraud or trickery, while keeping a fair distance from the towering man-like creature.

"Get on your knees and bow!" murmured Amena fearing Michael's wrath, should he be insulted.

"No, No . . . He is right not to bow. I am but a servant to The Lord. There is only one Master, and there is only one Father in Heaven. Refer to no man as father and call no man your master. Bow only to The Lord and no one else," Michael said.[21]

Amena remained on her knees with her head down, still too frightened to stand, while The Professor slowly stood up and drew the courage to speak and converse with the Angel:

"There were other Archangels on the front lines," and with the Professor looking down in sadness, he continued. "I saw many Angels fall to the forces of darkness . . . They seemed to grow stronger before my eyes."

"Yes . . . they would have," Michael replied. "You see, the power of Satan's army is in direct relation to the sin and hatred of Mankind . . . It's a kind of failsafe device created by God. As the sins of Mankind grow, so grows the power of Satan's army. Conversely, as the sins of Mankind diminish, and Man's deeds grow great through faith, then the serpent's powers are lessened.[22] Man is responsible for his own blessing or demise."

And as he slowly retracted his wings he continued:

"In the days before Grace, Man had only the Ten Commandments to govern his actions. But as Man broke each and every one of God's rules, the commandments ultimately became Man's damnation. In response, God unleashed his wrath. By the Order of God, I myself destroyed one hundred and eighty-five thousand Assyrian soldiers in one night.[23] But it wasn't until after Noah that God made a covenant with Man and every living creature, promising never again to destroy all life . . ."[24]

Amena slowly stood; shielded by the Professor she glanced at Numier to see if he was listening.

"But understand that when the world of Man provides enough fuel to the dragon, he will overcome the Angels who defend against him. Each and every Angel must be defeated, giving Satan enough power to cross dimensions and walk freely among Men, destroying the fortunate, and enslaving those who remain. The Bible refers to these events in The Book of Revelation . . . It is inevitable . . . The only unknown is . . . when?

The Cherubim Fields are neutral ground, as Satan draws no strength from Angels. Although it is true that Angels experience an array of emotions, they do not feel hate, envy, lust, or any other emotion that would evoke sin, but you . . . on the other hand . . ."

The Professor quickly interrupted:

"But I wasn't feeling any anger at all . . . only fear."

"It does not matter . . . the hate, greed, lust and all other flavors of sin that you've ever experienced, although forgiven . . . are carried with you . . . until the Lord, the Son of God, cleanses you of them. There will be a time in the end when Christ will gather His Church . . . taken to a place prepared for them . . . spared from the fate of the nonbelievers."[25]

"The rapture." said the Professor.

"But why would God do such things as described in Revelations?" asked Numier in true nonbeliever fashion.

"God does not. It is the choice of Men themselves that establish their destiny."

The Professor, still trying to cope with his responsibility in all of this, said:

"So you're saying that the evil forces were more powerful than usual because of my presence?"

"Yes," answered Michael. "They feed on your sins and gain strength from them. But fortunately . . . it was you and not the old one," as he looked at Numier, "or it would have been finished."

Numier looked to the corner of the room in shame and confusion, while Michael continued:

"The armies of my Brothers have held the evil forces at bay for eight thousand years. There have been times, in the history of your world, when Mankind chose to unleash Satan's fury, allowing the evil forces to gain ground. The Crusades, the World Wars, and the Holocaust are but a few recent examples of such times. But my Brothers are relentless and fight still for the protection of Mankind. I fear that your untimely presence on the battlefield may have hastened Satan's earthly walk."

"It was the accident . . . It caused an injury. We thought it all might have been a hallucination . . . I had to be sure!" pleaded the Professor.

"I understand . . . But now you must understand . . . There are no accidents. And now that Satan's armies have reached the tomb, there is very little time,"

Michael said, "as long as the tomb is in Cherubim control, it can be reached."

"But the book says that only God or . . ." the Professor paused as Michael opened his shirt revealing a large scar on his chest in front of his heart.

"It is the only place where it would be safe," he said.

He then inserted his index finger into his very flesh in the center of the scar line, separating the soft tissue as if it were a fresh wound, and pulled out a large skeleton key from his chest. Amena quickly looked away and covered her mouth.

"It is the key to Gabriel's Tomb," Michael said while wiping the blood onto his shirt.

"If you had the key, then why haven't you released him?" asked the Professor.

Michael explained:

"My Brother and I were on a mission from God, and when we returned to the battlefield, Satan was lying in wait. He lured Gabriel into a vast cave by imitating the cry of a child. By the time I reached the cave, it was sealed.

For one hundred years, the Cherubim and I tried to free him . . . but our efforts were in vain. For the first time, I experienced anger . . . The emotion overcame me, and for three hundred years, I destroyed millions of beasts driving Satan many miles away from the tomb.

The Cherubim weren't able to keep up with my killing, as I slaughtered my way deep into the Devil's domain. At last, I was within striking distance of the cowardly serpent ready to finish the job I'd started in Heaven, but it was not to be . . . I was ordered to spare him."

And while Michael proceeded to recall the sequence of events that led him to this place, his face took on a saddened expression as he painfully told his story.

"The Lord's instructions were clear and left no room for ambiguity . . . Satan was not to be destroyed. But for a fraction of a second, I paused . . .

I thought of Gabriel . . . I thought of hundreds of thousands of Cherubim and other faithful servants of God who had perished at the putrid hands of hell.

It was within that same fraction of a second that I clenched my fists, gripped my sword tightly, and considered freeing it from its sheath and ending my fallen brother's morbid life. And even though it would have resulted in a swift death for him, he was nevertheless exhilarated with the knowledge that he had me. It wasn't until I saw the sparkle in his dark pupil-less eyes, that I realized my impending disobedience.

It was still within that very same fateful second that I felt briefly the empty despair and horror of an existence outside the presence of God. It was then that I heard the cries of Gabriel. They were coming from deep within the tomb, three hundred miles away, reminding me of my immeasurable love and devotion to my Creator.

And as the second passed, and much to the disappointment of my dark sibling, I threw my sword to the ground, snatched the key from his talons, and vanquished myself from The Fields forever!"

"Why were you not allowed to kill Satan?" Amena asked stepping out from behind the Professor.

Michael craned his neck to one side to get a better look at Amena. He looked at her with curious familiarity, as if he'd seen her somewhere before. There was a noticeable uneasiness about him as he began to pace behind his desk.

Numier noticed the change in Michael's demeanor and turned to Amena:

"What did you do?!" he asked whispering loudly.

"Nothing . . ." she whispered back.

Michael stopped pacing, took a deep breath and addressed Amena:

"So . . . the Babylonian!" He said loudly once again shaking literature from shelves. "I see you've decided to overcome your fear and enter the conversation. Your question is inconsistent with scripture. I would expect more from you."

"Let us review," he said impatiently. "I was not created to question the Will of God, only to obey it. I can only turn to the Scriptures for answers, and the Scriptures are clear. God is always true to His Word . . . Satan will walk the earth for a period of years. And after his brief walk on earth, the world will again become paradise as it was in the beginning, and Satan will perish forever," Michael continued. "On that day, we will all rejoice. But until that day the serpent must live."

Amena slowly stepped back behind the Professor hoping to keep out of Michael's sight.

"Can't you go back?" asked Numier.

"No. My actions taught me that if the opportunity arose again, I might not be able to recuse myself from slaying the dragon, so the Lord obliged my request and removed my power to cross dimensional lines," answered Michael.

"Wow . . . So you've been protecting the key all this time," said the Professor.

"Yes . . . Waiting for the one who would deliver it back to The Fields and release Gabriel from His captivity. It's the only way to drive back the forces of evil."

"But what if this IS the end of times. What if it IS meant to be that the dark forces prevail?" posed Numier.

"No . . . It is NOT time. The Scriptural prophecies have not yet been fulfilled. The wall of Israel has not yet been completed. The Professor's presence shifted the balance in Lucifer's favor. Now it is up to him to shift it back!" Michael said in a firm tone.

Running on instincts and Faith, without the need for thought or deduction, the Professor volunteered:

"Tell me what I need to do . . . and I'll do it!"

"No!" Loudly whispered Amena with her face buried into the Professors middle back.

"We must act fast; you must go back to the exact place where you saw the tomb. Try to get as close as you can before you cross. The Cherubim can be fierce, and they won't know your mission."

"What if they spot me before I reach the tomb," asked the Professor.

"Show them the key . . . Every Angel knows of the key," answered Michael.

"How do you know it's not too late?" asked Numier.

"We're still here aren't we," said the Professor.

"Good point," said Numier.

"Here . . . take this," Michael said while removing a large gold medallion from around his neck. On it was inscribed, "Holy, Holy, Holy is the Lord."

"It contains the powers of dimensional travel and is the key to worlds beyond your imagination or possible comprehension . . . celestial worlds that you would not survive if entered into in your present form."

"It is the only device of its kind and must be guarded at all cost!" Michael said while placing it around the Professor's neck.

"Why are you giving it to me?" asked the Professor.

"For eight thousand years I've served the Lord . . . I serve Him still. When I asked Him to remove my powers of cross-dimensional travel, He obliged me and concealed them within this gold medallion. Exhibiting more faith in me than I have in myself, The Lord urged me to reconsider and to one day return to The Cherubim Fields. He allowed the decision to be mine. For sixteen-hundred years, I've resisted the temptation to access its powers."

"Fighting evil is what I was created to do . . . The battle beckons me with no end. In the quiet hours the night brings, I can hear the screams of Cherubim falling to the armies of Satan. If I close my eyes, I can see the battle raging and the bodies burning. I thirst and yearn for the very sounds and smells that haunt me. Before the temptation becomes too unbearable, you must take it to my brother Gabriel, where it will be safe and out of reach from me. You will be doing Mankind a service by removing this yoke from me."

"But what if I'm unsuccessful in my crossing and the medallion falls into the hands of evil?" asked the Professor.

"If Gabriel is not released, the Cherubim will not stand a chance, then Satan will not need it to cross," answered Michael.

The Professor felt weak from the pressure of the added responsibility, but after some quick reasoning, he deduced that getting the key to The Fields was all that mattered. The Angels would take care of the rest.

"You must keep it around your neck," Michael added. "When Gabriel sees it, he will know that it was I that sent you. Without it . . . he will show you no clemency. Now go! There is very little time."

The three hurried into the corridor and upon seeing Bohramee standing beside the coach holding its side door open, Amena stopped, turned back to Michael and said:

"Excuse me . . . But is there another way out? I mean, we were almost mauled by your lions on the way in here, and if it's all the same to you . . . I'd like to skip that part."

"Forgive me for frightening you. I chained the beasts upon your arrival, but your presence enraged them. You see, when I surrendered my sword, two of Satan's conjured beasts attacked me from behind and crossed along with me. I quickly subdued them . . . but rather than destroy them, I enslaved them and forced them to provide me with an unceasing supply of manual labor."

"The cave," said Numier.

"Yes. It took them several hundred years, but they dug it by hand as well as most of the castle construction. I will detain them long enough for you to pass. Controlling them has been easy until very recently . . . it seems that your presence has caused them much agitation."

"Clair!" shouted Amena.

"We left a young girl in our car . . ." said Goodwin. "Will she be okay there?"

"Oh yes . . . the Necrophim," said Michael.

The three paused and looked at each other, then back to Michael.

"The what . . .?" said Numier with lifted brow.

"She is a Necrophim," said Michael. "She's dead."

"What do you mean she's dead?! shouted Amena. "I knew coming here was a bad idea!"

"What are you saying?" asked the Professor. "I mean she looked a bit ill, but she was eating and drinking and . . ."

"She was killed two hundred years ago," interrupted Michael. "Suspected of being a witch, she was hung along with her family. She must have crossed when the portal opened.

Amena put her hand over her mouth and began to faint. The professor hugged her tightly as her knees buckled.

"There's a dead girl in my car . . .? said Numier.

"It appears so," replied Michael. "Caught between dimensions, her soul is unresolved."

But before Numier could depose the Angel for more information about this incredible phenomenon, he was immediately interrupted.

"Enough! Go now . . . stop for nothing. Be single-minded in purpose, and you cannot fail!" he shouted as the three hurried for the cave.

Bohramee wasted no time in escorting the trio back to the carriage. The team of horses stampeded straight through the oversized castle corridors, bouncing off walls and tearing through rooms with little effort. They skillfully sped their way through the labyrinth like bulls in a maze built of straw, collapsing walls and destroying entire rooms as they tore through the stone fortress.

Michael watched from the cave, perched by his feet high above the castle floor. By their throats, he held a beast in each hand. They were paralyzed into complete submission while dangling like lifeless puppies in the hands of a giant. The crumbling condition of the castle was of little concern to him as it was for this very day that it was built.

The Mighty Angel had waited over a thousand years for this moment, but it was bitter sweet at best. He felt the weight of the world alleviate from his shoulders . . . but felt extreme sorrow and compassion, in knowing that the weight had merely been transferred onto the shoulders of this mortal man.

Concerned that it might be too much for the Professor to bear, Michael tossed the beasts to the corner of the cave; spiraled down to the damp, musty, dirt-floor and dropped to his knees. He prayed to The Lord to bless this fragile, mortal man with the strength and speed of a thousand Angels.

CHAPTER XIV
THE REUNION

The coach busted through the double doors of the castle with ease stopping just short of the fountain. Steam released from its metal wheels as the three slowly exited the vehicle. They moved clear of the falling debris then stood still in front of the car. They could clearly see Clair. She was in the same position as when they left her, slumped over against the rear passenger door with her head against the window.

"Come on!" said Amena breaking the silence. "She wont hurt us."

With Numier at the wheel, they set-out for home. Fishtailing and spinning gravel at the crumbling castle, they raced their way down the long driveway.

The drive back from the castle seemed to drag on forever. The first hours were void of any substantive conversation whatsoever. Numier looked straight ahead at the road with Amena and Goodwin both looking out their windows trying not to look at Clair. There was a heaviness that surrounded them, as they'd become increasingly aware of the dangers that lie ahead. Up until now, there was some speculation as to whether the Professor's encounters were factual. But after meeting Michael, the Professor's hallucinations became horrifyingly real to them all.

For Amena, there was a deep sense of sorrow as she was deeply in love with the Professor and feared for his safe return. She thought of their possible future together. She thought of all the years she'd waited to see him again and wished she'd acted sooner.

Her concerns for the Professor were equaled by her sadness for Clair. Where had she been for two hundred years? What horrors had she seen? And why hadn't she crossed? Still leaning against the door, Clair's hand was visible at her side. Pale and cold, it rested lifelessly on the leather seat between them; Amena reached for it and gently squeezed it. Feeling Amena's warm hand and sensing that she knew . . . She turned to Amena and snuggled into her shoulder.

For Numier, it was not only the possibility of losing a friend that concerned him . . . but also the consideration of his own mortality. He'd lived most of his life convinced that God didn't exist, and that the idea of an afterlife was simply an illusion created by Man. But as the new information challenged his established beliefs, he felt a real sense of urgency to sort it out.

"Was it too late?" he thought. Would there still be time for him to change his ways and find salvation? Or had he in fact strayed too far from the flock, leading many innocent souls away with him? He thought of a first-year student he'd instructed many years ago.

He was little more than a boy, just out of high school, attending Numier's class as part of general education outside his major. He was an energetic, young buck, full of enthusiasm and promise. He seemed confident and cocky in presenting Christian views to Numier, challenging the seasoned theologian's knowledge of the Bible. But in true atheist and secular fashion, Numier ridiculed and bested the boy's budding knowledge of the Scriptures, posing arguments that a more learned Christian would have easily been able to refute. His mockery and contempt made his student feel small, and by the end of the semester, ultimately caused him to second-guess his newfound faith.

Some time later, while on a dig site, Numier received word, that the boy had lost a close friend in an automobile accident in which he was the driver. He had turned his academic interests to the secular study of searching within one's self and evolution for all of life's answers. And as depression set in . . . brokenhearted, and without faith . . . he took his own life.

At the time, Numier thought the boy weak . . . and that in some twisted Darwinistic mentality, the world was better off. That was . . . until today. Today his heart was heavy. For the first time, he mourned the boy. Silently and earnestly he hoped that the Lord not be too hard on the boy, knowing that it was he and not the boy who was responsible.

Although Numier and Amena had their own entirely different motives for the Professor's success, they were both nonetheless, worried and concerned that he might not return. And in true friendship, they silently vowed to stand by their friend . . . until the very end.

As they neared the last stages of their journey, the silence was broken by the sounds of the emergency broadcast system once again sounding off through Numier's AM/FM Radio.

The eastern borders of India had fallen to China's overwhelming mass of advancing troops. In an effort to neutralize the attack, India had released six Intercontinental Ballistic Missiles aimed directly at China's most populated cities.

In retaliation and in a preemptive maneuver, China released dozens of missiles, delivered toward India, Korea, as well as Russia.

The United States Government was now reporting that Missile silos throughout Europe and the Middle East were opening in anticipation of a worldwide conflict.

The broadcast went on to urge American citizens to remain calm, take shelter, and await the President's briefing, which would follow shortly.

"Oh my God!" shouted Amena. "It's happening!"

"What fools!" shouted Numier

"It may be too late!" yelled the Professor. "When I left The Cherubim Fields, the Angels were being overrun by the forces of evil . . . Even if I'm able to cross, there may not be anyone left to give the key to."

Upon reaching the base of the foothills, they quickly and dangerously traversed the winding hilly terrain. Their tires squealed on every corner as Numier pushed the limits of his vehicle. The Professor began to feel the panic, as his transformation was scheduled to begin at any time.

"Hurry Numier!" he shouted.

"Good God!" screamed Numier. "If I drive any faster, we'll all end up in a ditch!"

"Right here . . . "shouted the Professor as his voice cracked with fear. "Pull over!"

"No!" shouted Clair. "Not yet." Her head swung back and forth in a trance-like state. With her eyes closed, squinting tightly she shouted:

"There! By the large rock! Stop there . . ."

Numier stopped the car in the middle of the road and let Amena and the Professor out. "There should be a turn out just up ahead. I'll park the car and hurry back," Numier said. "Don't wait for me!"

Numier turned to Clair and looked at her for the first time since they left Canada:

"Aren't you going with him?" he asked, eager to get her out of his car.

"I need to stay here," she answered still nervously swaying her head back and forth.

Amena and the Professor ran to the side of Tollhouse Road where they could see the surrounding foothills. The grass was tall and the wildflowers gently swayed in the breeze, as the hills cascaded softly into the valley below.

It was early afternoon. The sun's rays poured quietly through openings in the puffy clouds that floated slowly by, loosely spotting the earth beneath them. Standing tall beneath a calico sky, the Professor took a deep breath and tried to gather the strength to slay a Dragon. He took two steps toward the hillside, stopped, turned back to Amena, and said:

"I'm so scared . . . I feel like a small child who has been given the keys to his father's car . . . What if something goes wrong? What if I fail? There's so much at stake."

She buried her face in his chest and hugged him with all her might.

"Michael said there are no mistakes, these things are happening to you for a reason. Jesus walks before you, and protects you every step of the way," she said with tears welling up in her eyes.

"I so want to see you picking flowers in your garden with grandchildren," he said, looking deep into her eyes for strength.

Amena took his face in her hands and spoke directly into his eyes:

"All my life . . . since I was a little girl . . . I've prayed to God to bless and keep safe the man that I would meet and love with all my heart. Don't be afraid . . . you will see me picking flowers . . . in OUR garden, with OUR grandchildren!" she said with tears streaming down her face.

He gazed at her beauty for several seconds . . . trying to freeze this moment in his mind forever . . . determined never to forget it. And although he wanted nothing more than to hold her in his arms on the soft shoulder of Tollhouse Road forever . . . he knew he had a mission.

"You're right," he said. "This couldn't have all been for nothing . . . "

And with renewed resolve, he turned and faced the hillside. Footsteps broke the silence as Numier came running up to greet them.

"She won't leave the car!" he shouted. "What did I miss?"

"Everything!" the Professor shouted as he walked down the embankment below the road.

He crossed the shallow stream and shouted over his shoulder:

"I'll be back with more stories for your notebook Numier. Don't leave! I'll need a ride home," trying to stay positive.

Reaching the other side of Granite Creek, he turned to look at Numier. And while walking backwards he lifted his hand and waved to his dear old friend.

Numier was reluctant to wave goodbye, being that he wasn't the sort to give in to failure, or even the possibility that he wouldn't see his friend again. So rather than wave, he threw both arms up, in a victory 'V' and shouted:

"Do it all, Don . . .! Do it all . . .!"

CHAPTER XV
THE CROSSING
❦

A few minutes passed while Numier and Amena intently watched the Professor walk slowly through the ravine. He stopped under a large oak tree, just yards from the base of a steep hillside where, if his memory served, was the approximate location of the tomb. His intentions were to hide in the thick underbrush and thistle beneath the oak, until it was safe for him to approach.

He took in the beauty and peacefulness of the foothills while he still could, knowing that in a few short moments, they would take on a much more severe and brutal appearance.

Standing still beneath the oak, he began to feel a tingling sensation in and around his head, and with a deep breath he thought to himself:

"Here we go."

Back at the road, Amena was fixated on the Professor's position, being that this was the first time she'd actually witnessed his transformation. She nervously watched him standing with his back to them, when suddenly it happened.

"Numier look!" she said quietly pointing in the direction of the Professor.

"Oh . . . My . . . God . . ." Numier said.

The Professor was crossing before their very eyes. It happened rapidly but in increments, with his image steadily fading until he had completely vanished. Numier was fascinated by the sight and quickly reached into his shoulder bag for his pad and pencil to accurately document the incident before he'd forgotten anything.

Amena, on the other hand, was horrified by the seeming finality of his departure. She scanned the hillside for him but saw nothing, only Clair a foothill away heading in the opposite direction.

"Clair!" she screamed, but there was no response.

She was several hundred yards away, just on the other side of the stream, walking in the direction where the Professor first had his accident.

"Clair!" again screamed Amena.

"Let her go . . ." said Numier. "She has to find what she is looking for."

And as Numier wrote feverishly, Amena fell to her knees . . . cradled her face in her hands . . . and cried.

THE FIELDS

The Professor's head throbbed as his blood pressure escalated and engulfed his brain with fluids. He closed his eyes and listened intently as he waited for his freakish transformation to conclude. Shutting down his sense of sight, he became acutely aware of his own physical condition. His knees were weak and trembled with fright. He could hear his heart pound loudly within the walls of his chest. He could feel the blood surging through his veins with the passing of each beat of his heart.

He made several attempts to open his burning eyes only to find his vision impaired by smoke. As the initial head rush began to subside, an awful and beleaguering stench all but overwhelmed him. His body violently resisted breathing, causing him to deliberately force air into his lungs one gasp at a time. And as he struggled to keep from losing consciousness due to the lack of oxygen, his mind drifted back to a time long ago.

His father had gone hunting with his older brother and had killed a wild boar. They were intent on roasting it whole on an open barbeque. They tried to explain that there was something primordial and

very manly about eating what they'd killed regardless
of how disgusting it may have been. The smell of
coagulating fat and burning fur filled the air as the
men hadn't fully cleaned and dressed the hog. He
recalled vividly his feelings of puzzlement at the
men's callus reaction to the foul odor while they
vehemently and indignantly denied their culinary
miscalculation. The pungent odor permeated his
clothes and stayed with him for months. He had
hoped never again to be subjected to such disgusting
stench.

Back in The Fields, he was overcome by the odor
as well as the memory of it, causing him to vomit
uncontrollably. His body convulsed as it fought
to expel the foul stench as quickly as it painfully
entered his nostrils.

He was completely mindful of the dangers that
surrounded him, and in an effort to remain
motionless he vomited upright through pursed lips
while struggling to fight back heaves. The sound of
his vomit splashing down around him indicated to
him that he was standing in liquid of some kind. His
eyes teared profusely as he reluctantly attempted
to assess his surroundings. He could faintly make
out that the tree under which he was standing,
had fallen, and that he was now standing within
its twisted and partially burned-out branches. The
heat radiating from the burning oak was almost
intolerable, but as its red-hot embers smoldered

and hissed, he knew that the cover it provided was invaluable.

The smoke began to clear as the Professor heaved intermittently. His nausea was exacerbated by the discovery of the origin of the horrible reek. The tree had fallen on top of two very large beasts, one in which the Professor was standing. It had apparently been severed in two at the torso, exposing its massive abdominal cavity. And as luck would have it, the Professor materialized inside the elephant-size beast, just below the rib cage. He was shocked and repulsed in discovering that he was standing shin deep in organs and entrails.

The Professor closed his eyes and thought of Amena and happier times he'd experienced as an instructor, while the vomit, bile and bodily fluids began to burn the skin on his lower legs. He struggled to remain still and calm with all his strength, employing everything in his power to keep from jumping out of the beast and running for fresh air.

As the smoke continued to dissipate, the Professor attempted to open his eyes once again. While squinting through watery eyes, he peered over the smoldering scaffolds of the burning oak and saw what looked like a multitude of bodies. There were countless beasts, dragons and Cherubim piled high throughout the arena. The sea of bodies blanketed the hillside and well into the valley where it appeared to have no end.

The Professor was concerned that he may already be too late, fearing that this had in fact been the Angels' last stand. He continued to examine the battlefield wreckage, and saw a hunting party of half-a-dozen-or-so beasts. They turned over boulders, cleared out caves, and sifted through the ashes of fallen trees, in an apparent search for survivors. They trudged along tirelessly, clearing paths for their master by tossing corpses into massive mounds, while torching levies of remains as they marched.

Deducing that there were no survivors, the Professor was compelled to begin strategizing his route to the tomb while teams of ghoulish troops headed steadfast in his direction. He stood paralyzed with fear, as he watched a hunting party stumble upon an injured beast. They pounced upon the lame creature, immediately tearing it apart, limb from limb, as it screamed and roared in pain.

The screams of the beast took the Professor once again back to his childhood. His heightened state of consciousness, now haunting, rendered him virtually powerless against the unwelcome recall.

He remembered vividly a time when his older brother had captured and tortured rabbits for fun. They came upon a trapped animal desperately trying to free itself . . . but it wasn't until the bunny saw them approaching that it began to scream.

The Professor recalled the horror he felt the moment he realized that the rabbit was not screaming in pain . . . but in terror. He later learned that a rabbit's scream was a rare occurrence. Unfortunately, this was no consolation; while as memories of images fade . . . sounds of memories do not. He now realized that such experiences as traumatizing as they were . . . helped prepare and somewhat desensitize him for this very day.

He watched as each beast pulled up a cadaver and sat down upon it, while enjoying their share of the fresh kill. But despite the horrors of such a cannibalistic feast, the break afforded the Professor valuable time to strategize. His plan was simple . . . He would make a mad dash for the tomb, hoping to reach it before they reached him.

As the time to run grew near, the Professor's breathing became shallow and deliberate while fighting back the fear-induced rigor. While still trying to build up the courage to run, a deep and powerful voice came from within the same oak tree:

"Speak and I will relieve you of your head."

The Professor began to turn toward the voice.

"Move . . . and I will commit you to join the rotting beast in which you stand."

The Professor remained absolutely still, fully aware that each and every creature he'd encountered in The Fields thus far was perfectly capable of carrying out such a threat.

"I don't know why you've come here . . ." the voice said in a low but powerful tone. "All I know . . . is that your presence has cost us the battle. Before you, lay twelve legions of Angels. Cherubim, Sparrows and Archangels of the Lord lay dead at your feet, all of whom fought bravely and valiantly and will be remembered. All that remain are three Archangels, a handful of Cherubim, and two squadron of sparrows . . . each of whom circle above awaiting my command. If this was your purpose, then you have succeeded," said the voice.

"You may speak now . . . but quietly while the beasts gorge."

Without turning his head, out of the corner of his eye, the Professor saw an Archangel. It was the one they called Maximus. He was standing not more than three feet to the Professor's left. With sword drawn, and intently focused on the Professor, he was ready, at a moment's notice, to make good on his threats.

"I never intended to come here . . . It was all a mistake," the Professor pleaded but was quickly interrupted.

"And yet you return . . .?" suspiciously asked Maximus.

"I bring the key to Gabriel's Tomb," answered the Professor.

Upon hearing the words that every Angel longed to hear for nearly two thousand years, Maximus' facial expression changed from intensely angry, to cautiously enthusiastic.

"Show it to me SLOWLY," ordered Maximus.

The Professor slowly opened his shirt exposing the key hanging next to the medallion. Maximus reached out and snatched the key from the chain with speed unseen by the naked eye, and wasted no time in saying:

"As before, your presence will stand against us in battle. Take this sword . . . It is possible that while they're busy killing you . . . I may be able to reach the tomb!" he said as he pulled a six-foot-long broadsword from the carcass of the slain beast.

He placed the sword into the Professor's left hand, and as the weight of it pulled him toward the ground, it became clear to the Professor that he needed two hands to hold it, let alone lift it!

"This sword is too heavy for me to carry! How will I defend myself?" pleaded the Professor fearing for his life.

"The sword you hold in your hands is called El Mórte. It belonged to a great and mighty Archangel of The Lord. He had slain millions of beasts for thousands of years . . . He gave his life many years ago in service to the Lord," Maximus said as only a true leader could. "You will wield it with honor . . . or you will die!!!"

And without warning, a squadron of sparrows descended onto the beasts cutting them down with surgical precision, providing the diversion Maximus needed to approach the tomb.

"But how will I fight? I've never fought anything before in my life!" the Professor shouted as Maximus took flight.

"Do your best . . . and let God do the rest!" he shouted while flying single handed into a patrol of beasts that stood between he and the tomb.

For a moment, the Professor considered hiding in the creature's remains until it was over and Gabriel was freed, but the words Maximus spoke were ringing loudly in his ears:

"Do your best . . . and let God do the rest!" He felt that God had a purpose for him, and it wasn't to remain hidden in the bloody entrails of one of Satan's conjured minions.

The Professor then squeezed the handle of the mighty sword firmly in his right hand and knelt to one knee now oblivious to the decomposing beast that surrounded him, and prayed:

"God please . . . If it is Your will that I may survive this day, please let it be so. Or if I should fall in battle, please let me to have fought bravely and honorably in Your Name. And if my passing is Your Will, please accept my soul into Your Heavenly Kingdom. This I pray in the name of Your Son, Jesus Christ."

Reaching deep down, and drawing strength from his conversation with Michael, "Be single-minded in purpose and you cannot fail", and with the words of Maximus "Do your best . . . and let God do the rest", the Professor took a deep breath, jumped free of the carcass, and ran toward Maximus' position, all the while keeping one eye on the tomb.

The beasts were surprised by the attack and were scattering in confusion awaiting instruction from Satan, making them easy targets for the Angels.

Unfortunately, for the Professor, two of the beasts spotted him and broke from their patrol to make short work of this small wingless Angel. The Professor was in full run, dragging the enormous sword behind him when the first beast jumped into his path. It roared like a lion in an apparent attempt to intimidate its victim, but before it could finish it's blustering, the Professor instinctively clutched the handle with both hands, and swung El Mórte with all his might in the general direction of the beast. He held on tightly to the sword as it took on a life of its own, gliding effortlessly though the creature severing it into two parts just above the abdomen. The gushing blood from the torso of the beast propelled the Professor backward like a fire hose.

The second beast charged on all fours like a raging bull. The creature was approaching much too quickly for the Professor to regain his feet, forcing him to fight from his knees. He deduced by the massive upper body, rigidity of spine, and speed at which the beast was traveling, that there was no way it could react to a sudden lateral movement.

As the beast reached his position in full run, the Professor rolled to his right and hurled El Mórte into its side like a javelin. The mighty sword punctured the creature's heart, killing it almost instantly as it collapsed, quaking the earth with its size and sliding to a stop several yards away.

It was no mystery that the creatures were evil incarnate; the very arms and legs of the Devil himself. But still, the Professor felt a warped sense of sadness as he watched the second beast struggle for its last breath while biting at the earth in pain.

Still on his knees and watching the creature die, the Professor was abruptly pounced upon from above. He was instantly pinned to the ground with a forearm pressed firmly against his throat. It was Maximus, angrily speaking with a growl into the Professor's face:

"Here in The Fields . . . your sword is your life! Lose it again, and you will surely die!"

And with that stern warning, Maximus pulled El Mórte from the quivering carcass of the dying beast, placed it firmly back into the Professor's hand, yanked him to his feet, and pushed on in the direction of the tomb.

As Maximus and the Professor rounded a large boulder a short distance from the tomb, a magnificent but frightening sight blocked their passage. It was HURON.

He was standing battle ready with his back to the tomb prepared and eager to do his master's dark bidding.

The Professor was worried about the success of their quest upon seeing such an impressive Angel of Darkness.

CHAPTER XVI
HURON

Huron stood close to thirteen-feet tall, enormously muscular, and equipped with heavy-duty battle attire, all but impenetrable to the average sword. Thirty-foot black wings expanded and contracted like a bird of prey initiating a war ritual. In his left hand, he held the rapier he wielded as an Archangel, and in his right, he griped Kismet.

His pupil-less eyes were deep set and sinister as they raked piercingly at Maximus, disregarding the Professor as no more than an annoyance.

Slowly circling the Mighty Archangel of The Lord, Huron clearly savored the tranquil moments before the strike while toying with Maximus:

"Well, Well . . . If it isn't Max," he said in a low gurgling sort of tone. "My dear, big Brother, who left me for dead in Tamera . . . all those years ago . . ."

Maximus, torn and heartbroken by the dark appearance of the once Mighty Archangel slowly uttered:

"You died . . . I felt it."

"Yes . . .! loudly hissed Huron. And by your own actions . . . Now the next thing you will feel . . . is Kismet!"

What kind of trickery is this?!" shouted Maximus.

Maximus had seen the results of Satan's black magic before, but never this complete, and never with the corpse of an Archangel.

"I can see by your black veins Huron, that you serve a new Master now. What exactly do you think to gain from that?"

Huron continued to circle while beasts and Angels alike instinctively cleared the perimeter in anticipation of the impending conflict.

"Satan is the one who will exalt me when I deliver him The Cherubim Fields. No longer just a drone . . . Soon I will rule over Mankind."

Maximus knew upon hearing his bleak testimony that Huron was no longer a Mighty Angel but rather a conjured beast with better equipment.

Satisfied that there was no hope for Huron, Maximus raised his sword and engaged The Dark Angel with vicious resolve. They took to the skies, thrusting and dodging fatal blows. Metal clashed and sparks flew as the giants fought like gladiators deeply immersed in a battle to the death.

The Professor seized the opportunity while all eyes were on the Generals, by creeping quickly and stealthily to the base of Gabriel's Tomb. Barely able to withstand the heat radiating off the tomb, he stood firmly in front of the massive metal door.

He looked to the skies and saw Maximus and Huron, just above the treetops, fighting to the death not far from the tomb. And after witnessing Huron's rage, he realized that Maximus might very well not survive the encounter. Upon acknowledging this, he felt he had no other option than to shout:

"Maximus . . . ! Throw me the key!"

The entire battlefield, Dark Angels and beasts alike, froze in their tracks, completely taken aback by what they'd just heard. In an instant, it became altogether clear to both sides, that it was no longer the battle . . . but the war, which was at stake!

The Angels took advantage of the confusion by summarily killing each and every beast in the immediate vicinity.

And as all remaining Cherubim rushed to form a wall around the Professor and the tomb, Maximus, swiftly and without hesitation, ducked under a grazing pass by Kismet, and threw to the Professor the key to Gabriel's Tomb.

Huron, still possessing the keen strategic mind of an Archangel, assessed quickly that with the Cherubim now in control of the skirmish and with two squadrons of sparrows quickly descending upon the tomb, pressing forward would be futile and sure suicide. Relinquishing his position, he hurriedly belly-crawled like a disjointed-salamander over and behind a large boulder, deducing quickly that it would be in his best interest to get as far away from the tomb as possible should Gabriel be released.

Maximus was disappointed in Huron's choice to surrender his position and flee the arena. Cherubim and Dark Angels alike knew that an Archangel would never back down from a fight. It was known throughout the fields that these Angels wore protective armor on their fronts only, to shield their vital organs as they pushed forward in battle, never turning their backs to the enemy in retreat. Even against insurmountable odds, an Archangel would fight to the death before conceding and compromising the success of his mission.

Dark Angels and beasts on the other hand were cowards, routinely fleeing engagement when the odds of battle turned against them. Even though Maximus knew that Huron was no longer a Mighty Archangel of The Lord, he was still sickened to see him acquiesce in such a cowardly fashion.

Maximus, satisfied that Huron would no longer be a threat, flew quickly and unhindered past beasts and Dark Angels who were momentarily caught off guard by the sight of the small wingless Angel. Joining the Professor at the entrance to Gabriel's Tomb, Maximus shouted through hissing heat that radiated off the giant metal door:

"Open the door quickly, the key will break Satan's curse!" he said while fighting off beasts as they began to morph.

"Show me where . . .!" the Professor screamed while franticly searching for the aperture.

Meanwhile, completely unaware of the events at the tomb, the Devil was behind the lines preoccupied with entertaining fantasies regarding his long anticipated domination of earth. He was in a makeshift, mobile camp riding atop a large beast that foamed at the mouth with its tongue hanging out in excitement. Satan was waving his hands in the air, eerily conducting a silent symphony in his head. He couldn't have been more pleased with himself for accomplishing in a few short days what he'd strived for thousands of years to achieve.

At that moment, a Dark Angel came running into the camp with news.

"Have you found the remaining Angels?" Satan impatiently asked. "They must all be destroyed before I cross," he added harshly. "There can be no survivors!"

"Yes, my lord . . . we have located them, but . . ."

"Good!" Satan anxiously interrupted. "Where did you find them?"

"They gather at the tomb my Lord!" the Dark Angel answered while cowering on one knee.

"What? Why must they insist on protecting it? Their efforts are idiotic!" he thought aloud.

"The man from the trench joins them," the Angel added. "He wears the medallion of Michael!"

The Devil turned to the Dark Angel with a confused look on what was left of his face, and peering deeply into the eyes of his quivering minion, thoughts streamed through his calculating mind. In his arrogance, he'd all but disregarded that Michael had snatched the key from his talons just moments before crossing dimensions. All this time he'd simply assumed that Michael had crossed into Heaven's dimension, rendering the key useless in the Hands of God, who didn't need it to open the tomb. But now, in an instant, it all made perfect sense to him . . . Why the man had returned . . . and why they had been protecting the tomb. His pride, arrogance, and excitement of impending victory caused him to underestimate the few that remained. Upon discovering their intentions, he dove into a fitful rage!

"NOOOOOOO!" He screamed franticly as he pulled the head off the beast beneath him.

On his way to the ground, and before the beast's head hit the earth, he unsheathed his black broad sword and cut the Dark Messenger in two vertically. He then immediately instructed every beast, minion, and Dark Angel to the tomb, while conjuring up millions of creatures from hell itself. The earth bubbled and boiled like a gaseous swamp with beasts popping out of the soil by the thousands. He realized full well that he'd been trumped and that all of his efforts could quickly be unraveled with one turn of the key.

"Kill them! Kill them all!" he cried, passing beasts and Dark Angels as he ran in a panic in the direction of the skirmish.

He screamed and cried like a child in a tantrum as he raced, dust billowing from under his cape, toward the tomb.

CHAPTER XVII
GABRIEL'S TOMB

Back at the tomb . . . after having located the keyhole, Maximus and the Professor prepared to open the gates to hell itself. The Professor could hardly stand the heat emanating from the two-story-tall, black, metal door.

At the instant he inserted the key, and before even turning it, the gigantic door violently burst open. The Professor was immediately thrown back by the force of what could only be described as a small nuclear explosion.

The entire battlefield shook from the quake created by the blast. Beasts and Angels alike were blown off the hillside, clearing a perimeter surrounding the tomb. The Professor was propelled backwards into the seemingly unaffected Maximus, who with one wing shielded the Professor, sparing him from certain incineration.

As he peeked out from under the wing of the mighty Angel, the Professor witnessed an incredible sight. The door to the tomb had been blown wide open, and in its place was a blazing inferno.

Fifty yards of blue flame torched out from the magma-like walls of the tomb. The fire was escaping the tomb like the exhaust of a jet engine in full afterburn.

Suddenly, an enormous figure walked out slowly through the inferno. It was completely engulfed in flames and only visible as an aberration as it moved slowly toward the outside world.

"Gabriel!" shouted Maximus as the silhouette of the liberated Angel grabbed the edge of the massive three-foot-thick door and slammed it shut behind him, sealing the tomb forever.

There, before Maximus, Steven, and a rag-tag army of surviving Angels, stood Gabriel. He was filthy from head to toe, blackened by two-thousand years of conflagratory killing. His wings were bright red with forging heat that made loud crackling sounds as they quickly cooled to a dull, ashy white. His body smoked and hissed as it cooled. He stood upright and erect and despite his outward appearance, seemed completely unaltered by his years of internment. He donned ancient, Roman, Gladiator-style attire with a full-metal breast plate and a pleated metal kilt.

Although most of the surviving Angels were present to greet Him, it was Maximus who was the first to embrace Him.

"It's been far too many years my Brother!" said Maximus welcoming Gabriel with a strong handshake at the forearm.

"I never abandoned hope for my release. How fares the battle?" snarled Gabriel, stepping quickly toward the hillside for a view of the theater.

"The battle goes poorly, my Brother. Our ranks are weak, and our numbers are few. The evil of Man has empowered the beast!" Maximus reported.

Gabriel looked over the foothills and on into the valley. He felt profound disappointment and sadness as his heart broke upon seeing the multitudes of Angels that littered the earth as far as the eye could see. And as he slowly turned to address his remaining forces, he peered over the shoulder of Maximus and spotted the Professor.

"Why have you allowed this man to live?!" he shouted while pushing past Maximus and raising his sword over the head of the Professor. "His presence will stand against us in battle!"

"He brings the key, and he wears the medallion of Michael!" quickly answered Maximus.

Gabriel paused for a moment, looked down upon the man, and saw the medallion hanging beneath his shirt and thought of his brother Michael. Not knowing all these years if he were dead or alive, he felt a strong sense of joy and relief upon seeing the medallion. He thought of how difficult it must have been for the Professor to have come this far. He knew that this man was one in several billion, a special breed of mortal human who possessed the rare ability to cross dimensional planes, as well as the innate ability to survive the harshest, cruelest and most evil environment that any human could ever endure. He was also aware that without such a man, his release might not have come in time to have made a difference; nevertheless, he was acutely aware that they were in the midst of a situation.

"This war is far more important than my freedom or any message from my brother for that matter," Gabriel said. "This man is no doubt the reason I see twelve legions of Angels lying dead before me."

And as he lowered his sword and turned back to the battlefield, he painfully said:

"Kill him."

The two Archangels standing behind the Professor each grabbed an arm and led him to his knees. Maximus drew his sword and raised it high above the Professor's head, pausing for just a moment to allow his victim the opportunity to pray. In an instant the Professor's life passed before his eyes. His heart rate and metabolism slowed to a near catatonic state, as his body fell into shock.

He thought of his mother whom he'd fallen out of favor with many years ago but oddly enough, was at a loss in recalling the exact reasons why. He perused memories of his father and brother and how their strength, however misplaced and twisted, could have been well used in this place . . . and on this day. He thought of his many shortcomings and unfinished projects and realized that they would all remain unrealized and incomplete.

He felt a brief sense of satisfaction and relief in knowing that he had been successful in delivering the key that liberated Gabriel. But most of all . . . he thought of Amena. Would she be alright without him? Would she marry and have children? Would she ever know how he truly felt about her? And with the pages of his life quickly passing before his eyes, he paused his thoughts on Amena, choosing that his last precious few thoughts . . . be of her.

But in the split second of Maximus' delay, and just before lowering his blade onto the Professor's vertebrae, something distracted him. Without warning and taking them all by surprise, a bright light illuminated from behind them.

It was a blinding light that more closely resembled a sustained burst or explosion. There were no shadows cast from the light, as its luminescence engulfed everything in its path. No Angel dared look directly at it, knowing that its brilliance would surely blind them. Many beasts too dumb to know better peeked into the light and were instantly blinded, with their brain tissue fused into a useless ball of tissue and nerves.

Upon seeing the light, the Angels immediately released the Professor. He fell forward onto his face and stomach fully expecting Maximus' sword to sever his head. Instead, he saw the Mighty Angel fall to the ground with his sword striking the soil beside him. Out of the corner of his eye, he saw Gabriel and Steven fall to their knees with foreheads to the ground without even turning to look.

The Professor managed to glance back, under his armpit, to witness beasts and dragons, who just moments before were in a stampede-like attack, stop cold in their tracks and cower in disgrace. They dropped their weapons and turned their heads in shame. Some Dark Angels closest to the light, committed suicide at the sight of It.

The Professor's heart raced, and his breathing shallowed when he realized that the light was emanating from his exact location. While laying flat on his chest, he raised his eyes just enough see feet standing right in front of him.

He looked upon a pair of sandals, in which were long and slender feet. Perfect in every way with the exception of a very large nail hole in each foot, positioned just below the ankle. Images passed before his eyes like an instant replay of his less then perfect life. He thought of the many good deeds he should have done . . . but didn't. He thought of the many sinful things he shouldn't have done . . . but did. Overcome with shame and a profound sense of unworthiness, the Professor began to sob uncontrollably at the feet of Jesus.

Paralyzed by the awareness of his shortcomings, suddenly, in an instant, all his thoughts and feelings of inadequacy subsided and were replaced with a deep sense of euphoria which surged and pulsed throughout his body. He became elated with the realization that he was in the presence of God as his head began to tingle with the good and positive energy radiating strongly off the body of Jesus.

As his tears of joy fell upon the feet of Jesus, the Professor felt a hand gently touch the top of his head. His body quickened and surged with electrical energy. Lifting several feet off the ground, he was suspended by a bright blue force that encapsulated him. His frail mortal body was barely able to survive the Celestial Hand of God, as he shook and flailed uncontrollably.

His shuddering subsided and was replaced with warm and comforting feelings of security and well being like those of a child when cradled in its mother's arms.

Along with the reassuring feelings, came understanding. In an instant, a deluge of information came streaming through the Professor's open mind. It was the knowledge of the universe. The beginning . . . the end . . . and everything in between, was all made clear to the Professor in a millisecond.

The information affirmed everything he'd ever known to be true. He saw the world through the eyes of God, and felt God's infinite love for Mankind.

Jesus slowly removed his hand from the head of the Professor, releasing him from the energy field and returning him softly to the ground. Jesus then turned his attention to The Cherubim Fields. His presence on the battlefield was truly a rare occasion, and by the reactions of the Angels, it was clear that there was purpose in his visit.

With the touch of Jesus, in an instant, the Professor became a member of a very elite group of warriors in service to The Lord. On the one hand, someone the Cherubim would protect with their lives, and on the other, one whom Satan would desperately wish to destroy.

Jesus then, without so much as a word, lifted His Hand and motioned to Steven, who at the time of Gabriel's release had been standing near the bottom of the ravine, guarding the outer perimeter. Upon being summoned, Steven lifted his war-tarnished wings high above his head and released his precious cargo. The Professor, still on his knees, turned to look as all eyes were now on Steven. The Fields surrounding Steven were again vibrant with color and filled with life. Each tree in the immediate vicinity, regardless of how badly scorched, was bursting with new limbs, leaves, and branches, returning to their original beauty.

Again the Professor's heart began to beat rapidly within his chest, only this time it was with both joy and sadness as a dozen-or-so small children ran out from under the protecting wings of Steven and toward the outstretched waiting arms of Jesus.

They were barely more than toddlers, in a myriad of shapes and colors. They smiled ear to ear with laughter as they frolicked waist deep throughout the wildflower-covered hillside. The Professor's eyes welled up with tears of joy when he saw the happy and excited expressions on the children's faces, as they raced past him on their way to Jesus.

After only a brief separation, they were finally being reunited with all that was familiar to them and more. And without ever taking their eyes off Jesus, they were running home.

With the children all safely in the arms of Jesus, Steven followed slowly up the hillside. He was carrying a small infant, no more than a few minutes old. And as he walked by, the Professor could see that it was the newborn from the hospital. The Professor smiled at her and was immediately taken by the elated expression on her face as she looked up the hillside, in the direction of Jesus. Instinctively, the Professor glanced sheepishly up the hill.

There on the knoll, standing next to Jesus, was the young mother from the hospital. Tears of joy streamed down her face as she reached out and held her daughter in her arms for the first time. She hugged and kissed her baby, knowing they would never be separated again. Then Jesus, Steven, and the small group of beloved souls, turned and moved slowly up the hillside.

And while all eyes in The Cherubim Fields watched, Gabriel turned to the Professor and said:

"There is no greater gift . . . than to sacrifice one's life for the lives of others . . ."

The two spoke briefly of things to come . . . and how all the dimensions will merge into one glorious kingdom of God with no memory of evil or sin,[26] but that for now, there was work to be done in this dimension. He explained how the Angels hadn't ever really understood their foe, as they'd never experienced sin. The Professor, on the other hand, had.

Neither of them knew exactly why Jesus had come to The Fields on that day. Was it to spare the Professor from the fateful sword of Maximus . . .? Was it to see his faithful servant Gabriel again . . .? Or was it to collect Steven and his precious passel of souls . . .?

Gabriel looked at the Back of Jesus as He walked up the hillside and said:

"He wants you to stay here, with us. But as always . . . the choice is yours."

"How could I go back now?" thought the Professor. "Knowing what I know."

"Satan will no longer exploit your sins, for the Son of God has cleansed you of them," said Gabriel.

The Professor was speechless and in awe as he gazed upon Jesus on the hill.

Then, with the Professor still on his knees, Gabriel drew his massive broadsword and placed it onto the Professor's left shoulder and said:

"Do you swear allegiance, loyalty, and complete obedience to The Lord God in Jesus' Name?"

"Yes . . . Yes I do," the Professor answered. "I'll take my place . . . here in The Cherubim Fields . . . for as long as The Lord Wills it."

"So be it then!" said Gabriel pulling the Professor to his feet and giving him a firm handshake at the forearm. The remaining Cherubim all lifted their swords in celebration to their newest brother.

For a moment, the Professor was saddened by the realization that having become a soldier in the Army of The Lord, returning to his dimension was no longer an option. He thought about Amena and the future they could have had, but having seen the full picture, he realized that time is not a limitation in God's dimension, and that thousands of years of believers will simultaneously be brought before God at the very moment the world was created. And although his mind understood . . . his heart still ached . . . for her.

As Jesus neared the top of the hillside, Satan himself was just cresting the bluff on the other side of the ravine. He was in an animal-like rage with his hate levitating him well over the burning funeral pyres.

Flying quickly to the tomb, he screamed at his subjects:

"Why are you hiding like children?! Why are you not fighting?!! Kill them . . . Kill them all!!!"

CHAPTER XVIII

SATAN FALLS AGAIN

When Satan departed Buchanan Hollow, he hurriedly made his way across the foothills, flying high above the battlefield like a wingless falcon kept aloft by nothing more than pure and unadulterated hate. He couldn't believe that the beasts he'd created from the very ugliest and darkest part of his being were apparently stopped cold in their tracks by the presence of Gabriel.

This enraged him even more as he'd trained them all to kill each and every Angel on sight regardless of how meek or powerful.

While approaching the area of the tomb, Satan noticed a blue-light emanating from just beyond a medium-size foothill. It was bright enough to produce a silhouette of the foothill in front of it, but faint enough to allow those in the immediate area to gaze into it unharmed.

Satan discounted its origin assuming that it was the afterglow of Gabriel's release.

But upon reaching the top of the hill, Satan saw something that he thought he would never see again. It was Jesus. He was walking slowly away, up the adjoining hillside on the other side of the ravine, with his back to The Fields. Satan shuttered and wheezed deeply at the sight of Him. He brandished his razor-sharp, jagged-teeth, and with a hateful scowl, anticipated engaging the Son of God. Satan, after all, had been incorrectly referred to by Man as the antichrist, and believing this to be the case, led him to the misconception that he was some sort of threat to Jesus.

All this time . . . and for thousands of years . . . he had deluded himself into believing that he would have something to say . . . or a voice at all in the presence of God. But when given the opportunity, all he could do was crouch down and hide like a frightened child. Making every effort to remain undetected, Satan cowered behind a large rock at the top of the hill, silently turning his face away in an attempt to conceal his ugliness.

But as curiosity got the better of him, he slowly lifted his eyes to gaze at the Back of The Lord, hoping desperately that Jesus would quickly return to Heaven, leaving The Fields to him, to do with what he pleased . . . But it couldn't have been further from the truth.

Jesus knew of Satan's presence on the hill. Beasts and Dark Angels alike watched anxiously in a state of suspended animation as Jesus stopped and slowly looked over his shoulder directly into the eyes of the cowering Devil. Suddenly two beams of light came streaming out of the eyes of Jesus, illuminating Satan with the blinding light of God.

The force of the rays tore Satan's cloak and stripped it from his body, revealing his repulsive nakedness for all to see. He was burned from head to toe, resembling a leper with open wounds that refused to heal. His body was a lucid manifestation of the hate that emanated from within.

Snakes, worms, and a superfluity of insects passed in and out of his abdomen. He was an operational corpse, partially decomposed and propelled by pure evil. He was an amalgamation of all of Man's sin and darkness on display for all to see.

Exposed, disfigured by the rigidity of his rigor-mortise, he gambled greatly by leaping atop the rock behind which he'd been hiding. He stood as tall as his crippled body would allow, and peered directly into the eyes of God in complete and total irreverence to his Creator.

It was at that moment that it happened . . .

Suddenly his scars began to fade . . . his burns and open sores smoothed over and healed instantaneously. He opened his eyes widely as his hair rapidly grew and flowed magnificently behind him. Rodents and vermin scuttled out from within him when the pink and rose-colored blood began to surge once again through his collapsed veins.

As his body healed, his posture became erect, and he stretched his arms out wide to soak in the cleansing light of God. The skeletal remains of what once were glorious wings filled with life as they unfurled stunningly behind him. He leaned forward indignantly, facing steadfast into the Light.

He was transforming back into the Angel that God had intended him to be. And in seeing that his metamorphosis was nearing completion, Angels and beasts alike stood in astonishment and awe. There before them stood the most beautiful Angel ever created by God . . . Lucifer . . . The Angel of Light.

He stood a full fifteen-foot tall, with the sculpted body of Adonis, and the skin of milk and honey. The features of his face were drawn with perfection, reminiscent of the works of Michelangelo, beautiful and yet masculine. His eyes were as blue as the skies of Eden. He was adorned with jewels the likes of which had never been seen on earth. His wings were a brilliant white and spanned thirty feet from tip to tip. Tears streamed down his face as he ran his hands over his smooth skin and silky hair. And although he vaguely remembered his time in good standing with The Lord, he'd all but forgotten the feelings of dignity and splendor that being in his presence brought.

He was whole again. Strong and vibrant with every ounce of his being filled with the glorious bounty of the Lord.

For a moment it seemed as though it all would be over. The evil, the sin, the fighting, and the world of Man . . . all finished by the transformation and reunification with Lucifer.

But it was not to be . . .

Satan was in absolute awe of himself and wasted no time in capturing the moment.

"See me . . .!" he cried as his restored vocal cords filled and permeated the hills and on down to the valley floor. "Behold the Angel of Light! Look upon me and see my beauty! Give me your praise, and I will lead you to victory!"

Inevitably, in true Satan accord, his self-adoration turned to pride, which was his downfall from the very beginning. He could never be satisfied with the blessings bestowed unto him from God . . . He wanted more. He wasn't content in his original role as praise collector for the Lord. He wanted it for himself . . . He wanted it all.

"Bow down before me!" he cried as he pointed to the smaller and less prominent Cherubim. "Praise me . . .! The Angel of Light who stands before you! All Angels and beasts shall kneel in worship to ME . . .!" he shouted while defiantly raising and shaking his fists toward The Lord.

Dragons, beasts, and Dark Angels alike jigged in victory and danced with perverted madness at the sight of their leader.

And as Lucifer stood preening and loving on himself, in the full indulgence of self-adulation, a single tear of pity and disappointment ran down the cheek of Jesus.

For the Compassion of Jesus is limitless, and His Heart breaks for even the most foul of creatures.

Upon seeing the tear, Satan knew that his moment had passed. Jesus closed his eyes and turned, slowly continuing his walk up the hillside, leaving Satan once again in darkness.

"Noooooo . . .!" screamed Satan, as he quickly began to crumble.

Absent from the Light of God, and with no internal goodness to sustain him, his body erupted into a flaming inferno. His outward appearance quickly began to revert back to the hideous creature that so represented the being within. He screamed in pain as he was once again burned beyond recognition. The wings that spanned gloriously over The Fields were engulfed in a whirlwind of fire. It was a swift but powerful blaze containing the force that could destroy an Angel as mighty as Lucifer.

In a matter of seconds, his regression was complete, leaving only the wretched, charred, smoldering remains of the being that he was, just moments before. Screaming in shame and disgust with himself, he scurried back down the hillside, back toward his camp, killing beasts by the hundreds in his rage and frustration.

Upon reaching the camp, he opened the dark box of damnation and instructed beasts and Dark Angels to begin devouring the human souls of the condemned like never before. And with unfettered hate, he continued his reign over his realm of nonbelievers.

Back at the tomb, Gabriel looked out upon The Cherubim Fields and saw Satan, along with hundreds of thousands of beasts, minions, and Dark Angels, as they fled in terror from Jesus. Watching with the excitement of a child on Christmas morning, Gabriel turned to the Professor and said:

"Come my wingless brother . . . Let your training begin!" And with a gleam in his eye, he pulled his broad sword and pointed it toward the fleeing masses.

"Today we will kill deep into Hell itself before we rest!" he shouted, with all remaining Angels lifting their swords in confident allegiance.

The Professor remembered his conversation with Michael and the temptation he faced when given the opportunity to rid the world of Satan. It worried the Professor to think that Gabriel might not be as disciplined as Michael and might ultimately be tempted into disobedience to The Lord.

"Could this be my purpose now?" he thought. "To ride herd on 'Gabriel's Revenge' . . . To make him aware of Michael's brush with insubordination and the self-inflicted fate he suffered as a result?"

And what of Satan? Despite the knowledge that had been bestowed onto the Professor by Jesus, he was still unclear about the transformation of Lucifer. Was it a second chance? Was it to remind the Darkest Angel of his place as a created being powerless in the presence of his Creator? Was it to remind Satan of just how far he'd fallen from the cleansing Love of God? Or maybe Jesus transformed him so that the innocent souls he'd collected wouldn't have to witness his wretchedness. Possibly, he thought, as he recalled Amena's junk food analogy . . . God simply couldn't look upon evil or accept it in His presence.

These answers would all be revealed to him in time, but for now . . . all he could think of was Amena.

He walked slowly to the place where he last saw her. It was across Granite Creek, at the edge of the battlefield, halfway up the hill where the road would have been in his world. He stopped at the exact spot where she would have been standing. And peering sadly and solemnly into the hillside, he closed his eyes and thought of the first time he saw her sitting in his class room . . . a student visiting from another school so confident and yet so vulnerable. He smiled as he remembered what a beautiful woman she'd become and how her personality and dry sense of humor often times made him falter for words. He

recalled their night together at Johnsey's Station . . .
He would never forget the smell of her hair or the
warmth of her touch.

He struggled to remember every moment they
shared in their short time together. If it were up to
him, the images and memories that were engraved
into his very soul would be carried with him into
eternity.

But it was not to be . . .

Sadly they were memories and emotions that could
not be kept with him in The Cherubim Fields, as he
thought of his conversation with Michael:

"Be single-minded in purpose and you cannot
fail . . ."

He knew that his heartache would stand against him
in battle, as Satan would surely use it against him,
jeopardizing everything they stood to gain.

CHAPTER XIX
SAYING GOODBYE
⟡

Back at the car, Amena waited at the roadside. She had faithfully remained there for several hours, watching the hillside hoping for even the slightest sign of his return. Numier shuttled back and forth from Johnsey's Station with supplies preparing for an extended vigil. While pulling his car off the road with a fresh supply of bottled water, Numier shouted:

"He did it! The Chinese have pulled back and the ICBMs were diverted and detonated over the ocean. Missile silos are gearing down throughout Europe and the Middle East. I can't wait to tell him!"

It was late afternoon. The sun was setting and the cool evening breeze blew gently against Amena's face. The sky was purple to the east, looming ominously over the Sierra Nevadas. From the west, the setting sun projected its majesty of vibrant color onto the muddy ridge that blanketed the San Joaquin Valley.

The calm and serenity of the countryside complimented Amena's stunning beauty as she sadly gazed upon the foothills below. She slowly walked to the shoulder of the road and closed her eyes. Standing still, while mentally taking-in the empty hillside on the other side of the stream, she turned to Numier and said:

"He's not coming back . . ."

"Why do you say that?" he asked.

"I just know . . ." she answered. "But I still feel him . . ."

And as she turned back to the hillside, she reached out her hand as if to wave to him . . . or maybe to touch his face if it were there. Like a statue she stood, waiting for something . . . anything.

Back in The Fields the Professor stood still, his heart was breaking as he stared at the empty hillside.

Suddenly and without warning, just before disappearing into the hillside with Steven, Jesus stopped and turned his head briefly into the direction of the Professor.

A simple glance from Him was all it took. Directly in front of the Professor opened a port-hole back to his dimension. It was a circular breach slightly larger than a doorway . . . an opening between two worlds. And there in the center of it, standing not more than two feet in front of him . . . was Amena.

Her hair was flowing gently in the cool breeze of the Sierras. Her radiant beauty permeated The Cherubim Fields. Green grass and wildflowers sprang up across the scorched earth at the sight of her. Archangels and Cherubim looked upon her with wonder and delight, as she was a living testimony to God's creation.

Peering into the portal, Amena gasped. She saw squadrons of Angels circling in formation, ready at a moment's notice to drop down into battle. She saw levies of funeral pyres burning throughout the valley, which echoed their flames onto the low-lying crimson and tangerine-stained skies. She saw disfigured Dark Angels wielding whips of fire violently striking hideous beasts in various states of confusion and retreat. She saw haunting silhouettes of dragons circling the arena awaiting their chance to rejoin the engagement and strafe the battlefield. She saw Archangels of The Lord standing battle ready, watching with curiosity and amazement the scene in which they themselves were in no way created to experience.

She saw many magnificent and horrifying images, but most importantly of all, standing right in front of her . . . she saw the Professor.

She'd waited a lifetime for him in her world. He was the man she'd hoped to spend the rest of her life with, the children, the picket fence . . . the dog. But it was not to be.

He was here now . . . in the realm of spiritual warfare, pledged to do battle against evil in service to The Lord. Sworn to protect the very world he could no longer return to.

She looked at him with unconditional love.
He seemed the same, but somehow changed.
His hair was longer and more radiant. His eyes
were deeper and wiser, his face more wrinkled
than she remembered. He wore the tattered
clothes he had on when he first injured himself.
He was filthy from battle but somehow seemed
stronger. He stood tall and healthy despite the Hell
breaking loose all around him. He held tightly to a
large broadsword as the blood of hell beasts dripped
thick from its blade. In his eyes, were the Seven
Wonders of the World and the knowledge of the
universe.

She was looking at a man who had seen God . . . and
she knew it.

The one thing that had not changed was the way
he was looking at her. He stood breathing-in the
beauty that he wished would have no end. Her
hair, her skin, her breath. The love he felt for her
was pouring through the portal. She felt its force
pounding against her chest as all of his love was
flowing out of his soul and into hers.

Unafraid, she reached through the doorway-sized
opening and gently touched his face, shutting out
the sights and sounds of fighting and dying that
engulf this dimension. She felt overwhelmed as she
saw herself from his eyes and realized how much he
loved her. Sensing the brevity of the moment, . . .
she held his face in her hands:

"I love you with all my heart Don Goodwin," she said through tears that flowed uninhibited down her face.

"All my love for you . . . I give to you . . . You must carry it for us both . . .!" said the Professor as he purged his love onto her, where it would remain hidden in the world of Man . . . safe and innocent forever.

She shuttered as the full torrent of their love passed through them. Somehow she understood that he couldn't take it with him where he was going . . .

Though powerful, the moment was brief.

And without another word, as quickly as it opened, the portal closed . . .

Amena stared briefly at the empty hillside before falling to her hands and knees. Overcome with emotion, exhaustion, and shock, she wept beneath tangerine skies on the soft shoulder of Tollhouse Road.

Numier had been standing several yards away from Amena, down the road a bit, near the car. From his vantage point he couldn't see the Professor, but was able to glimpse into the portal. He saw a massive door at the base of a foothill that hissed and smoked as it cooled. He saw Archangels standing battle ready while silhouettes of sparrows swiftly circled above

He made the observation that the skies appeared
unaffected by the dimensional vortex. And that
each evening, our worlds collide in a very brief but
significant way, sharing the sunset for just a few
short moments as it reflects the pain, suffering,
and sacrifice of Man's great protectors, a celestial
dimension away . . .

And as the skies transformed to a deep cobalt-merlot,
Numier and Amena walked silently to the car and
made their way slowly down the loosely paved foothill
road with one less angel among them.

BOOK 2 "THE LAST CHERUB"

CHAPTER XX

A NEW LIFE

❧

The portal closed, and Amena was gone. The Professor franticly searched the vacant hillside for any sight of her, but she had vanished. He closed his eyes and held tightly to the images of her face, her eyes, and her hair. He filled his lungs with the sweets smells of unspoiled air that faintly lingered across the hillside. His soul felt hollow. The deep and profound feeling of loss was overwhelming. His love for Amena, as new and powerful as it was, left a sizable void in his heart. It was a void that would be filled with something very different in this place. Something contrary to everything he had known.

He struggled to pull his concentration off the empty hillside knowing that he must clear his mind and focus on this strange celestial world, and his newfound God-given responsibilities . . . whatever they may be. He realized quickly that he was in a dangerous place now. A place where he would be under constant attack from all types of evil. He needed to be stronger than he was before. Faster, and more determined, like a soldier . . . like a warrior.

Now, separated from his earthly fears and trepidation, he could feel his soul changing. The anger and hate of this place slowly crept in. His head tingled and his ears felt hot. A slight electrical current shot up the side of his neck as he began to succumb to the rage. The old Professor was gone . . . and the new one was ready for combat.

Turning his attention to the battlefield, he could see the Archangels assembled a hilltop away. Less than half a dozen, they summoned what was left of their forces. With Gabriel's release from a two thousand year incarceration in a tomb-like abyss, there was optimism in the fields. Together with the remaining Cherubim, they expected to make headway against Satan's armies of darkness. Though hopeful, the Angels showed no emotion, only duty, as they prepared for battle.

The only emotion in this place came from the evil side of the battlefield as Hell-beasts and Dark Angels circled the small wingless Angel, waiting for their chance to pounce.

Suddenly a ten-foot-tall, hell-beast roared inches from the Professor's face. It was a creature known by the Cherubim as a Leatherback. Assembled from the backside of a rhino, the upper body of a hairless Grizzly bear, and the horned-head and neck of a large man. Though not as fast or agile as a screamer, this two-ton behemoth was a formidable adversary for any Angel let lone, a man.

"NOOOOO!!!" screamed Gabriel not wanting to loose his newest recruit.

The beast's massive claw grazed the Professor's chest tearing his shirt and opening his epidermis. He took a step back, and with one pass of the mighty sword, El Mórte, the creature was disemboweled. With a second pass, he cut the beast in two halves from its collarbone to its hip.

Instantly, a Dark Angel standing behind the Leatherback pulled a large cleaver from its sheath and swung it at the flailing minion. With swift precision, the beast's arm was severed at the shoulder-socket and tossed into the air above the Professor. Cherubim rushed the Professor's location, as the Dark Angel caught the lifeless arm and claw.

Apparently more interested in it than the Professor, he tucked it under his shield, turned his back to the advancing Cherubim, and ran quickly into the dense cluster of burned-out oaks that skirted the battlefield.

The sounds of clashing metal and gnashing teeth filled the combat zone as the Professor was immediately greeted by three more Leatherbacks spitting and foaming in their rage. He stood his ground and engaged the onslaught. Before he could lift El Mórte for another pass, he was joined by a squadron of Cherubim who, like sentries, threw their bodies between he and the monsters.

The screams of death rang loud as the small platoon of Cherubim made short work of quartering the brain damaged man-beasts. With the battle reigniting, the Professor made his way back to the Archangels. Beasts and Dark Angels fell in droves by the swords of Maximus and Gabriel slaying shoulder to shoulder with the remaining Cherubim fighting at their side.

As an incredible sense of excitement and exhilaration overcame the Professor . . . Gabriel turned to him and said:

"Welcome to The Cherubim Fields . . . my small, wingless brother. Come now . . . and let us show you how it's done!"

CHAPTER XXI
AM I DEAD?

Gabriel, the Professor, and the remaining handful of Cherubim slaughtered well into the night. Beasts and Dark Angels were no match for Gabriel as bodies of the undead were cut down in droves. Cleansed of his earthly sins, the Professor's presence would no longer cause the beasts to morph. Wingless dragons fell from the skies like rain hitting the earth with rumbling thunder. The hillsides rang with a ghoulish requiem as thousands of beasts and Dark Angels cried out to the skies, mourning their dying comrades.

With the three-headed dragons neutralized, progress was steady. Though outnumbered, the Angels pushed forward. Gabriel and the remaining Cherubim backed Satan's forces well beyond the cliffs of Buchanan Hollow allowing time to regroup and await reinforcements.

The Hollow, a strategic stronghold, was a preferred location to reestablish base camp. Its elevation, steep hillsides and jagged rock face made it almost impenetrable to ground forces.

Gabriel was pleased with the day's advancement. Beasts and Dark Angels were much easier to kill now that he had room to stretch his wings. For almost two thousand years, Gabriel endured constant attack while inside the tomb . . . never stopping and never resting. His mind and body were in continuous motion with his heart racing beneath his breastplate. Even in the days when no beasts came, his mind was keenly focused on the outstretching abyss.

Resting was foreign to Gabriel, but with the skirmish presently in hand and a new arrival to the fields, he took the time to stop. He summoned Maximus while pacing at the top of the jagged rocky-foothill.

"Tell me of his progress," growled Gabriel to Maximus, while glancing over his shoulder at the Professor.

The two Angels stood near the top of the stony fortress like cathedral guards. Thirteen feet tall, their muscular bodies shimmered against the night sky.

"He is a man . . . He comes from a place where competency is rare," answered Maximus with a stern, less than satisfactory look on his face.

"But yet he lives," replied Gabriel with furrowed brow.

"He fights bravely, but sees only what is in front of him," said Maximus. "Unlike our kind, he lacks the ability to sense the location of beings in his vicinity. Many beasts have I killed as they flank him . . ."

"It is unprecedented to have a man among our troops," said Gabriel, now peering at the Professor.

"Surely, there is a purpose for his presence . . ." replied Maximus.

Gabriel turned his attention from the Professor to the combat zone.

"It is not our place to question the Will of God," replied Gabriel redirecting his focus to the broader picture. "Only to serve it."

And as the two walked to the edge of the steep hillside, they could see millions of Satan's forces in various stages of retreat. Fearing the sword of Gabriel, they ran to the East. Beasts were quicker than their partially crippled handlers as they ran over the tops of Dark Angels only to be beaten ruthlessly from behind. The Sierras were their destination and their refuge. The closer they got to safety, the more desperate they became.

Once at the base of the mountain range, beasts and Dark Angels stopped short of intruding on their commander's encampment. Wings of fallen dragons served as canopies under which the gruesome generals congregated. Now well behind their previously accomplished front line, they assembled on ground that had seen battle for centuries. Most of the vegetation was gone with the exception of several dense clusters of charred Oaks, lifeless and black.

Leatherbacks and screamers regrouped and took positions along the base of the mountain range. Ten million strong, and growing with every passing minute, they blanketed the foothills as far as the eye could see.

"This War is far from over brother," said Gabriel as he quickly calculated how outnumbered they were.

As the two enormous Angels discussed battle strategy, Goodwin watched with intrigue. The Professor knew not to stray too far from Gabriel. If there was anyone in the fields who could keep him alive, it was him. Seeing the hilltop meeting, the Professor remained patient. He waited for instructions.

He paused for a moment and took inventory of his physical condition. He felt no pain. His legs weren't cramped. His sword wielding arm felt surprisingly fresh after swinging an over thirty-pound hunk of metal relentlessly for the last ten hours.

There was no exhaustion or fatigue, and he wasn't hungry or thirsty.

The killing and dying that surrounded him seemed less gruesome than before. He felt indifferent to everything other than the desire to proceed. He anxiously buttoned his shirt where the beast had grazed him, not wanting to reveal his vulnerability.

"Am I dead?" wondered the Professor, believing that in this place, anything is possible.

He took the opportunity to speak to the Cherub standing closest to him:

"Why is it that I don't feel tired . . . Why aren't I hungry . . . And why aren't I thirsty?" he asked, eager for conversation.

The twelve foot tall Cherub did not respond, nor did he indicate that he heard him at all . . . but Maximus did:

"Do not speak to the Cherubim!" barked Maximus from the hilltop. "I am your commander; direct your questions to me."

Maximus was a large Angel. He stood close to fourteen feet tall and at least five hundred pounds. Even in the blackest of night, Maximus' face glowed with a dim white hue. Somewhere in battle he'd lost his breastplate. A metal and leather paneled kilt and roman style ankle-strapped sandals were all that was left of his uniform. He carried a large, straight broadsword in his right hand and a two-sided axe in his left. Thick leather straps protected his forearms that overtime contoured to his rippling muscles.

As the mighty, war-torn Angel approached the Professor, his battle scars could clearly be seen. His upper left arm and shoulder swirled darkly with burn scarring. The unscathed flesh of his lower arm and half midsection outlined the shape of a shield that caught the brunt of the fiery attack. Across his face, beneath his left check-bone, was a deep scar that, upon healing, tightened his skin into a permanent smirk.

At first glance, those in the fields who were present on that day thought that Maximus was uninjured by his encounter with Huron. But when the Professor screamed for the key, Huron swung Kismet, the evil sword of doom, with all his might delivering a fateful strike. Maximus ducked the brunt of the blow but was grazed just under the left eye. The evil carried by Kismet for so many centuries crippled and blackened one side of Maximus' face.

The Professor thought back and remembered that none of these scars were present the first time he'd met Maximus.

Maximus walked up to the Professor and said sternly:

"Gabriel wishes a word with you."

As he reached the top of the hill, the Professor could only stare at Gabriel whose size was more fully appreciated in close proximity. He stood at the edge of the cliff with his back to the man. Though not as large as Maximus, he had a more solid appearance. His body was dark and smooth. The Professor noticed the lack of scaring on Gabriel, and considered the possibility that, in fact, there was no part of him that hadn't been scarred. His wings were retracted revealing the rippling muscles beneath the thin, metal-tunic that draped loosely over his upper back.

The pre-morning sun crept slowly behind the Sierra
Nevada's casting swirls of deep purple over Buchanan
Hollow. In the skies above, over the massive shoulder
of Gabriel, the Professor could see Seraphim by
the thousands flying in with much needed supplies
from the rear. With six wings and hundreds of
eyes constantly assessing the battlefield, they glided
stealthily through the night sky. Now in full battle-
armor, it was clear that these Angels would be taking
a much more physical role than simply observing.

Still looking into the skies, Gabriel said:

"Seraphim can be fierce warriors when their ranks
are needed." The tone of his voice dropped as he
watched them fly towards the mountains knowing
that they were barely out of boot camp.

"Why am I not tired?" the Professor asked. "And why
aren't I hungry... or thirsty?"

Gabriel turned and faced him:

"You are one of us now."

"You mean I'm an Angel?" he answered curiously.

Sneering, Gabriel looked down upon the Man,
merely half his height and a fraction of his weight:

"No . . . you are NOT an Angel. Here in the fields,
you will feel pain and fatigue, but with less severity

than in your world. And you will not feel hunger or thirst in the same way as in your dimension."

"It seems that feelings are in short supply here," replied the Professor as he looked out at the blank stares of the Cherubim.

"Your insight into feelings and emotions will serve us well to understand the enemy," Gabriel said looking over the hordes of raging beasts plodding and pounding at the earth, angry and frustrated by retreat.

"Strangely, I'm not feeling much of anything," replied the Professor.

"No . . . you wouldn't. Many of your feelings have been removed," said Gabriel. "But your memories of these . . . feelings . . . have been left intact. Surely you must have knowledge of many emotions."

"Besides the overwhelming desire to press forward, the only thing I feel is anger."

"You are absorbing that from the dark side," said Gabriel. "But that emotion is well documented here."

The Professor was unsure of what the mighty Angel was getting at.

"There is one emotion I am most interested in," Gabriel took a step closer and looked straight into the Professor's eyes and surprisingly said:

"Tell me of Love."

"Love . . .?" questioned the Professor looking up at Gabriel. "What do I know about love?" he added looking down at his tattered shoes, surprised they were still on his feet.

"In the vortex, the way you looked at the woman . . . your passion was evident. For a moment the two of you seemed to be as one . . . as if nothing else mattered. Tell me of this."

"Amena?" asked the Professor.

Gabriel did not mince words as his request struck right at the heart. He wanted insight into Man's emotions, and he was in no mood to wait.

"Yes, Amena," impatiently barked Gabriel. "Your emotions appeared to overcome you . . . Was this love?!"

"Surely, it must have been," replied the Professor as he searched the skies for inspiration. "The feelings are all a memory now, like a dream I had as a child. Curiously, I can't accurately recall the thing you ask about, but I do remember her . . . her beauty . . ."

Goodwin turned and faced into the soft breeze that escorted unsoiled air from the Cherubim side of the arena as he continued:

"Subtle wafts of perfume . . . a faint glimpse of the side of her face. Her hair. Her porcelain skin . . . The sapphire rim that surrounded the emerald-green-irises of her almond-shaped eyes.

If I could still feel her . . . I'm sure I could tell you more. It seems like forever since I last saw her, although I know it was only yesterday."

Their conversation was broken briefly when a medium-size beast, constructed of mostly sloth and man, appeared suddenly among the Cherubim. Without hesitation, they dismembered it as it screamed in pain and confusion. Gabriel only glanced at the mêlée as his focus was on the Professor.

"What about you?" asked the Professor. "Surely you must know about love. You're an Angel. I thought Angels were loving-beings . . . There must be love somewhere behind all that armor."

Gabriel paused . . . "There are many different kinds of Angels," he said. He stopped pacing just long enough to look over the battlefield and down upon all the bodies that lay strewn. It was a reminder of many years of combat and sacrifice. Miles and miles of Angels, hell-beasts and dragons littered the bloody landscape. He lowered his eyes and looked back to the Professor.

"I was not created with Human emotions," he said. "I serve The Lord . . . and honor my duty. But what I witnessed through the portal was different.

"You're one of the oldest Angels," said Goodwin. You must be over eight thousand years old. Surely this wasn't the first you've seen of love. Scripture speaks of your interaction with the human world, surely . . ."

"Yes . . ." interrupted Gabriel. "There was such a time."

Gabriel turned to the rising sun, looked straight into it, closed his eyes and remembered:

CHAPTER XXII
CHINERETH

There was a time . . . early in the history of Man when Human kind was caught between the flesh and the spirit. Demons roamed the earth with little resistance, entering and inhabiting humans at will. Mutations and deformities were commonplace as many were physically crippled by the demons that possessed them. They began speaking in languages unrecognizable to humans . . . the language of demons . . . the language of Satan. Some recognized the ailments as possession but had no tools to vanquish the parasites.

Technology was at a standstill. Buildings were made of earth and straw. Roads were dirt and rock. It took many days to travel short distances on foot or atop small riding animals. There was no refrigeration for the food that rotted quickly. Animals were slaughtered and eaten in the same day to avoid disease and pestilence. For most, sanitation was a luxury, not a priority. It was an unclean world . . . a time before salvation . . . a time before grace.

In such a time I was sent on a mission . . . not one of combat, but of diplomacy. Once in your world, I would need neither sword nor shield. In your world, there is no physical threat to me.

In the time of my mission, a sorcerer named Harrod was the ruler of The Garden, or The Middle East, as you would know it. His ruthless treatment of his friends and enemies caused him to be known by many. He gained stature in the underworld by ordering the killing of each first-born child throughout Egypt. The cries of mothers were heard in every dimension. He, along with those who carried out the act, confirmed their reservation in Hell.

High above the earth, in the celestial realm, there was a different kind of ruler– a much more sinister one. He was known as The Evil Prince of Persia. He was a fallen Angel. One who, in the beginning, helped Lucifer conspire against The Lord. Though their plan was futile in nature, they managed to summon a great deal of evil in their coo-ish attempt. When the serpent was defeated, Satan took a third of the Angels and fell to earth.[27] Much of that evil was taken with him to govern over The Garden where he ruled with an iron hand. Very little restraints were placed upon the Dark Angels in his command, who in your world, are called demons.

Prior to entering your world, there was much opposition from the Persian Prince and his army, but being that this was not our first meeting . . . I was ready. I employed the aid of a brigade of Sparrows. Unmatched in the air, their speed and agility made them an unbeatable force. Ten thousand strong, the diversion held the evil forces long enough for me to enter the earth's atmosphere unimpeded.

Upon entering your world . . . my mission was
all that mattered. It was a mission to deliver a
message. A mission where, for a moment, I found
myself in the presence of beauty. And it was in that
moment, serving as a vessel between two worlds, that
I experienced a rush of powerful emotions. They
were feelings. Feelings that were quite foreign to
me. Initially I was confused, until I reasoned that the
feelings were not mine.

The experience lasted only a few minutes . . . but as
brief as it was . . . I carry it with me always.

Gabriel turned and faced the Professor, with his back
to the battlefield. He stood tall on the edge of the
cliff overlooking the valley below. The early morning
sun lit the mighty Angel's face as he began to recall
the precise details of his experience in Man's world.

The Professor sat on a knee-high boulder, looked up
at the mighty Angel, and listened.

CHAPTER XXIII
THE ASSEMBLY

At thirty thousand feet, I soared. Flying high above the earth where the air is cold and thin. It was late afternoon, and the heat of the desert was sending plumes of thermals upward, cutting through the bitter chill and rocking my flight. I descended quickly, circling at speeds of twelve hundred miles per hour, twice the speed of sound in your world. But even at that altitude, I was able to see clearly the scene in a small village just west of the Sea of Chinereth.

I am not always versed in the particulars of my mission, sometimes only the message and subject. But on this day, I saw a human . . . It was a man. He was walking toward the center of town, where another man was speaking.

As the villager approached the town square, I could see that he had a child in tow– a girl, most likely his daughter. She was holding his hand as they walked.

A short distance behind shuffled a tall elderly woman. She stopped at the inside edge of an apple orchard while the others kept walking. Blossoms softly fell around her in the slight breeze. Pale pink and white pedals mixed whimsically with the thick strands of grey in her hair.

"Eli, where are you taking her?" she yelled to the man.

"We won't be gone long. We'll be back before dark." He replied with a smile.

The woman did not retreat. She wrapped herself snuggly in her thick, off-white, cover-up and stood still as if to wait for them there.

"Where ARE you taking me, Papa?" The girl asked in a soft voice.

I could see now that the girl was older than a child but not yet a woman.

"I'm taking you to the town square Aziza (Aramaic for sweetheart). There we will find a man who speaks of the prophecy," he answered.

"You mean the prophecy of the Messiah, Papa?" she asked

"Yes, my love. The prophecy of the coming King."

"But Papa . . . you have spoken much about this King. What will this man say at the square that we haven't already heard?" curiously she asked.

The man just smiled and softly laughed.

"There is still much we do not know about our Messiah," he answered with the patience of a father.

As they dew nearer to the center of the village, the Rabbi's voice could clearly be heard:

"And there will come a Man. Not an ordinary Man, but a King. He will come from the House of David, and He will deliver us from our oppression."

The townspeople continued to gather at the square near a large cobblestone water well. The Rabbi stood and faced the crowd with his back to the well. Many holding their goat skin bags and empty clay pots stopped to hear his message. I couldn't help but notice how attentive she was. Others at the square were busy visiting with friends or shuffling about, but not this one. She stood still as a statue at her father's side, firmly holding his hand while listening to every word and inflection of the Preacher's voice:

"He was given authority, glory, and sovereign power. All peoples, nations, and men of every language worshiped Him. His dominion is an everlasting dominion that will not pass away, and His kingdom is one that will never be destroyed."[28]

It was only minutes before the Romans came to break up the assembly. I could see demons all around them, but they could not. Trying to protect the Rabbi, two men from the crowd rushed toward the troops. The first Roman guard closest to the Rabbi saw the men approaching and quickly positioned the back of his spear onto the base of his foot and carefully aimed the tip of the spear at the attacking crowdsman's neck. It entered just below the chin and stopped at the inside of his upper skull lifting him several feet off the ground. The weight of the man on the spear settled the slender weapon deep into the soft sand, hanging him by his own head.

"It was a clever move, even by my standards," said Gabriel.

"Stop!" yelled the Rabbi. "There must be no violence here! This will not be the way of the coming King!"

"What other way is there?!" screamed a voice from the crowd. "We cannot even gather without them killing us!"

The second guard grabbed the Rabbi.

"Control your crowd or more blood will be shed!" yelled their commanding officer.

Eli swept the girl up and ran swiftly from the scene as the crowd began to disburse. He knew that being shorter than the villagers in front of her, she would not have seen the violence at the well, and he wanted to get her far away before the hanging body became visible.

"What happened to that man, Papa?" she asked as he ran.

"It's not your concern child," he panted as he turned down an empty side street.

Moving quickly, still dangling to one side, tucked safely under her father's armpit, the girl looked up. Down a narrow alleyway she could clearly see a Man. She did not recognize him from the village, but gasped at how perfect he was. Tall and thin, His golden-brown-hair swayed in the gentle breeze. The complexion of His skin was much lighter than the villagers. His veins shown through His thin, opaque skin. His long slender face was anchored by His piercing but compassionate blue eyes.

She felt a warm calming sensation when she saw him. It was like he was telling her that everything was going to be all right. She smiled at him, and he softly smiled back as if he knew her. Just before passing the alleyway, He lowered His head. Suddenly, wounds appeared, as blood trickled down his forehead. Tears streamed down his face and blood flowed from holes in his hands and feet.

"Papa!" the girl cried as she buried her face into her father's underarm.

"It's OK . . . we're almost home," he said replacing her to her feet.

Together they ran back to the safety of the apple orchard and into the waiting arms or her mother.

"Are you Shidana (Aramaic for crazy)!" the woman shouted from the edge of the apples. "How could you have taken her to the assembly? You know how dangerous that is!" she scolded.

"She is old enough to know and to hear!" he shouted.

"Let her hear it from you . . . not from the square," she said.

"Yes, Anne," he said sheepishly still shaken by the sight of the man's body hanging on the spit.

"Mama, I saw a man," said the girl.

"What man?" she answered quickly turning her furrowed brow to Eli.

"She didn't see anything, I'm sure of it," he said.

"Not at the well, Mama. In the alley, just over there," pointing in the direction of the bleeding man. "He was hurt and bleeding, Mama."

The woman looked in the direction of the empty alleyway:

"There's nothing, Aziza . . . Now enough of this talk of bleeding men. Let's get you inside and cleaned up for supper," she said still fuming at Eli.

She wrapped the frightened girl in her shawl, and still bent to the girl's height, they hurried towards the safety of their cool mud hut. A red, clay-tile roof and straw-covered porch shaped their rectangular, thick-walled adobe home.

With the three safe inside, still descending from high above the earth, I turned my attention back to the square. I could see the guard still holding firmly to the spear as the last quivers of the dying man made for a tight vertical plant.

Letting go of the spear, he yanked the Rabbi from the hands of the other soldier.

"Please, sir!" he urged to his commanding officer. "Let me take this sorcerer to the rooftop and put a stop to this foolish blasphemy."

The guard was a young, over-zealous Roman soldier whose allegiance to Caesar drowned out all tolerance. His ruthless treatment of all followers of the Prophesy earned him the name, "Paul the Persecutor".

"Settle yourself soldier!" barked the commanding officer. "You've collected enough blood on your spear today."

"But he speaks out against Rome," Paul added. "Let me take him to the roof, and we'll see if his GOD softens his fall."

The remaining crowd was now in an uproar.

"Silence!" said the officer:

"This man's words are not a threat to Rome," pulling the Rabbi from the clutches of Paul. "The Man he speaks of . . . your Prophet . . . your Messiah. Let him come, and let Harod deal with him!"

After forcefully returning the Rabbi back into the arms of the waiting crowd, the officer turned his attention back to Paul, and while leading his troops away from the well, he said:

"Be patient Paul . . . Let them have their ideas of salvation. In time, these false prophesies will only serve to increase their suffering."

CHAPTER XIV
THE GIRL

Night had fallen, and the village was quiet. Wild dogs quietly roamed the empty desert streets. They searched for discarded food set out at the ends of the narrow alleyways. Though diligent in their search, they were careful to avoid traps laid by Bedouins on the outskirts of the village.

Designed to lure and destroy desert wolves, sharp knives were dipped in goat's blood and set deep into the soil with several inches of blood-soaked blade exposed above the earth. Wolves would come from miles away. Finding the blood irresistible, the hungry carnivores would begin licking the blade until the goat's blood mixed with their own. The bloody combination would send them into a feeding frenzy sealing their fate and hastening their death.

Slowing my flight to treetop speed, I descended onto the village and entered the home of my subject. Quickly crossing dimensions allows for seamless passage through solid objects. After creeping undetected by several sleeping humans, I reached the final destination of my mission.

I stood hunched over in a small, low-ceiling bedroom. To my left was a box with drawers used to store clothes. On top of this box was a slowly burning candle, dimly revealing the rectangular-shaped room. On one side of the wall, opposite me, was a small window, far too small for a human but large enough for moonlight. Against the other side of the wall, tucked into the corner where two walls meet, was a narrow bed. There slept the recipient of my message.

It was the girl from the square. Not more than thirteen human years old, she lay peacefully sleeping in the home of her parents. Together, the moonlight and candle illuminated her clearly for me to see. It was a cool-night, and she was bundled-up to the neck with only her face visible. I could see from the outline of her sheets that her tiny stature covered less than half the bed. I remember being quite surprised at how beautiful she was, even for a human. Her hair was brown with golden highlights. Her face had gentle features, oval-shaped eyes and long eyelashes. Her skin was fair, much lighter than the villagers. Even in her sleep, she had a quiet, peaceful look on her face.

I looked upon her as she slept. With each breath she drew, my chest tightened. It was a feeling of vulnerability that I was not familiar with. I'd spent six thousand years surrounded by Angels and beasts darkened and filthied from battle. These new feelings were foreign to me.

The feelings did not subside but intensified. My heart pounded behind my armor breastplate, and my breathing grew shallow. I could hear the blood surging through my arms with each beat of my heart. Initially, I considered the possibility that I'd sustained some sort of wound upon re-entry. Realizing the improbability of injury, I kept my focus on my subject and my mission as a mild sense of panic-like euphoria mellowed into a profound sense of compassion. The feeling was powerful . . . much more so than I was capable of feeling for anything . . . let alone a human. I deduced quickly that passing through me . . . in that small, dimly lit room on the outskirts of Chinereth . . . was love.

It was a love that could not have originated with me . . . It was a love that was not mine . . . but His.

An innocent Love . . . The purest and most uncontaminated kind of Love . . . It was the Love of God.

I hesitated for a moment. Knowing that my presence in her room and the message she was about to receive might be too much for her. Nonetheless, this was my mission. So softening my voice as much as a Mighty Angel could . . . I spoke:

"MARY"

CHAPTER XXV
THE MESSAGE

The room shook from the vibration of my voice. Plaster fell from the walls and resting pigeons flew from the outer eves of the home. Startled by the sound, with her heals, she pushed herself into the corner of the room and pulled the sheets over her eyes. She immediately began to tremble and shake, but despite her best efforts, she was not able to scream through her fright:

"Greetings, you who are highly favored! The Lord is with you." I said.[29]

In a mild state of shock, too frightened to speak, she lowered the covers to the top of her nose and slowly looked up at me. The sight of me has caused many humans to loose consciousness, so I spoke quickly.

"I am an Angel of The Lord, and I've been sent to deliver a message to you."

"Do not be afraid, Mary, you have found favor with God.[30] You will be with child and give birth to a son, and you are to give him the name Jesus. He will be great and will be called the Son of the Most High. The Lord God will give him the throne of his father David, and he will reign over the house of Jacob forever; his kingdom will never end."

Her fear turned to puzzlement, as she lowered the sheets to the base of her chin, and with a trembling voice, she spoke:

"How will this be," Mary asked, "since I have not been with a man?"[31]

Then I said to her:

"The Holy Spirit will come upon you, and the power of the Most High will overshadow you. So the Holy One to be born will be called the Son of God[32]. Even Elizabeth your relative is going to have a child in her old age, and she who was said to be barren is in her sixth month. For nothing is impossible with God."

Despite the message being far too large for any human, and despite my war-torn, ominous appearance contradicting everything she'd ever seen or heard, she showed surprising courage and devotion to God:

"I am the Lord's servant," Mary answered. "May it be to me as you have said."[33]

It wasn't until after I delivered the message that I became truly aware of the importance of my mission. For this was no ordinary home . . . And this was no ordinary girl. The young woman whom I was looking upon was the one chosen from eight thousand years of women. She was the one . . . who, among so many, found favor in the eyes of God. She would be the one to bring God's Son into Man's world. The one to, from her body, bring perfection into an imperfect world.

Just before departing her room, she looked up at
me and smiled. I smiled back with mixed feelings
knowing that the next time I would see her . . . she
would be crying.

Gabriel paused and looked at Goodwin:

"The Lord honored me to deliver such a message.
The experience changed my perception of Mankind
as a whole. Before that day . . . I slaughtered beasts
and Dark Angels in service to God . . . blindly
fulfilling my mission as directed. But since that day, I
see my purpose through different eyes."

"How so?" asked the Professor.

"He cares for your kind, more than any creature
created. He loves your world more than any other . . .
and this is why we fight and die."

Maximus abruptly interrupted the conversation from
halfway down the hillside:

"Gabriel, a storm approaches!" pointing to the East.

Gabriel ran to the edge of the steep ravine and
peered carefully at the unforcasted dark-cloud
formation. Originating from the base of the
mountain range, rolling over foothills like a thick
black mist, it came. Too far for the Professor to make
out, Gabriel could clearly see:

"Dragons!"

CHAPTER XXVI
THE STORM

It was not a storm cloud at all, but hundreds of thousands of three-headed dragons mounted by Dark Angels brandishing whips of fire that cracked loudly as they rode the army of beasts directly at the surviving Angel's location. It was a Hell-storm, with all the forces of evil pushing for one final assault.

"Call down the Seraphim!" yelled Maximus.

But Gabriel, with his eagle-vision, could clearly see tens of thousands of Seraphim wings and appendages hanging out of the mouths of the oncoming dragons.

"They already know . . ." he said.

Satan, riding the largest dragon, screamed with crazed laughter, violently waving his sword while flying through plumes of smoke and body parts of Seraphim shouting:

"Kill them! . . . Kill them all!!"

Maximus shouted, "But how can this be . . . the Man has been cleansed!!?"

Gabriel turned quickly to the Professor and noticed the dried blood forming the outline of a large claw-scratch beneath the Professor's shirt.

"The Medallion!!" screamed Gabriel.

CHAPTER XXVII

SARAH

Earlier, back in Auberry, it had been an exhausting seventy-two hours. Three ordinary people embarked on an extraordinary quest, finding a way to bridge the gap between two dimensions. They pushed themselves to their physical and emotional limits. Sleep deprived, they overcame their fear, and said goodbye to a loved one. After watching the Professor walk bravely into the unknown, Numier drove an emotionally spent Amena back to the doublewide mobile home where she had been staying with a friend.

Sarah, Amena's roommate, was a young and vibrant, nineteen year old, junior college student and lifelong resident of Auberry. Being American Indian, she belonged to the local Mono tribe and had never left her native lands. Her nurturing spirit filled the hearts of all who came in contact with her. And although not a student of Numier's, he knew of her from campus.

Numier pulled slowly into the long, decomposed-granite driveway of Sarah's doublewide. Trying not to wake Amena, he turned the car off and carefully walked to the passenger door.

Sarah came running out from the mobile:

"Oh my God! Where have you been? I've been worried sick," she yelled.

The passenger door opened slowly.

Amena couldn't speak, with her hair veiling her face, she leaned out of the passenger seat on her way to the ground.

Sarah pushed passed Numier as Amena fell into her arms.

"Is she OK?" asked Sarah looking at the unfamiliar Numier with suspicion.

"Yes and no . . ." said Numier, trying to catch his breath.

"She's not physically hurt, but she may be in shock." he added.

"Come on . . . let's get you inside," Sarah said while helping shuffle Amena across the loose driveway toward the front porch.

Numier took a step toward the Mobile when he realized Sarah didn't know him.

He shut Amena's door and walked slowly around the front of his car. He paused for a moment and felt his age as he leaned his body against the hood of his car. He waited awhile until they were both safely inside. He thought of just sitting for a bit in the comfort of his well broken-in driver's seat. But with the sun setting in his rear view mirror, and the foothill breeze picking up, he knew he ought to get home.

He knew Amena needed rest and would be fine with her friend. He slowly pulled onto Auberry Road and began to coast downhill toward the elementary school. Although there were no students present, he reduced his speed out of habit as he drove over the painted yellow crosswalks that striped the street in front of the chain link-lined sidewalk. He looked out the passenger window to see the swings slowly rocking and the tetherballs tapping softly against their poles in the breeze. He could almost hear the sounds of children playing at recess. Laughing and hollering, chasing and throwing, ticking away the carefree minutes of their tiny days. He could almost see long, wavy-blond hair tossing in the wind as the boys passed for another goal. Without having any children of his own, on any other day, these sounds and images had gone unnoticed, but today, as he passed slowly by, he longed to hear them once again.

He scanned the roadsides for a lonely girl. Was she wondering the foothills . . . searching for something in this dimension? Her family . . . her old home-site . . . something at all familiar.

After slowly negotiating the windy foothills, he returned to his log cabin just off Tollhouse Road. Worn out, he spent very little time tidying up his nine hundred square foot home. He fed the cats, watered his flowering succulent, and laid his head back on his pheasant-hunting-patterned couch. Exhausted, he tried to relax, but couldn't get Don out of his mind.

"How could he survive in such a place?" he thought over and over.

He shook his head in disbelief as he thought of the adventure they shared and how after so many lonely years, Don seemed to have found love. Knowing how Goodwin felt about Amena, Numier felt a strange obligation to help her in any way that he could.

He'd planned on checking up on her after a couple of days, giving her a chance to rest and recharge her batteries, but after a troubling and restless night, on his otherwise comfortable couch, his plans changed.

He awoke before dawn with a feeling of despair and urgency and was quickly back in his car, speeding up the road on his way to Auberry.

CHAPTER XXVIII
SLOTHMAN

It was early morning on Tollhouse Road. The rising sun lit up the foothills. The warming earth unsealed the aromatic countryside releasing the smells of manzanita, wild sage, and lavender. Numier rolled his window down and tried to enjoy the foothills, but nothing seemed pleasing to him today. Fidgeting with nervous worry, he reluctantly turned on his radio. He hoped to hear some soothing jazz or interesting talk radio that would take his mind off his concerns. Instead there was a prerecorded message from the President playing on a loop, on every station.

"Overnight, China deployed one million troops across its borders into India, and in an unprecedented act of aggression, The Republic blanketed India with countless nuclear warheads killing its own soldiers along with millions of innocent Indian civilians. The United States and its allies have officially declared war on China . . . God help us all . . ."

"Noooo!" screamed Numier as he put his foot down on the accelerator.

It took less than ten minutes for Numier to reach Sarah's place on Farris Road. His car skidded to a stop in the front drive, as a thick cloud of grey dust swirled-up and surrounded him. Exiting his car before it had stopped, Numier ran to the front and knocked loudly against the aluminum screen door. Despite the racquet, there was no answer. Hoping they were sleeping, he ran to the back porch and looked in from the breakfast-nook window.

His heart began to race when he discovered the trailer ransacked. Tables were over-turned, bookshelves were torn down and simulated-wood-grain-paneling was pulled away from the walls.

"Amena!" he shouted as he picked up a gardening fork from the terracotta pot nearest him and pried open the thin aluminum door.

Numier rushed hastily through the unstable, mobile home, all-the-while shouting:

"Sarah . . . Amena!"

He searched franticly under disheveled mattresses and toppled couches.

"What could have done this?" he thought as he inspected a large, three-fingered claw mark on the hallway wall. There was a green, coagulating gel-like substance dripping from the claw opening in the wall that went all the way to the studs. Numier held his hand over his mouth.

"That stench!" he muttered as his eyes began to water.

"Amena!" he desperately shouted.

When the echo of his voice subsided, he heard a faint whimpering sound coming from the master bedroom. He slowly moved toward the source of the sound now keeping absolutely silent.

He heard the sound again and slowly pressed open the master bedroom door:

"Hello . . . is there anybody here?" he called softly.

Just then a muffled scream let out from beneath the floor in the closet. Numier quickly opened the closet door and pulled back a hatch in the floor, accessing the crawl space beneath the trailer.

There he saw an elderly woman curled up in a ball beneath the sub-floor. Her hair was long and white. Her hands were wrinkled, liver-spotted and arthritically curled. Her face was buried into her knees as she whimpered.

"It's O.K.," Numier said softly as he extended his hand towards her.

"Everything's going to be alright Mamm . . . My name is Numier."

And as she slowly extended her hand to him, she lifted her head to face him.

"Oh my God!" he shouted, as he jumped back from the crawl space.

"Sarah!" he said as his heart sank at the sight of her.

Her face was heavily wrinkled; her eyes were opaque, without pupil or iris. Unable to focus, completely blind, she reached franticly for Numier's hand. The once beautiful and lively young girl now appeared to be close a hundred years old, as she struggled for every breath.

She weighed almost nothing as he effortlessly pulled her withered body from the opening. Her white flannel pajamas were completely soiled from tears, body fluids, and moisture from the sub-floor. Numier scanned her filthy clothes searching for signs of blood or injury. He found it curious how the odor of Sarah's garment was inconsequential compared to the stench still filling the room from the claw mark in the hall.

"Sarah . . . Oh my God Sarah . . . What happened to you?"

But Sarah didn't answer.

Numier'd been around the elderly before and could clearly see that Sarah was fading.

"What happened here?" he said loudly, concerned that her condition might not improve.

She struggled to speak through her deeply wrinkled and chapped lips.

"Diablo," she said softly with a crackling voice.

"Diablo?" he responded.

"Where's Amena?" he asked.

But she did not answer. Her body was failing as she continued to age before his eyes. Now little more than a corpse, there was no time left for pleasantries:

"Sarah!" he yelled startling her back to consciousness.

"Where's Amena?" he shouted.

She opened her eyes widely revealing tiny images. And with the backdrop of her whitened eyes, the events eerily unfolded as Numier watched in awe.

There was no knock at the door; no forced entry. Amena sat at the breakfast-nook table staring into a cup of steaming liquid, while Sarah shuffled busily in the kitchen.

"You're going to be alright," Sarah said as she put a box of Celestial Seasonings, sleepy-time tea and a thick honeycomb of bee's wax, back into the cupboard.

"I've had my heart broken a time or two," Sarah added. "Remember that guy with the black Harley . . . Oh what was his name . . .? You see, I can't even remember his name for crying out loud, and I was ready to ride away with him."

Amena didn't answer.

What we need is to keep busy," Sarah said. "We need to cook! That's what we need."

Amena's eyes were glued to the tea bag floating in her cup. Peculiar the way the surface residue runs from the bag.

"We'll make Posole!" Sarah shouted. "We'll start with pork. Then we'll add . . ."

"That stinks," said Amena, as her eyes began to water.

"OK then . . . no pork. We can make it with chicken . . ." said Sarah while sitting down at the table with her tea.

Slowly coming out of her semi-coma like state, Amena looked up from the tea cup and straight into Sarah's eyes and whispered:

"Run."

Sarah tilted her head in confusion.

Amena jumped to her feet as her chair flew back behind her.

"What!?" shouted Sarah, struggling to stabilize her tea.

"Run!" Amena screamed grabbing Sarah by the arm and pulling her toward the hall.

"What's that horrible smell!?" shouted Sarah.

"Move!" screamed Amena, now sprinting down the hall with Sarah right behind.

Pictures fell from hallway walls as they slammed the master bedroom door.

"Quickly!" said Amena in a whispered shout as she yanked open the bi-fold master closet doors.

"You're scaring me!" Sarah shouted.

"Keep quiet," loudly whispered Amena digging past shoeboxes and dirty laundry.

"What's going-on?" asked Sarah as Amena opened the crawlspace.

"Get in here!" said Amena. "You should be safe in here!"

"Safe from what?" loudly whispered Sarah as she crouched down and looked up at Amena.

"Just don't move!" said Amena.

The mobile home began to shake and rock violently. Mirrors shattered as toiletries flew out of medicine cabinets. Religious relics fell from shelves while dishes crashed out of open cabinet doors.

"Earthquake . . .! shouted Sarah.

"I don't think so . . . Now stay down." ordered Amena as she shut the crawlspace door.

"Where are you going . . . are you crazy?" shouted Sarah from beneath the muffled sub-floor.

Amena instinctively ran back into the living room to divert attention from the master closet crawlspace. Screams filled the mobile as she discovered the origin of the stench.

Although she saw terrible things when she glimpsed into the portal, nothing could have prepared her for the sight of what was standing in her living room.

The back of its shoulders pressed firmly against the doublewide's cottage-cheese ceiling as an enormous sloth thrashed and writhed.

Its fur was blackish-green, oily and crusted with the dried blood of other beasts. Centipedes and flying insects traversed in and out of the crevasses in its fur. Although at first glimpse it had the head of a sloth, it was clear that the face was dead skin of a sloth hanging loosely as a mask. As the creature roared with painful anger, the loose pelt shifted, revealing the deceased eyes of a man starring straight at Amena.

As the sloth-face fell to the floor, the decomposing man-face became visible. The head and neck were haphazardly sewn onto its shoulders with the dried entrails of other beasts. Soot and dried blood mottled the beast's face accentuating the strong, deep, hate-lines from its permanent scowl. Just above its ears were large holes where horns once protruded. Its close-set eyes and low hanging, drooling, lower-lip indicated that it was as stupid as it was ugly.

Nevertheless, it had half of a sheetrock wall and a lazy-boy recliner griped tightly in just one of its massive and lethal claws.

The sight of the creature and the thought of her impending death caused Amena to scream uncontrollably. The deafening sound of Amena's high pitch, combined with the sloth-man's primordial roar, were all but drowned out by the sound of another creature standing directly behind her. It was a low and thundering voice that nearly shook the mobile home off its foundation.

"Ahhhh . . . such a beautiful creature to waste," said the voice.

Amena turned and shuttered . . . It was Huron.

Fraught with panic, Sarah was still safely tucked into the crawlspace just beneath the sub-floor when concern for Amena got the better of her fear. She crawled to position herself under a floor-furnace-vent that had been shaken away from its ducting and peeked through to the scene in the living room. There she saw Amena standing waist high to an enormous man. He was dressed in solid black, ancient Roman battle garb. His ankle high sandals and metal studded battle kilt gave him an almost pious appearance. His face was hardened and defined with a seriousness of a man on a mission. His backless chest-armor exposed his rippling muscles glistening with pale, clammy moisture.

Sarah quietly watched like a small mouse peeking through a crack in a wall.

With his left hand, Huron grabbed Amena, and with his right, he held a large medallion up to the hallway wall. Again the mobile shook and a low frequency hum filled the air.

Instantly, a large double-door size opening appeared, cutting through the wall and burning at its edges. Through it, Sarah could see thousands of other large, winged-men in white Roman battle attire. The earth rumbled as they sprinted, with swords drawn, past the opening.

Seeing the Cherubim supply-line through the portal, Huron knew his forces had lost ground with Gabriel on the battlefield. He needed to get back to base camp which was now well to the east, but he couldn't carry both Amena and the beast. He released Amena just long enough to grab the sloth-man by the throat and kick him through the closing portal. He then yanked Amena off the ground and clenched her tightly against his breastplate. But just before flying straight up through the roof with Amena in tow, he abruptly turned over his left shoulder and looked straight down into the eyes of Sarah.

Amena screamed, "Nooo!!" as she reached out for her childhood friend.

Numier grimaced and turned away from the eyes of Huron as even the replay of his evil-stare would have surely blinded him as well. And as the curtain closed on her memory, she drew her last breath, and in a whisper, she painfully sighed:

"Forgive me."

With tears in his eyes, Numier softly laid her lifeless body onto a pile of clean white sheets.

Fumbling for his cell phone, with burning eyes, he made his way past the stench of the claw and back to his car. He dialed 911 and intended to report the incident to the police but realized that they wouldn't believe him if he tried, so he simply said:

"There's been a death at 20 Farris road in Auberry." and he hung up the phone.

After seeing the events unfold on the cloudy corneas of Sarah's blinded eyes, he knew there was only one person who could help Amena now, and for that matter, the world. Speeding dangerously down Auberry Road, he called information and asked for Yosemite International Airport and said:

"I'd like to book the next flight to Canada."

CHAPTER XXIX

PRATHER

✥

Amena hated flying. This night was no different when the only thing between her and the ground was Huron. The Dark Angel's tractor-tire size arm pressed Amena firmly to his left side as she fought his grip to breathe. The terror and panic of her abduction quickly gave way to her fear of heights. She stopped struggling and held on tightly as they cleared rooftops and power poles. Dangling beneath him, facing downward, they accelerated over small foothill towns and cattle ranches. Unable to draw enough breath for a decent scream, she kept quiet and franticly scanned the ground for help.

Over treetops they flew. She could smell the redwoods and pines as the tips of the giant trees slapped against her dangling ankles. Ascending higher still, oddly, she noticed how quiet Auberry was on a dark Sunday night. She spotted a janitor roaming the empty halls of Auberry elementary, pushing a cart from room to room, preparing for the next day's classes. The market and sheriff substation were closed for the night, and Sunday night bingo at Auberry First Baptist was all cleared out.

While trying desperately to focus on life on the ground, the loud hum of Huron's wings was a constant reminder of her bleak situation. She didn't know where he was taking her, only that they were heading East toward the Sierra's. There was a brief bit of comfort and hope when she saw the lights of Prather. The local pharmacy and hamburger dive were just closing down. The neon lights of the video store and pizza parlor turned off one by one. Amena watched helplessly as the late crew got into their cars and pulled out of the parking lot. She tried to scream but couldn't. They flew past, unnoticed.

The small-town lights faded in the distance as Huron dove back to the treetops. He strafed down Lodge Road and pulled up sharply at the high school. Though the stadium lights were on, Amena couldn't see anyone at the school. They climbed quickly to the top of Black Mountain where Huron hovered for a moment gathering his bearings of the surrounding foothills. He quickly regrouped and made a beeline toward the small-town of Tollhouse.

Amena dangled helplessly as Huron accelerated. She strained against the wind to see Huron holding up a large circular medallion. Even in the dark, Amena recognized it as the one given to the Professor by Michael. Her heart broke, knowing that if the medallion was in the hands of Huron, Don must surely be dead.

She began to cry with sadness and despair as a hole appeared in the sky in front of them. No larger than a doorway, it was a bright orange tear in the otherwise deep-purple sky. They entered the celestial dimension with a bang. The battlefields resonated with the high pitch sound of her scream as she realized the horror of leaving her dimension.

CHAPTER XXX
The Fields
❧

The atmosphere seemed heavier. The heat and humidity acerbated the awful stench of decaying bodies. Though there were no city lights to illuminate the skyline, battle fires and burning oaks cast an eerie reddish glow onto the low-lying layer of soot and smoke lighting up the horizon. Trying to avoid the scene beneath her, she scanned the mountainsides searching for familiarity. She could faintly see the outline of Black Mountain and the ravine between two hills that would have been Tollhouse Road. She searched for anything that would take her back to the world she knew, but the foothills would offer her no comfort in this place.

As they cruised above the oaks, she closed her eyes and prayed to God to take this cup from her. She kept her eyes closed hoping to avoid seeing the horrors that surrounded her. With destination in sight, Huron set his wings to glide mode. Gusts of wind and heat from the fires beneath whistled and whirled through his blackened feathers. Without the deafening hum of Huron's flapping wings, the morbid sounds of battle began to ring loudly in her ears.

She could hear the clang of war hammers pounding molten iron into sharp axes and battle hatchets.

She heard breaking and snapping of large trees as scaffolds fell to the ground. She heard the moaning and heavy breathing of beasts and crippled Angels as they pushed and prodded toward the front lines.

Reluctantly, she opened her eyes to see funeral pyres burning all about the hillsides. Fatty-flesh of the dead and dying hissed and popped as hell beasts tossed casualties into large piles of burning remains. Large, dense wafts of guttural odors entered Amena's lungs like sludge. She tried to resist vomiting by pressing her hand against her mouth, but it was no use. Her screams and heaves pushed past her hand as she shook her head in terror.

Dark Angels cracked whips of fire onto the backs of myriads of creatures all horribly disfigured but each performing some sort of battle-task.

They flew through the pork-rind smelling plumes of cremation smoke as they descended to their final destination. It was a clearing of trees and bodies where several makeshift tents were erected. Eager to rid himself of the screaming, vomiting woman, Huron swooped past a gathering of Dark Angels and dropped Amena several feet from the ground. She tumbled and slid on the dry scorched earth until she stopped at the base of a thick black cape.

Unharmed but mortified, she looked up to see what no Christian woman was ever meant to see. Condemned, Dark Angels gathered in a semi circle around her position. Blackened by eight thousand years of battle, and crippled from burn scarring, they shuffled and moaned in pain and discomfort.

Their faces were twisted and disfigured with oversized black weeping eyes. They protected their location by striking whips of fire onto the chests and faces of crowding beasts that surrounded the assembly. They lifted their weapons in a show of unity and groaned out a cheer for Huron's arrival.

Her high pitch screams of terror and confusion were interrupted by the bustling of rodents beneath the thick piece of fabric she was laying on. Slowly she lifted her eyes to see a being towering over her at the center of the gathering. Though not as tall as a healthy Angel, the creature was much taller than a human. Long and slender, his robe rattled with the sounds of insects traversing within it. He slowly craned his spinal cord and skull to look down at his newest captive, but remembering the fate of Sarah, Amena closed her eyelids tightly and quickly turned away.

Without introduction, she knew instantly who he was. Her fright sent her spiraling into shock as her eyes rolled back and her body went limp. All was still but her lips as she began to chant:

"Even though I walk through the valley of the shadow of death, I will fear no evil, for you are with me; your rod and your staff, they comfort me."[34]

Now on the ground, Huron approached his commander:

"Well done," said Satan wide eyed with excitement.

Wasting no time, Satan grabbed the semiconscious Amena by her hair and lifted her high off the ground showing her to his armies of darkness:

"The hour is upon us . . .!" he screamed.

Startled back to consciousness, she fought through the pain and grasped for the boney wrist of her capture. Slightly lifting herself by the skeletal claw relieved some pain from her scalp while fleas and crawlers tickled her tightly griped fingers. With her face aimed at the battlefield, suspended several feet off the ground, she couldn't avoid the scene that was before her.

Hideous hell beasts began to morph thousands at a time. Three headed dragons leapt into the air with Dark Angels on their backs whirling whips of fire against their leathery scales. They stretched their massive wings while flapping with great force. They circled as their numbers increased until the sky became an enormous funnel cloud from Hell. Within minutes, the ghoulish army was airborne and heading strait for Buchanan Hollow.

Their flight was slowed briefly by thousands of Seraphim descending onto the battlefield from above. Armed with swords and arrows, normally intended for hell beasts and Dark Angels, they aimed their weapons primarily at the vulnerable riders, but were no match for the napalm spewing dragons.

Some were snatched-up in the talons and sharp teeth of dragons being ripped apart before ever firing a shot. Others were caught in streams of fire plummeting to the earth like fireballs. Still valiantly, they attacked.

Satan tossed Amena to the feet of Huron, and with tuffs of her hair still clinging to his skeletal fingers, he pointed at Huron and said:

"When you see Gabriel fall . . . Kill her!"

He then mounted a fully morphed dragon and took to the blazing sky shouting orders and obscenities with his cape billowing long behind him.

CHAPTER XXXI
FINAL ASSAULT
⚬⚭⚬

Back at the Hollow, the storm cloud descended quickly. Gabriel, on point, began slaying three-headed dragons by the hundreds. Hoping to avoid sure death by Gabriel's unmerciful sword, their riders ditched at the last moment. Jumping from their three-story high beasts, Dark Angels hit the ground running. They screamed in horror as they scurried toward the oaks in search of shelter. Their fear was short lived as waiting Cherubim butchered them without hesitation.

Through the flames and tumbling wings of falling dragons, Gabriel looked across the hillside and saw Huron standing tall beside a small creature. It was a human . . . a female human. She held her face in her hands trying to avoid the awful scene that unfolded before her. And although her identity was concealed from most, Gabriel knew who she was.

"She's here . . .!" yelled Gabriel.

"Whose here?! shouted Maximus through the flames.

Suddenly, there was an eerie silence on the battlefield.

Gabriel looked over the Fields and hillsides that surrounded him. He thought of the eight thousand

years he'd been in service to The Lord. He thought
of all the Angels, both pure and fallen, who had
lost their lives in battle. He thought of his life as an
Angel and how honored he was to have served in
this cause and how every moment of his epic life was
spent in preparation of this day.

He turned to face the Cherubim side of the conflict
and drew in a deep breath of clean, unspoiled air.
He filled his lungs with the lifeblood of the Fields.

With no shield to set down, nor helmet to remove,
he slowly took a knee and placed his sword on the
ground in front of him.

"Gabriel . . .!" shouted Maximus.

Beasts and dragons alike wasted no time crowding his
position. With arms stretched out wide he stood in
the face of the evil army . . .

"What are you doing!?" shouted Maximus as he
rushed to Gabriel's position, slaying dragons and
screamers from behind.

"Holy, Holy, Holy is The Lord . . .!" Gabriel shouted,
laughing as he leaned into the onslaught.

Huron watched from a distance Gabriel's actions on
the battlefield. He was very familiar with the Angel's
combat procedures and knew it was not in Gabriel's
nature to surrender or retreat.

"Noooo!" shouted Maximus through the inferno that separated him from Gabriel.

The remaining Cherubim and Dark Angels alike turned to look as Gabriel's shoutings were muffled beneath thousands of hell-beasts that rained down upon him.

The Professor couldn't see Gabriel from his position but knew something was wrong.

"Where's Gabriel?" Shouted the Professor from behind the protection of a small platoon of Cherubim. Maximus did not answer.

Confused and distraught, Maximus and the remaining Cherubim continued fighting against the raging army. Shouting orders and slaying beasts, they held the line.

Above the battlefield, well out of danger, Satan laughed with a sinister madness. He circled the blazing skies watching his troops converge on Gabriel's position. A heavy shadow of black smoke followed behind him as his invigorated evil set fire to the sky, searing the oxygen he passed through.

Huron flew at treetop height with Amena in tow to a place called Whispering Springs. It was a scenic area of the Fields where Cherubim would come to drink water. From deep beneath the surface, clean fresh streams would flow naturally from artesian wells. But on this day, the increased heat from the earth caused the water to spout upward in plumes of steam adding to the already humid conditions. Closer to the front line, the Springs provided an excellent vantage point for Huron as he kept his eye on the exchange between the Dark Angels and Gabriel.

Huron eagerly watched as a mass of hell-beasts and Dark Angels plunged off a steep cliff with Gabriel beneath them. All that was left on the hillside was Gabriel's sword lying still and alone atop the blood and entrails of many fallen beasts.

"This is a good day . . ." yelled Huron, yanking Amena to her feet.

"Look!" he said pointing her face by the back of her neck.

She reluctantly opened her eyes to see the slaughter in full tilt. Dragons snapped up Angels seemingly at will. Dark Angels showed no mercy beating whips and large battle-axes onto the backs of un-morphed beasts that pushed forward destroying everything in their tracks. Many dragons with no Angels left to kill swooped down and took position in the middle of the battlefield. Incensed by the open wounds created by the Dark Angels' ruthless beating, they began tearing, ripping and eating as many hell beasts as they could get their teeth into.

"Gabriel is dead . . ." said Huron while forcing Amena to her knees. "And now it is your turn . . ."

CHAPTER XXXII
STEVEN

❦

Across the ravine, at the base of Buchanan Hollow, the Professor sensed a change on the battlefield. From his position, he couldn't see over the three-story high dragons and needed to get a better vantage.

He yelled to the Angel fighting nearest him:

"Steven! Help me get to the top!" as he pointed up the steep crag.

Steven flew up the face of the rocky knoll, killing dragons as they tried to land on the jagged hillside preventing the Professor's ascent. Feeling invigorated by Steven's progress, Goodwin stepped forward and engaged Dark Angels as they fell from their flailing beasts. He made short work of slaughtering many minions while pushing his way to a high point to get a glimpse of the arena.

Scaling his way to the top of the rocky knoll, the Professor pulled himself onto the ledge of a steep cliff. He looked down and noticed that his hands were covered with blood . . . but it was not his. He stopped his upward climb and looked down the length of the ridge. There, on the shallow shelf was Steven. He sat with his back to the jagged cliffside with one leg dangling over the edge. The other was gone.

"Steven!" called the Professor.

There was no answer. Fearing that Steven was all that was left of the Cherubim army, the Professor rushed to his side to see if he was still breathing.

"Steven!" he yelled.

Steven's eyes were open. He was looking across the battlefield. He gazed over hilltops and burned-out oaks with a loving, compassionate expression.

Confused, the Professor stood and looked across the battlefield.

Now, near the highest point of Buchanan Hollow, he could clearly see the devastation that ensued. He searched for help on the Cherubim side of the conflict but saw only Maximus backing slowly into the base of the Hollow with a thousand dragons converging on his location.

"Where's Gabriel?" asked the Professor. But Steven just shook his head.

"How can we win without Gabriel . . .!?" shouted Goodwin.

Again Steven just shook his head.

He wasn't sure if there were any Angels left besides Steven and Maximus. Knowing their chances were slim to none, he looked for answers on the dark side of the conflict.

"You were right . . . she is beautiful," said Steven as the Professor's eyes finally saw what Steven was looking at.

His heart sank when he discovered the object of Steven's gaze and the source of all the morphing beasts . . . It was Amena.

Two hillsides away, she knelt at the feet of Huron. Her head hung low as he taunted her with pointed sword. Even among so much evil, the Professor was taken aback at how beautiful she was. Her hair, her skin, it was all that he'd remembered and more. Her beauty was striking. His heart stopped for a moment, and his abdomen felt heavy. He struggled to breathe as he deliberately forced air into his lungs one gasp at a time.

"How could something so beautiful be in such a horrible place?" he thought, "and why was she here?"

The Professor's heart began to beat stronger than ever. Seeing her somehow changed him. His heart was full again. Free to feel all the range of emotion known to man– the love, the passion, the happiness . . . but most all, the anger.

His rage increased as he thought all the hate
and wickedness he'd witnessed in his life. All the
death, and all the cruelty inflicted by Satan's grip
on Mankind was made clear to him on that rocky
foothill.

Though physically the same, he had also morphed.
The passion brought to the Fields by Amena
empowered him with super human strength and
hate-based resolve. His body tingled as his head
grew hot. His ears began to ring and buzz, as blood
pounded into them. With Gabriel gone, he knew he
had to stop Huron.

She was all he could see now. Consumed with the
thought of her, he turned to Steven.

"Steven, I have to get off this mountain."

There was no answer. Steven was failing fast.
Although he'd tied a tourniquet around his upper
thigh, he'd lost a lot of blood and was slipping into
unconsciousness.

"Steven please . . .!" pleaded the Professor.

Steven silently lifted his head toward the blackened
sky as a ray of light passed through the darkness and
illuminated his face. He took a deep breath and
slowly opened his wings as he looked at the Professor
and said:

"Get on my back"

Steven rolled off the ledge into a free-fall. With the Professor on his back, he dove straight down the cliff face.

"Pull up!" screamed the Professor as they plummeted toward the earth nearing terminal velocity.

With all his might, Steven lifted his head and fully extended his wings, leveling-off just feet above the battlefield, narrowly missing the mass of beasts that had taken over Maximus' position. Goodwin looked as they quickly passed to see nothing more than Maximus' sword laying still and alone on the scorched earth.

Unable to land with one leg, Steven and the Professor rolled and tumbled to a stop in the middle of the cannibalistic feast. Still with ground to cover, Steven yelled to the Professor:

"Run!"

As the Professor sprinted straight into a herd of frenzied leatherbacks, he looked over his shoulder to see Steven. Of all the Angels that could have been on the battlefield on this day, Steven was the most loyal. He was a carrier; an Angel given the task of escorting souls to Heaven. Souls that otherwise would not have had a chance to know Jesus. On most days, Steven would have been in possession of such a soul, but on this day, he was without cargo. He was without the one thing that made him invincible in battle . . . a child.

He fought bravely and without fear, but the numbers were far too great . . . He tried to keep up with the Professor, but his injury was too severe. Loyal to the end, he stopped and stood his ground, drawing many beasts away from the Professor. Slowly sinking back into the armies of darkness that surrounded him, with sword still swinging, Steven fell beneath the oncoming hordes.

Seeing Steven fall angered the Professor even more. He ran towards Amena with all his might. Running faster than he ever thought possible, his feet struck the earth with immortal speed. With a feeling of invincibility and the strength of a thousand Angels, he engaged the three-headed dragons in his path, still gorging themselves on the wounded and dying hell beasts.

Plunging straight into the mouths of dragons, he severed them from within. Heads separated from scaly necks and organs hit the earth. He ran with all his speed forward, toward Amena, hacking and butchering anything and everything in his path. With sword blazing, body parts of beasts and dragons tossed into the air behind him like rooster-tails. Single minded in purpose and driven like a madman, Goodwin made his way toward Amena. Never stopping and never resting, he wielded El Mórte like an Angel possessed.

CHAPTER XXXIII
GIDEON'S BIBLE

Back in Auberry, the airport answering service informed Numier that all non-military air-travel was grounded until further notice. With no flights available, he knew there was no time to drive to Canada. Sarah was dead, and Amena had been taken. This was one of those rare instances in Numier's life where he felt utterly helpless. Reluctantly, he turned his radio on to hear the emergency broadcast buzzer followed by a pre-recorded message from the President:

"Fellow citizens of The United States of America. Diplomatic efforts have failed with China. Nuclear warheads aimed at America's most populated cities have been launched. Regretfully, we have no choice but to retaliate. You are encouraged to seek shelter immediately. May God bless us all . . ."

Speeding down Lodge road, he swerved to avoid accidents and speeding vehicles. He saw the looks of fear and panic in the eyes of passing motorists. He hadn't put much thought into the lives of others . . . until today. He wondered were they heading for high ground? Did they have friends to be with at a time like this? After hearing the news, were they going home from work to be with loved ones? Children, maybe?

He passed a silver Volvo and thought of Don. Was he still alive? Something must have gone very wrong to have caused everything he'd accomplished to unravel so quickly? He thought of the good times they shared overseas on archeology expeditions. He almost smiled remembering how excited Don would get upon discovering the remains of a clay pot, or an arrowhead. It all seemed so trivial now.

Realizing that he had nowhere to go, he drove slowly down the narrow, tightly wound, foothill road eventually coming upon the empty parking lot of the High School. His first instinct was to pull-in and head for the office to work on his to-do-list and tidy-up a bit.

"No . . . I've put my time in at the office," he thought as he slowly rolled passed the place where he'd spent most of his adult life. It seemed oddly peculiar to him that the cows were still grazing behind the goal post of the stadium, happily unaware of the events unfolding around them. And how, despite all his intellect and academic accomplishments, today, he secretly envied the cow.

Not far past the school, he rounded a tight corner as traffic came to a standstill. People were yelling and horns were honking as panicked worshipers waited to get into the parking lot of Foothill Lutheran Church.

Still struggling with his own beliefs, Numier passed his chance to turn into the parking lot, and eagerly sped passed. He could still hear their horns honking as he rounded the next corner and pulled into his driveway.

He walked in slowly, leaving the front door of his tiny log cabin wide open.

He walked into his empty house and stood for a moment, taking-in the cozy home that he'd lived in for so many years. He visually surveyed the cabin, taking a mental inventory of the few worldly possessions he'd managed to accumulate.

He looked across the room and noticed the deerskin lamp that one of his students made for him many years ago. Her name was Angie.

Her older brother had taken World History from Numier but dropped-out before completing his class. Angie knew, when she saw Numier's name on her class schedule that she had to do something to make-up for her brother's disrespect. She worked hard to complete the construction process in time for Christmas.

She scavenged the skin from her brother who'd enjoyed a successful hunt. She waited for an opportune moment to make off with the prize as she watched him in his post-hunt ritual.

Upon returning with his kill, he hung the deer by its back hooves in the open carport and made an incision in its neck, allowing the blood to drain into an old blue Rubbermaid pail. He skinned and quartered the buck leaving the pelt and organs behind to be buried out back. The head and horns were to be buried as well, allowing the worms and decomposing organisms to clean it to the bone. Later he would dig-up and mount the skull and horns intact on his bedroom wall.

She noticed that when he was skinning the deer, the abdomen area was relatively furless and semi transparent when held up to the light.

"What a perfect skin for a lamp shade," she thought.

"Be careful Angie . . . it's not clean," warned her brother.

"I know," she said. "I learned how to cure in Home-ec class."

Numier remembered how she'd explained the whole ordeal to him as he corrected papers in his office. Where the buck came from, how she cured the hide with salt and vinegar, and how she found the base at the Prather craft fair. He struggled to process who that man was that couldn't spare the energy to look up and thank her. It was a missed opportunity at kindness in the face of a thoughtful student that oddly he remembered so vividly today.

"Was I always that bad?" he thought as he remembered back. His eyes panned the cluttered cabin and came to rest on a small piece of art in the corner of the room. Standing-out against the light-honey, knotty pine, tongue and groove wall sat a small wooden chair. Made of solid eucalyptus indigenous to northern California, and hand carved with ancient Aztec motif, sat the three legged chair. Numier smiled and thought of David.

It was late autumn, nineteen-ninety two. Numier made his way to the street to pick up his Sunday morning paper. He was startled by a man standing in his driveway just off Tollhouse road. Timidly not wanting to enter the long drive uninvited, the man spoke:

"Pardona-me Boss, ju-need-a new roof? I have-a lot-a hungry."

Numier looked at the man with cautious suspicion. The man was short, maybe five feet tall. His face was brown and small. In his early fifties, he was clearly Mexican, through and through. His hair was long but coarse enough to stick straight up and back. His shirt was a light blue, pinstriped, thrift-store dress shirt, which was thoroughly soiled. His pants were faded jeans, several sizes to big, held up by a piece of cotton rope tied to one side for style. His work-boots were separated from the sole exposing his sockless toes on both feet. The tar on his pants and hands indicated that he had in fact been working with roofing materials.

Numier was not the kind of man to extend generosity, especially to a stranger.

"Do you live near by?" asked Numier.

"I live in my limousine," eagerly replied David while gesturing to an automobile parked a few yards down the road.

Numier looked curiously at the jalopy parked under the defoliating pomegranate trees. It was an early seventies, half primed, half painted, dark blue Toyota Corolla hatchback.

"You live in your car?" asked Numier.

"Oh, jes boss; it's good . . . runs real nice."

"What if I just give you some money to help you on your way?" said Numier as he reached for his money clip.

"No, No boss . . . I no take money. I like-a the work."

Numier felt more respect than pity for any man willing to work rather than accept handouts.

"How much?" asked Numier.

"Two . . . three hundred," said David.

"A day?" said Numier.

"No, No Boss. Por ju roof!" said David wide eyed with excitement.

Numier extended his hand and said:

"Call me Gene."

"Nice to mee-ju Yeen. My name is David Limone.

The days passed by quickly with David around. Numier found himself coming home straight after work wondering what kind of crazy thing David had been up to besides the roof. Sometimes he would make something out of a hand full of feathers. Sometimes he would carve a little figurine out of a piece of pinewood. It was not uncommon for David to break into dance. Shuffling and stomping across the driveway, he would twirl himself into a cloud of dust while circling around an imaginary hat or sombrero. The song he sang while he danced was unrecognizable to Numier, but quite entertaining just the same.

At the end of each day, David would sit on the very tallest peak of the roof and stare into the sky. Numier often wondered what he was thinking as he gazed at the setting sun while making coyote crying sounds as loud as a human could.

"David!" yelled Numier across the back porch as David slowly made his way down the ladder.

"Jez Boss!" answered David, filthy from a hot, twelve-hour day on the roof.

"Cerveza?" said Numier sliding a Dos Equis toward an empty seat at the back patio table.

"Oh, jez Boss . . . pretty nice."

After each sip, David would hold the cold bottle tight to his chest and look up into the star-lit sky.

Fraught with curiosity, Numier had to ask:

"David . . . Why do you howl at the sky each night?"

David paused and slowly took in a deep breath, savoring the aromatic foothills before answering:

"Anna Rosa," he said as his eyes welled up.

Numier paused for a moment before asking the next question; wondering if he was ready for the answer:

"Who's Anna Rosa?"

"OOOhhh . . . Anna. Cheese my love . . . my gwife. De love de my life, Boss"

"You didn't tell me you were married," said Numier.

"Oh, jez Boss . . . In nineteen-seventy-two. I live in esmall village near Durango. Every day I see de most beautiful girl in de worl. She was seventeen, I was thirty-two. I work for my father, cutting the hair por the sheep."

"Shearing wool?" interrupted Numier.

"Jez, Boss, de-cheering de-wool. She pass de house de my father everyday. I go to house de father de Anna Rosa, but he say no marry my Anna Rosa.

"Why?" asked Numier.

"Por que, David Limone no have no money to give to father de Anna."

"Like a dowry?" said Numier.

"Jez, Boss. Money por de crazy father de Anna Rosa. He say no marry, so I take a little gun from closet de my father and I go to house de crazy father de Anna Rosa, and I take her."

"You kidnapped Anna Rosa?" said Numier.

"No, No Boss. I love her . . . she love me. De father de Anna Rosa es mucho crazy."

"Por three days I hide in corn field with Anna Rosa. We talk about everything Boss. She want many

children and little house. Every nigh, we watch
de sun go down together. In the arms, we sleep
together until morning. On day nombre four, many
village people come to cornfield. Anna say run . . .
por-favor mi amore . . . please run or they will kill
you. I tell her I come back some day for my Anna."

"Is that when you came to America?" asked Numier.

"Texas, Boss. I have-a lot-a family in Texas."

"So did you go back?"

"Three years . . . I work hard in the fields. Cotton,
cantaloupe, tomato. I save three thousand dollars
por de crazy father de Anna."

David paused for a moment and finished the last half
of his beer.

"Then what?" asked Numier.

"My brother came from Mexico, to Texas, to work
de cotton with me. He say . . . my Anna . . . marry
somebody else. He say, she real happy." David just
looked away.

David stayed on through the spring of the following
year. On a warm April morning he packed his things
and danced his way down the long gravel driveway
to his waiting limousine. He said he was on his way
to seasonal work in Oregon. The only thing he left
behind was the hand-carved chair, and on it, a note.

"To my bess frend, Yeen . . . David."

The memory of David made Numier smile. He laid his keys down on the knotty-pine entry table and made a beeline to the wine rack where he selected a vintage he'd been saving for a special occasion. He pulled a 1989 Silver Oak Cabernet Sauvignon, white label, black bottle. He poured himself a glass, grabbed a cold bottle of Dos Equis and walked out onto the redwood deck behind his cabin. He sat on a black-iron patio chair and looked around at the dense clusters of pines and oaks. He opened the cerveza and slowly slid it across the table to an empty chair.

Of the hundreds of books he owned, only one seemed suitable on this occasion. On his lap sat a complimentary, pocket size, emerald-green colored Gideon's Bible. He'd kept it out of respect for his childhood sweetheart who gave it to him all those years ago.

The memory of her was vague. It seemed like many lifetimes since he last saw her. She had blonde hair and blue eyes. Her skin was less than white. She had pouty, red lips that stood out against her pale gaunt complexion. It was no wonder, she came to visit from Paris France where sunny days are a rare commodity.

The young Numier, knew her grandparents from odd-jobs he did for them for extra money. Even though they were well into their eighties, he would often stay and talk to them for hours. Babbette came to visit her grandparents for the summer. They were concerned that she might not have anyone to play with and since Eugene was the only kid her age they could trust, they asked if he could come over for bologna sandwiches. From that day they were inseparable.

She spoke little English, but at age twelve, not much conversation was necessary. They walked together along the sycamore-lined dirt roads of Auberry while kicking rocks and holding hands. Much of their time spent together was in the front yard of her grandparents. Babbette was mesmerized by how big the trees were here in the foothills. They would lie on their backs for hours. Side by side on a carpet of green grass, speckled with dandelions and small purple flowers, they would look up at the swaying pale, green-leafed branches, and talk about everything and nothing.

Their innocent love story was fleeting as the summer ended all too soon. He watched from the dirt driveway of her grandparent's home as she stood next to the car to leave. She extended her small white skinned hand as the goose-bumps raised beneath the shimmering blond hair of her forearm. She handed him the Bible. He took it reluctantly having made his feelings clear regarding religion, but he didn't want to be rude. He leaned in and thought of kissing her for the first time, but she had braces on her teeth, and he thought she wouldn't like it . . . so he hugged her goodbye and watched the car drive away.

He never heard from her again in all these years. He'd often wondered about her but never got up the nerve to try to locate her. He held tightly onto the small imitation leather Bible, realizing that in all these years, he'd never actually understood or appreciated its value . . . or the courage it took for her to give it to him . . . until today.

He reclined back and slowly sipped his finest wine while looking into the skies above. The trees surrounding his log cabin converged to a narrow opening where he could see blue sky. Between the clusters of Oaks and Pines he watched the vapor trails of dozens of fighter-jets as they headed towards the Pacific.

CHAPTER XXXIV

AMENA

"Face me and take your death with honor!" Huron shouted with a thundering voice while towering over Amena.

A soft rain began to fall on the battlefield. Steam rose from the scorched earth as each raindrop hissed to the ground. With the rain, came peace for Amena. The fear and shock fell away. The skies seemed alive as they swirled and flowed with currents of orange and red, illuminated by the fires beneath and the electrical storm above.

Dragons descended slow, cutting through the clouds like B-52 bombers, their metallic scales still shimmering from the storm above. They glided low with wings fixed over the shoulder of Huron on their way to the valley below. Their wings made a thundering hiss while cutting through the thick atmosphere of heat and decay, but Amena couldn't hear them. The sounds of fighting and dying faded in the distance as Amena tuned everything out.

She felt calm for the first time in a long time. She thought of her Mother and how hard she'd worked to provide food and shelter after immigrating from the Middle East. After perfecting her English, her mother attended school at night to become a social worker. Despite many set backs, she passed her tests and gained full-time status working for the County. Though slightly above the poverty line, it was enough to pay the rent and Amena's school expenses.

She thought of her Father and how proud he would have been of her had he lived past her eighteenth year. He'd worked as a civil engineer for a global firm building schools and bridges across the Middle East. His hopes and dreams after returning to the states quickly gave way to alcohol. His drinking outlasted his liver, and he died alone in the streets of Fresno. She always thought fondly of him even after the creditors came to her mother's door. Although she was only six when he left, she wondered if there was anything she could have done differently.

She thought of the Professor and how she wished she could spend just one more moment with him. To hold his face in her hands once again . . . and to feel his soft but leathery touch against her skin. She felt regret for the years she spent away from him. She didn't know herself well enough to recognize that she'd been in love with him all along. She wondered what their lives could have been together if they'd had more time.

But most of all . . . she thought of God. She'd put Him first in all things in her life and despite the grim surroundings, today was no different.

On her knees, she sat back on her heels with her toes pointed inward and lifted her hands. Facing Heaven with the rain falling softly on her face, palms upward at shoulder height, she began to pray the Lord's Prayer.

Her serenity and devotion to God took Huron by surprise. With sword raised high above her head, he paused for a split second and looked at her . . . For a moment time stopped . . . Everything stood still. Dragons, hell beasts and Dark Angels stopped in their tracks. The Professor and the beast he was slaying froze like ice sculptures. Even Satan himself, while circling to descend upon the Professor's location, was suspended in mid air.

It was at that moment that he saw it . . .

"This cannot be . . ." Huron grunted.

Somewhere within the blackened heart of Huron remained microscopic residue of the once Mighty Angel of The Lord. Looking down upon Amena and witnessing her unwavering devotion to The Lord, blindsided him. It was enough to briefly remind Hell's newest minion of just how far from Grace he'd fallen.

He paused, tilted his head in confusion and squinted his eyes to see what had been hidden:

"I know you," he said with his sword frozen in the sky like a statue.

He dug deep into the oldest tissues of his deceased brain from when he was in good standing with The

Lord. He closed his eyes tightly and strained to recall his acquaintance with her.

Two thousand years ago on the mount of Golgotha on the outskirts of Jerusalem . . . people gathered by the thousands. Dark storm clouds circled the city and evil was everywhere. Demonic-Dark Angels walked the streets inhabiting souls at will, causing them to do unspeakable things. People's minds were confused into performing an act of evil that would survive the ages.

Fighting broke out in the streets. Brother against brother, sister against mother, and families torn apart. Screams of torment echoed through the narrow streets and alleyways, as death was everywhere. The walls of the city bled as dark forces prepared the city for treason.

He entered Jerusalem on the back of a donkey. It was an inauspicious arrival for the Man many called King. He wore no gold, no silver . . . no jewelry at all. He came unarmed and without guards, ill-equipped to defend Himself against the hordes of sedition that awaited Him. As He slowly rode through the streets, people laid palm leafs at His feet. Crowds followed behind like parishioners, loyal to Him on any other day . . . but not today.

It was a grim day for Mankind. Accused of a crime He did not commit and left to the mercy of the tainted crowd, the Man many called King was sentenced to death. It was a day that would transcend generations. Dimensions, worlds, and galaxies would change forever. On this day, God's only Son was on the cross. Hung by the very hands that would heal the world, He was left to die like a common thief. Disciples, who had been followers from the start, denied any and all acquaintance with Him . . . but He was not alone.

Angels assembled by the millions. Stacked high into the clouds, they waited for his command. They gathered twelve legions strong, more than enough troops to annihilate the world and all who lived in it. All they needed was a Word from Him, and the Angels would remove the Son of God from the cross and clean an unclean world.

The Angels were prepared to perform an act of Genocide that God himself promised never to unleash again on Humanity. But this time it was different . . . this time it was up to Jesus.

The Angels sat for hours waiting, patiently anticipating fulfilling their mission. Armed with shields, swords, sicas and crossbows, they perched. They waited for their orders, a Word, even the Will alone would send them into action. They were eager to carry out righteous vengeance on a world that had turned its back on a Perfect Being . . . But the order never came.

Gabriel hovered over Jesus' right shoulder and Huron, over His left. People could not see the celestial army, but the Angels could see everything. Swords drawn, they waited. Even the Angels were surprised and taken aback when Jesus uttered the words:

"Father forgive them . . . They know not what they do."[35]

While lowering his sword, Huron looked at Gabriel with curiosity as the Mighty Angel took particular interest in a woman in the crowd. She knelt at the base of the cross. She had been there since the beginning and would not move for the soldiers who kept the crowd back.

Her name was Mary, the Mother of Jesus, and the Woman with whom The Lord was well pleased. It was the same young girl who showed such strength in the presence of Gabriel thirty-four years earlier in the small village of Nazareth. Sensing that there was something special about this Human, Huron looked at her as well. He noticed curiously that she never took her eyes off Jesus, not even for a moment.

Though there were three crosses on that day, the crowd congregated around this one. They assembled for different reasons. Some knew Him and many had only heard of Him.

The centurion was there. He stood a good distance from the cross, trying not to be noticed by the Roman guards. A year ago he'd traveled a great

distance to ask Jesus to return with him to heal
his dying servant. When he finally caught up to
Jesus and begged him to heal his servant, Jesus told
him that his faith had already healed him. Upon
returning to his village, he discovered his once dead
servant alive and awaiting his return. The centurion
believed that surely this was the Messiah.

The rich man was there. Not wanting to loose the
respect of his wealthy peers, he too stood on the
fringes of the crowd. Some month's prior, he'd
arrived at the house of one of the chief Pharisees to
offer aid to the new, grass-roots movement lead by a
Man called Jesus. He proposed items of comfort to
help Jesus and his followers in their arduous journey
through arid lands. He pledged his political loyalty
as he had many contacts in the Senate. He offered
all this to the Man who had clearly won the hearts
of the People. But when Jesus asked him to give all
his money to the poor and come follow Him . . . he
could not. He returned to his village believing that
this Man was surely the King of Jews.

Some looked up and saw a King, and some looked up
and saw a Messiah . . . but not Mary. Mary was at the
cross for an entirely different reason.

She wasn't looking up at a King . . .

She wasn't looking up at a Messiah . . .

She was looking up at her Son . . .

With each expansion of his chest and with every breath that he took . . . she remembered Him as a child.

She was a young mother; barely old enough to bare children let alone have one. She walked humbly through the town square, where as a child, she and her father would go to listen to the Rabbi preach of the coming Messiah. Close behind her followed a toddler. The unpaved streets leading to the town square billowed under the feet of thousands of shuffling townspeople. Through the dust He toddled, hanging loosely to his Mother's garment. With His Shoulders and Head barely above the dust line, Jesus made his way toward the center square. She remembered how at times the crowded square would overwhelm Him:

"Mama, Mama . . ." he would call.

"I'm right here my love . . . I'm right here," she would answer.

Even at the tender age of four, he was under constant attack from the evils that surrounded him. Protecting the young Jesus was an important task. Keeping him safe and alive was paramount for the success of his mission. Powerful Cherubim kept evil well out of sight of the Boy King as they pulled demons from the humans they inhabited.

The years flew by for Mary. She watched her Son grow as a normal boy. Running and jumping along side His friends. They assembled every day after school, many times in front of the home of Mary and Joseph. They played Harpa, a soccer-like game played with a goatskin ball.

"Mama, Mama!" shouted the ten-year old Jesus, running into the house with a furry, filthy goat pelt, followed by a group of muddy boys. "We won, Mama, we won!"

The boys grabbed the ball from Jesus and ran out for another round of Harpa. Before Jesus could reach the door, Mary swept him up off his feet and kissed him on his muddy face.

"You're a good boy Jesus," she said. "But don't go too far . . . I want to see you outside my window!"

"I won't Mama," he said.

At times the boys played rough. Not knowing Jesus' deity or destiny, they treated Him like any other boy on the field. Pushing and checking, He often ended up on the ground. With the wind knocked out of Him, struggling to catch His breath, He looked past the running boys and found Mary's window.

"I'm right here my love . . . I'm right here," she said.

The rain began to fall softly onto the people who gathered at the cross. One by one, many left . . . but not Mary.

She looked up at the cross. Never moving, and never turning away, on her knees she sat back against her heels and with toes pointed inward she lifted her hands. Facing Jesus with the rain falling softly on her face, palms upward she prayed the Lord's Prayer.

The rain fell onto the body of Jesus and then splashed onto the face of Mary. Never flinching and never wavering . . . the blood of her little boy mixed with tears streaming down her face.

As He drew His last breath, He searched the crowd and found Mary. Through tear stained eyes, he looked at his mother as she said:

"I'm right here my love . . . I'm right here . . ."

CHAPTER XXXV
WHO ARE YOU?

Huron hit the ground with a rumble. Displaced by blackened steel, earth and water splashed as Kismet hit the ground. Huron knelt on hands and knees in front of Amena with his head hung low in shame.

As his mind's eye shut on the scene in Jerusalem, he tried to process the moment.

"It's you . . ." he said in a soft voice. "I remember you from the cross."

Speechless and confused, the frightened Amena began to push herself slowly away from the giant creature kneeling before her.

"Do you know who you are?" he said lifting his head to face her.

"My name is Amena," she said sheepishly.

Huron took a moment to consider her response.

"Of course . . ." he said.

He strained to recall the scene at the cross. Mary was not alone. She had other children with her on that day. Much younger than Jesus, they too were present at the cross.[36] Behind the safety of the crowd, they wailed and mourned the crucifixion of their half Brother along with the rest of the family. Through their tears, Huron could clearly see that their flesh was that of Mary and Joseph.

"You are the image of someone I knew a long, long time ago . . ." he said marveling at the resemblance.

"I don't understand . . ." she said.

"I can see the faith in your blood . . . Thousands of years of Christianity flows through your veins. You carry Noble Blood. The Blood of the Royal Family." he said.

"I don't know what you're saying," she said.

"You are the last of the daughters of Mary," he said.

Amena paused.

"Oh my gosh . . ." she said as her mind went back to her childhood.

She had few memories of her childhood. Her mother married while still living in the Middle East. The first years of Amena's life were spent traveling throughout the region. Her father, who was a civil engineer, specialized in building bridges. Syria, Iraq and Kuwait were just a few of their short-term homes.

Her father managed to bring her mother's family to America. Aunts, uncles and grandparents all lived under one roof. Shortly upon returning to the states, her father left the two of them alone in a foreign land.

Amena brought back her earliest memory of her grandmother. She sat on the lap of a woman in her eighties and listened to stories of the old country.

"We come from a dying people, Aziza," said Amena's grandmother.

"We aren't dying Gummy," said the six-year old Amena in a soft, horse voice.

"No my love . . ." Gummy giggled, hugging Amena and kissing her on the forehead. "We have no country . . . We are all that is left of the Hittites, the Babylonians."

"What is a Hittites, Gummy," asked Amena.

"We are a proud people . . . descended from Priests and Patriarchs. We are the first Christians my dear. From the base of the cross we've believed. We were there when St. Peter formed the Church. We were fed to the lions for four hundred years before Constantine brought Christianity to the world."

"Lions, Gummy?"

Amena's tender memories of her grandmother were interrupted by a loud, low growl. She looked up and saw Huron. His face was again filled with hate as he struggled to stave off the evil flesh he inhabited. He grabbed Kismet by its razor sharp blade as it began to slice into his hand. Blood dripped from his tight grip, as he offered the sword, handle first, to Amena.

"What are you doing?" she said.

"Take the weapon . . ." he snarled.

"What?!!" she replied.

"Kill me . . .!" he yelled as the battlefield came alive. "Quickly, you haven't much time . . ."

Satan screamed with renewed energy as hell beasts roared in the talons of dragons.

With a painful grimace, Huron tried with all his might to keep his focus and not give in to the darkness.

"I don't kill," she said

"If you fail . . . I will kill you!" shouted Huron on his hands and knees with head hung low exposing the vertebrae of his powerful neck.

"Take it! Do it! Then release the sword quickly."

Amena looked down at Huron. He seemed so humble, so vulnerable. She looked up at the battlefield and once again saw the horrors that awaited her.

"Can I do such a thing?" she wondered as she extended her hand toward Kismet.

"No!" she said. "I will not!"

She realized that her refusal, valiant as it may have been, would surely cost her, her life. And as she pulled her hand back, she placed it on the shoulder of Huron.

"Do what you must," she said. "I cannot kill you."

Huron exhaled loudly and sighed. As he slowly looked up at her, she could see that his face had changed. The hate fell away from him. The darkened veins that once transported the blackened blood of hate and distain were blue again. His pale, ash-grey skin had a lightly tanned, pinkish hue. His hair turned from jet-black to a vibrant, golden brown.

He was whole again. Restored to the mighty Angel of The Lord that he was intended to be.

"Your blood carries power in this world . . . let's hope its enough," he said as he gently helped Amena to her feet. "Come . . . we have much work to do,"

Much of the battlefield was in front of Huron. Dragons and beasts alike had run out of Angels to kill and began turning on one another. It was a Hellish free-for-all as Dark Angels whipped violently, desperately trying to control their dragons. Satan circled the Professor's location preparing to end his short visit to the Fields.

None of Hell's minions would ever question Huron's authority, so they weren't remotely concerned with the events unfolding at Whispering Springs.

"We haven't much time before Satan sees us . . . quickly you must take the sword," said Huron still offering Kismet with bloody hand.

"I don't know how to use a sword," she said in a panic.

"Your presence has caused the beasts to morph more powerfully than ever. I cannot kill what is behind me," he said.

"I told you, I don't kill," she replied.

"The beasts are already dead," he whispered loudly. "Besides, do you wish to save the man . . . or do you not?"

"The man?" she said.

"Yes . . . the one you call the Professor," as Huron pointed to an adjacent hilltop.

Till now she'd assumed he was dead. She looked in the direction of the hilltop and saw the Professor. He was standing alone. Slaying dragons one after another. He fought like a madman, advancing steadily in Amena's direction.

"Donald!" she screamed.

The conflagration spewing from the mouths of dragons made it impossible for him to hear her as he continued moving in her direction.

Amena turned quickly and reached for Kismet.

"Careful, this weapon carries much evil . . . you may only wield it for a short time . . . then it WILL change you," Huron warned as he handed the sword to Amena.

She grabbed it tentatively, fearing its power, she softly gripped its handle. Instantly her hand was pulled into it. The pain was intense. She held back screams by gritting her teeth and growling hard. Fused like molten steel, her hand turned black instantly as the darkness crept slowly past her wrist and up her lower forearm. She instinctively tried to release it, but it was no use. She and the sword were one now. Realizing that there was no turning back, she turned to Huron and said:

"Show me what to do."

CHAPTER XXXVI
KISMET

࿇

Satan sensed Huron's treason as he circled the Professor's position:

"The girl!" he shouted.

Dark Angels launched their dragons into the skies while partially devoured hell beasts fell from their roaring mouths. Ground forces rushed toward Whispering Springs while Huron and Amena moved in the direction of the Professor.

"Stay behind me and swing the blade at anything that gets in your field of vision," screamed Huron, as heads of dragons began to roll past Amena.

"What do I do?!!" She screamed when a large hell beast crossed into her space.

"Just lift Kismet off the dirt . . . and hang on tight."

She moved quickly in reverse, while dragging Kismet behind her. The Grizzly-bear-beast lunged toward her with both claws. She pushed herself into the backside of Huron while trying to escape the oncoming beast. She remembered the sloth man in her living room and how her last memory of Sarah was of her face and eyes burning at the sight of evil.

Anger welled up in her soul and her head began to tingle. Her muscles felt tight and her jaw clinched.

She dug her heels into the scorched earth for balance and held on to the sword.

She screamed as she lifted the heavy blade off the ground in the general direction of the beast. The sword had a mind of its own. After many centuries of being fused to the hand of Satan, Kismet knew exactly what to do.

The first pass severed the massive garden-rake size claws of the beast. As it paused to roar at its bleeding stumps, the second pass cut off its head ending its shrill and sending a gush of rank maroon blood onto the face and front of Amena.

Curiously she felt powerful. Her legs were stronger and her feet moved faster. Kismet was no longer heavy. She whipped and twirled it like a baton as she prepared for the next attack.

The second beast was not so lucky. She swung Kismet at the advancing Leatherback's charging legs and severed it at the midsection. With centrifugal force, its massive shoulders and single-horned, man-head hit Amena square in the chest. She fell backward, rolled to one side, and returned to her feet just in time to engage a Dark Angel that darted out from behind the beast's flailing carcass. She took a step back, recognizing that this one looked even more like a man, she hesitated for one second.

The minion pulled a large double bladed axe, referred to in the fields as a war-hatchet, and swung it at Amena's head. She tried to duck but was taken off guard by the Dark Angel's speed and accuracy. She received a grazing blow to the upper forehead, which only served to anger her further. She lifted Kismet and struck the Dark Angel between the legs. The blade entered at the pelvis and exited out the clavicle, cutting the demon in two vertically.

She then reached down and picked up the war hatchet with her left hand, and before the butchered Dark Angel hit the ground, she ran in front of Huron and pushed toward the Professor.

CHAPTER XXXVII
THE FINAL CHERUB

An enormous dragon hit the ground in front of the Professor. Dirt, debris, and the charred remains of Angels fell off the creature while the earth shook beneath it. Turning toward the Professor, all three mouths spewed a barrier of napalm, circling and encapsulating his position. Halted by the inferno, through the flames he saw a dark figure dismount the scaly beast. He could see that it was Satan . . . more confident and more animated than ever before. Goodwin grimaced, as the stench of eight thousand years of decomposing flesh was almost unbearable.

The Professor stepped forward and swung El Mórte with all his might, hoping to inflict enough damage to buy time and save Amena. He remembered his conversation with Michael and how killing Satan was not part of the master plan. But it was either he or Amena.

Unfortunately, even with his enhanced abilities, he was no match for the Devil. Satan dodged the swing and swiped El Mórte from the Professor's hand.

The Professor screamed in frustration while helplessly watching El Mórte tumble through the air. He remembered Maximus' advice. "Your sword is your life here in the fields . . . loose it again, and you will surely die." He watched in desperation as El Mórte came to rest blade first, handle-up, and well out of reach. The Devil picked the Professor up by his throat and lifted him high off the ground:

With more rage than fear, the Professor faced the serpent and looked straight into his eyeholes as Satan read his mind.

"You think you hate me now," Satan said in a loud rumbling hiss.

"I invented hate!" he yelled as he threw the semi-conscious Professor into the side of a large boulder.

"This will be a slow death for you," he said, levitating inches off the ground. Field mice, roaches and snakes fell out from under his cape. He'd planned on enjoying this kill, but his plans were short lived.

"Hey you!" came a voice from behind.

Satan turned quickly in the direction of the voice giving Goodwin a chance to catch his breath.

It was Amena. She stood high atop an adjacent foothill. She was covered with cremation soot and coagulating blood of Dark Angels. Her hair was tousled and disheveled. The skirt she wore was ripped to the upper thigh exposing her muscular, scuffed–up leg. She stood tall and strong . . . ready and willing to do battle with anyone who stood between her and the Professor.

In her left hand she brandished a large, war- hatchet. Its blade dripped with the blood of beasts. In her right, she carried Kismet. Her hand and arm were blackened by the evil of the sword. Dark lines that were once veins crept up her neck to the base of her jaw. Welcoming her morphed physical condition and accepting her new role as butcher, she pointed Kismet at Hell's Darkest Angel and shouted:

"You took something from me a long, long time ago . . . Not this time!"

She ran towards Satan, with all her might killing beasts at will as she flew passed them. With blind determination, she focused on the Professor and the job at hand. Although her rage gave her the strength to push forward, it caused the beasts to morph more violently than before.

Huron sprinted behind. Using feet and wings, he tried to keep up with her. He killed beasts in droves as they stormed her position, giving her the time she needed to fulfill her mission.

Satan tilted his head back and laughed with a fanatical madness.

"What a day this is!" he shouted as he extended his open hand toward Amena.

Kismet responded to The Devil's summon, pulling toward his skeletoid claw with Amena dragging behind it. Refusing to let go of the only thing keeping her alive in this place, she found herself face to face with the Devil himself. He grabbed Kismet by its blade and ripped it out of her hand. Instantly her evil infused power was gone. Exhausted and sapped of her strength, she fell at the feet of Satan. Once again, hair in hand, he dragged her to the Professor's side.

"Now . . . you may watch . . . while AGAIN, I will take something from you," he said raising Kismet high above the Professor's head.

"Noooo!" screamed Amena as she reached out for the Professor.

Before he could lower the fateful blade onto the back of the Professor's neck, a cry rang out from beneath a pile of beasts and dragons. Satan paused briefly, being caught off guard by a loud scream in the distance.

Overpowered by the onslaught of beasts, Huron's final breath marked the end of an era. With his death, everything on the battlefield stopped. Dragons, Dark Angels and hell beasts all paused . . . awaiting word from their leader:

"The Last Cherub . . ." growled Satan.

The Fields came alive with a Hellish celebration. Dragons stopped their gorging and took to the skies with drunken bliss. Hell beasts tossed body parts of fallen Angels high into the skies like graduation caps. Dark Angels jumped for joy and paused their beastly whipping to scream into the air with a victory howl.

But their gala was short lived as Huron's death ushered in a thunderous sound that echoed across the Fields.

"NOOOOOOOOOOOO!!" screamed Satan, shielding his ears from the deafening sound. His face disfigured and his lower jaw opened widely. Insects and rodents flew from his mouth hole as he screamed loud in agony. Kismet spiraled through the air; striking the earth and coming to rest, handle up, beside El Mórte. The two swords hissed as they cooled while leaning against each other, forming an X in the earth.

Dark Angels' celebratory screams turned into horrifying shrieks of pain and fright. The skies rang out with the moans of dragons and Dark Angels falling from the skies like rain. Armies of hell beasts burst and vaporized by the frequency of the sound.

Insane with shame, Dark Angels hung themselves by the thousands as orchards of blackened Oaks were ornamented with their dangling and swinging bodies.

The earth shook and the ground began to rumble. Charred trees and underbrush burst into flames, and the skies became a firestorm. Amena buried her face into the Professor's chest:

"What's happening?!" she screamed.

"I don't know!" shouted the Professor, shielding Amena with his body.

Their clothes began to burn and tear away. The Professor strained his eyes to look into the inferno. He looked to the East to see the mountains that would have been the Sierra Nevadas in his world sinking into the horizon. They burst into flames and continued to crumble until they vanished in the distance. Burning boulders from Buchanan Hollow fell onto the foothills that flattened into the undulating valley floor below. Devastation ensued as far as the eye could see.

Satan, kept upright by self-pride alone, indignantly leaned into the flames while struggling to stay on his feet. Staggering and stumbling he looked into the skies above and finally spotted the source of the sound . . . It was Michael.

CHAPTER XXXVIII
THE RAPTURE
❧

Numier couldn't sit still any longer. It had been more than half an hour since the Emergency Broadcast reported missiles had been launched. But for the moment . . . everything seemed quiet.

Curiosity got the best of him. The trees surrounding the cabin limited his view of anything and everything.

Numier left the shelter of his cabin and walked down the long driveway, then onto the shoulder of Tollhouse Road. He tentatively looked down the windy lane. Between two hills, he could see the skyline of the densely populated valley below. He looked onto the thin layer of dust and smog that usually blanketed the cities beneath . . . and didn't see anything out of the ordinary.

"Everything seems ok here," he thought.

He felt compelled that he should be with others at a time like this. He remembered all the people lining-up to get into Foothill Lutheran Church. Maybe they'd heard something . . . anything. It wasn't far up the hill, and he could use the walk.

As he slowly headed up the road, he felt a slight rumble under his feet. Being a native Californian, he'd been through earthquakes before. He instinctively held his hands out beside him for balance, preparing to surf the quake . . . but the quake never came.

"Just a tremor," he murmured as he started back up the road.

Suddenly, the hair on the back of his neck stood on edge. A rush of wind came from behind pushing him off balance. He turned to look at the truck or passing motorist . . . but there was nothing.

The wind turned into a slight breeze that swirled around the faded, blacktop road. He thought it curious that the breeze was not blowing past or around him, but upward . . . vertically. The long comb-over on the top of his head lifted exposing his bald-spot. Loose grass, leaves and small tumbleweeds, slowly lifted into the air, then flew straight up.

"Tornado . . .?" he thought suspiciously, since twisters were uncommon in these parts. He braced himself for more . . . but no more came.

He held his forearm over his head and again turned towards the Church. He noticed that the foothills were quieter than usual. The hawks weren't screeching, the cows weren't mooing, and he hadn't seen a car on the road for sometime.

Feeling an increased sense of urgency, he picked up
his pace and approached an area where Dry Creek
bends close to the road.

Passing a large sycamore tree, he came upon an
unusual sight . . . three horses standing together
on the opposite side of the stream. They stood
knee high in the tall grass facing Numier. They
were not strapped or tied to anything, but yet, they
didn't run or even move. He found it odd that they
were completely saddled . . . blankets, saddlebags,
everything . . . but no riders.

Spooked by the abandoned horses, Numier began
to jog up the road, looking back over his shoulder at
the horses looking at him.

Rounding the last corner before the Church, he
noticed a truck driving erratically in his direction.
He dove to the side, narrowly avoiding the speeding
pick-up that careened off the road and into the
stream.

"Hey– take it easy . . .!" shouted Numier from one
knee.

Through the dust, he spotted the backside of the
truck when he heard engine noise behind him. He
turned to oncoming traffic and ran quickly to the
center of the street, while dodging another car. It
slowly rolled past Numier and onto the soft shoulder,
coming to rest against a barbed-wire fencepost.

He ran to the passenger door of the car, and looked in.

"Are you alright," he called, but there was no answer . . . because there was no driver.

He craned his head for a better view and saw into the cab of the pick-up . . . empty.

Confused and bewildered by the scene, he looked up toward the Church. The structure appeared unchanged. The quaint, high-steeple chapel, nestled into the base of Black Mountain, appeared normal. But still . . . no people.

"Oh, my God . . ." he said, as he watched several unmanned autos rolling and turning about the parking lot.

He ran towards the Church and found piles of clothes, each bunched together with a pair of shoes or boots. A floppy hat, resting atop a colorful floral-pattern dress and old high-heeled shoes. A dusty-grey hairpiece, sitting beside a suit and black wing-tip shoes.

Numier spotted an old man on his knees. He seemed to be dressed-up to go somewhere . . . but not today. He held the sleeve of an old dress that lay in a bunch on the ground in front of him.

"What's going on here . . .? he asked the old man. But there was no answer.

Beyond the crunching sounds of colliding metal, he heard a cry in the distance. He looked up the road and saw a woman standing alone. Franticly she screamed, holding an empty baby blanket as a rattle, little hat, and tiny socks fell to the ground at her feet.

"Oh, no . . ." he whispered immediately recalling scripture and fearing that this was much more than odd.

Feeling a sense of urgency, he ran passed several of the bewildered, slowly shuffling toward the church. They were in a trance-like daze, as though they'd all been part of something none of them could grasp or explain.

As he ran up the stairs to the Church, he flung open the double doors and gasped. There before him, littering the pews and isles of the Chapel, were piles and piles of clothes. Purses, watches, and jewelry were everywhere.

Slowly he walked, carefully stepping over worthless earthly possessions; he made his way to the altar. He noticed a small girl kneeling alone. With her head hung low and her hands folded together in prayer, she remained motionless. As he slowly approached, he recognized her:

"Clair!," he whispered loudly. But there was no response.

After pausing a moment he gathered the strength to overcome his fear and apprehension and slowly and quietly approached the altar.

Tired from his long journey, and in a new state of understanding . . . Numier slowly went to his knees next to Clair.

He thought of all the Christians he'd known and how many of them tried . . . but he didn't listen. He thought of all the opportunities at salvation God had sent to him . . . but went unaccepted. He thought of what a fool he'd been that, even after meeting the Archangel Michael . . . he still couldn't surrender.

He hung his head low as the ground began to rumble and shake. Clair flinched next to him as explosions rang loudly on the valley floor, echoing and reverberating throughout the hills and mountains. Bright bursts of light flashed through the stain glass windows of the Church, lighting-up the walls around him in a myriad of colors.

Out of the corner of his eye he could see shadowy images hunching and crawling abnormally about the pews. He began to hear moaning as shards of broken glass swirled around him reflecting images of twisted faces.

He felt the shaking of the young girl next to him as he realized finally that although trapped in an undead body, Clair had a soul just like his. So he reached around the shoulder of the trembling child and held her close as she began to cry.

He then took a deep breath . . . looked up at the large wooden cross on the wall . . . and said:

"Forgive us . . ."

CHAPTER XXXIX
CREATION

Michael descended quickly through the clouds. He ripped across the skyline, blowing a large golden trumpet[37]. Behind him followed a thousand newly created Cherubim. Just minutes old, their wings were clean and white. Their swords were drawn, and their shields shown brightly through the blazing skies.

The Professor and Amena tucked snuggly into each other while a cloud of decomposed granite, dust and ash covered their position.

As suddenly as the noise began, it stopped. The quaking had subsided, and the flames were gone. The skies began to clear, as new rays of sunlight burst through openings between tuffs of thick dust and smoke. Small flakes of white ash fell softly onto the barren soil. The Fields were quiet for the first time in eight thousand years.

Amena and Don slowly stood and scanned the silent Fields.

"Are you OK?" Goodwin quietly asked.

"I'm fine," said Amena inspecting her body white with ash.

"Why weren't we burned?" Amena whispered.

"I don't know," said Goodwin looking down at the pile of smoldering cinders that used to be their clothes.

As the dust and smoke settled around them, the images began to appear. The terrain was a lunar landscape as far as the eye could see. Everything was charred, flat and devoid of life. The piles of bodies were gone. The odor of the dead and dying was gone. There were no signs of Satan, Dark Angels or Hell-beasts of any kind . . . only Michael.

He stood silently in the distance on the only remaining knoll. He appeared larger than before. His hair was longer and his body glowed. Like an ancient Olympian, he wore white fabric that draped over one shoulder and wrapped to a gold studded kilt. He fully extended his thirty-foot wings and flew high above the topography.

The Archangel opened his arms widely as bright rays of light burst through the parting skies above. The earth quaked again. Goodwin and Amena went to their knees as the ground rumbled beneath them. Deep canyon-like chasms formed, filling loudly with rushing water. Great lakes appeared where the Sierra Nevadas once stood. The valley floor rose thousands of feet into the sky then settled to form mountains slowly stepping downward to the foothills. The skies swirled with shades of blue replacing the blood-red-orange that had been the ceiling for thousands of years.

Redwoods, Oaks and Deodara Cedars covered the newly created mountains forming vibrant forests. Grass, plants and flowers sprang up as far as the eye could see. Oak trees, sycamores and Alders burst up through the soil propelling earth into the skies like geysers.

"What's happening now!?" shouted Amena with her head buried into the Professor's chest.

"I don't know!" he yelled through the deafening sound.

Slowly the earth stopped shaking as giant redwoods settled into position. The ripping and exploding sounds of moving earth subsided and the fields were quiet again . . . Slowly the dust settled and wildlife began to emerge.

Through lush fields of waving green grass, creatures new and old appeared, speckling the landscape as far as the eye could see. Birds glided in, flapping their wings though the pure clean air. Geese flew in formation, whizzing and honking as they passed by overhead. Stags, does, and fawns, pranced through blossoming wildflowers and abundant spring meadows.

Birds of all kinds flew fast, perching and hoping in and out of treetop branches surrounding the meadows. They chirped and squealed as they scurried in and out their new tree-nests. Chubby ground squirrels and bunnies popped their heads in and out of the soft earth, hunting for choice locations as they hurriedly burrowed their new homes.

The Professor and Amena couldn't believe their eyes:

"I've never seen anything so beautiful," she gasped as new life sprang up all round them.

Michael landed, and turned to Amena and Don. He retracted his wings and slowly walked toward them with the newly created terrain still settling behind him. An exhilarated Amena ran up and hugged the mighty Angel with all her might:

"We were almost killed," said the Professor excited to see Michael.

"Yes . . . I know," said Michael. "But now you are safe."

Amena smiled and returned to the Professor. While holding on to Goodwin for strength, Amena turned to face Michael and sheepishly asked:

"Is it true . . . what Huron said about me?

"Yes . . . Huron spoke the truth," Michael said.

"Wow," she said. "Wait till I tell my Mom."

Amena paused and looked at the Professor.

"I'm ready to go home now . . ." she said slowly and tentatively.

The Professor turned to Michael.

Goodwin remembered teaching his class about the rapture. The mighty Archangel will sound his trumpet and the dead in Christ will rise first, followed by the living. He looked around and realized.

"We can't go back . . . can we?" he asked.

"No . . . you cannot," replied Michael. "Mankind has been harvested, and Satan's armies have crossed . . . Your world is no longer suitable for believers."

"Oh my God!" cried Amena burying her face into the Professor's chest.

"My mom . . . my friends . . ." she said as she began to cry.

The Professor thought of his students while holding Amena tightly.

Michael pointed high into the skies above.

The Professor looked up as Amena peeked up from under his chin. Just above the hilltop, heading for the clouds, flew millions of newly created cherubim. They each carried hundreds of tiny lights in their arms and under their wings, speeding across the skyline like meteors.

"Are those people . . .?" said Goodwin.

"Souls," said Michael."This day has been prophesized for thousands of years," continued Michael. "Believers of all ages, shapes, sizes, religions and nationalities. They're all heading to a place where there is no sin . . . no sickness, pain or death," said Michael.

The Professors felt overwhelmed and humbled to be alive to witness this epic event.

Amena gasped and said:

"Look!" pointing to a cloud in the distance where the Angels were all heading.

It was Jesus, standing in the sky, larger than the clouds, welcoming his church into his open arms. Together they streaked across the sky, crossing dimensions on their way to Heaven.

"They're safe now too," said Michael. Reminding them of scripture. (1 Thessalonians 4:16)

"This day marks a new beginning," said Michael smiling down upon the two of them. "For them and for you."

"Are we going with them?" asked Amena.

"No . . . you have a new mission now." Michael answered.

And as a fully-grown, fruit-bearing fig tree shinning and sparkling with new life sprouted up behind them, Michael turned to them and said:

"You have all you need to flourish here . . . For this is the new Garden."

The animals came to the base of the foothill where Amena and Don were receiving instruction from Michael:

"God has created these animals to be pleasing to you . . . give them new names and govern over them."

Somehow they understood why they were brought to this place, how they'd survived, and what was being asked of them. Amena and the Professor lifted their hands and waved as they watched Michael and his army of Cherubim fly through an opening in the sky . . .

Amena looked at Don, then out across their newly created world and smiled. The two of them were alone in Paradise.

Together they stood . . . holding hands beneath the tree of life . . . innocent in the Garden . . . without sin and without shame . . . only love.

The Beginning

Endnotes

[1] (Isaiah 6:2) 2 Above him were seraphs, each with six wings: With two wings they covered their faces, with two they covered their feet, and with two they were flying.

[2] (2 Chronicles 3:11) 11 The total wingspan of the cherubim was twenty cubits. One wing of the first cherub was five cubits[g] long and touched the temple wall, while its other wing, also five cubits long, touched the wing of the other cherub. 12 Similarly one wing of the second cherub was five cubits long and touched the other temple wall, and its other wing, also five cubits long, touched the wing of the first cherub. 13 The wings of these cherubim extended twenty cubits. They stood on their feet, facing the main hall.

[3] (Mark 15:22) 22 They brought Jesus to the place called Golgotha (which means The Place of the Skull).

[4] Manica- Scaled armor worn by Thracian gladiators up the left arm for protection.

[5] Sica- curved short sword use by Thracian gladiators.

[6] (Ezekiel 1:10) 10 Their faces looked like this: Each of the four had the face of a man, and on the right side each had the face of a lion, and on the left face of an ox; each also had the face of an eagle. 11 Such were their faces.

[7] (1 Kings 6:29) 29 On the walls all around the temple, in both the inner and outer rooms, he carved cherubim, palm trees and open flowers.

[8] (Revelations 12:7-9) The above is the passage from the NIV.

[9] (Daniel 10:13) 13 But the prince of the Persian kingdom resisted me twenty-one days. Then Michael, one of the chief princes, came to help me, because I was detained there with the king of Persia.

[10] (Acts 4:12) 12 Salvation is found in no one else, for there is no other name under heaven given to men by which we must be saved.

[11] (Dt 18:11) 10 Let no one be found among you who sacrifices his son or daughter in [a] the fire, who practices divination or sorcery, interprets omens, engages in witchcraft, 11 or casts spells, or who is a medium or spiritist or who consults the dead. (Isa 8:19) 19 When men tell you to consult mediums and spiritists, who whisper and mutter, should not a people inquire of their God? Why consult the dead on behalf of the living?

[12] (Mt 7:23) 21"Not everyone who says to me, 'Lord, Lord,' will enter the kingdom of heaven, but only he who does the will of my Father who is in heaven. 22 Many will say to me on that day, 'Lord, Lord, did we not prophesy in your name, and in your name drive out demons and perform many miracles?'

23 Then I will tell them plainly, 'I never knew you. Away from me, you evildoers!'

[13] a condition called hematidrosis

[14] (Luke 11:23) 23 "He who is not with me is against me, and he who does not gather with me, scatters.

[15] (Genesis 19:1-29) 1 The two angels arrived at Sodom in the evening, and Lot was sitting in the gateway of the city. When he saw them, he got up to meet them and bowed down with his face to the ground.

[16] (Colossians 1:18) 18 And he is the head of the body, the church; he is the beginning and the firstborn from among the dead, so that in everything he might have the supremacy.

[17] (Colossians 3:3) 3 For you died, and your life is now hidden with Christ in God. 4 When Christ, who is your[a] life, appears, then you also will appear with him in glory.

[18] (Matthew 26:26-29) 26 While they were eating, Jesus took bread, gave thanks and broke it, and gave it to his disciples, saying, "Take and eat; this is my body." 27 Then he took the cup, gave thanks and offered it to them, saying, "Drink from it, all of you.

[19] (John 14:20) 20 On that day you will realize that I am in my Father, and you are in me, and I am in you.

[20] (John 3:16-21) 16 "For God so loved the world that he gave his one and only Son,[f] that whoever believes in him shall not perish but have eternal life. 17 For God did not send his Son into the world to condemn the world, but to save the world through him. 18 Whoever believes in him is not condemned, but whoever does not believe stands condemned already because he has not believed in the name of God's one and only Son.[g]

[21] (Mathew 23:9)) 9 And do not call anyone on earth 'father,' for you have one Father, and he is in heaven.

[22] (Luke 10:18) 18 He replied, "I saw Satan fall like lightning from heaven.

[23] (2 Kings 19:35) 35 That night the angel of the LORD went out and put to death a hundred and eighty-five thousand men in the Assyrian camp. When the people got up the next morning—there were all the dead bodies!

[24] (Genesis 9:11) 11 I establish my covenant with you: Never again will all life be cut off by the waters of a flood; never again will there be a flood to destroy the earth."

[25] (1 Thessalonians 4:16-18) 16 For the Lord himself will come down from heaven, with a loud command, with the voice of the archangel and with the trumpet call of God, and the dead in Christ will rise first.

[26] (Revelation 21:3-5) 3 And I heard a loud voice from the throne saying, "Now the dwelling of God is

with men, and he will live with them. They will be his people, and God himself will be with them and be their God. 4 He will wipe every tear from their eyes. There will be no more death or mourning or crying or pain, for the old order of things has passed away."

[27] (Luke 10:18) And I said unto them, I beheld Satan fallen as lightning from Heaven..

[28] (Daniel 7:14) And there was given him dominion, and glory, and a kingdom, that all the peoples, nations, and languages should serve him: his dominion is an everlasting dominion, which shall not pass away, and his kingdom that which shall not be destroyed.

[29] (Luke 1:28) And he came in unto her, and said, Hail, thou that art highly favored, the Lord is with thee.

[30] (Luke 1:31) And behold, thou shalt conceive in thy womb, and bring forth a son, and shalt call his name JESUS.

[31] (Luke 1:34) And Mary said unto the angel, How shall this be, seeing I know not a man?

[32] (Luke 1:36) And behold, Elisabeth thy kinswoman, she also hath conceived a son in her old age; and this is the sixth month with her that was called barren.

[33] (Luke 1:38) And Mary said, Behold, the handmaid of the Lord; be it unto me according to thy word. And the angel departed from her.

[34] (Psalm 23:4) Yea, thou I walk through the valley of the shadow of death, I will fear no evil; for thou art with me; Thy rod and thy staff, they comfort me.

[35] (Luke 23:34) And Jesus said, Father, forgive them; for they know not what they do. And parting his garments among them, they cast lots.

[36] (Matthew 12:46-50; Luke 8:19-21) 46 While he was yet speaking to the multitudes, behold, his mother and his brethren stood without, seeking to speak to him. 47 And one said unto him, Behold, thy mother and thy brethren stand without, seeking to speak to thee. 48 But he answered and said unto him that told him, Who is my mother? and who are my brethren? 49 And he stretched forth his hand towards his disciples, and said, Behold, my mother and my brethren! 50 For whosoever shall do the will of my Father who is in heaven, he is my brother, and sister, and mother.

(Luke 8:19-21) 19 And there came to him his mother and brethren, and they could not come at him for the crowd. 20 And it was told him, Thy mother and thy brethren stand without, desiring to see thee. 21 But he answered and said unto them, My mother and my brethren are these that hear the word of God, and do it.

[37] (1 Thessalonians 4:16) For the Lord himself will come down from heaven, with a loud command, with the voice of the archangel and with the trumpet call of God, and the dead in Christ will rise first.

Made in the USA
Charleston, SC
10 September 2010